Dancing

with

COVID

DANCING WITH **COVID**

One of the first coronavirus survivors and her quest for answers

Laurel Valvano
Fischbach

www.dancingwithcovid.com

info@dancingwithcovid.com

This book was printed in the United States of America.
Copyright © 2021 dancingwithcovid
ISBN: 9798590505432
Imprint: Independently published

As citizens worldwide wait for their vaccine, healthcare professionals have been risking their lives to bravely battle COVID-19 daily.

This book is dedicated to all:

Healthcare Workers, First Responders, Hospital Staff, and Scientists

In memory of:

Roman A. Malecha

Eileen Elizabeth Dorson Williams

Author's Note

In writing this memoir, I've strived to be as factual as possible, referencing text messages, emails, letters, photos, and my personal calendar. I've asked friends to recount their conversations with me, and I've tried my best to turn memories into sentences. *Dancing with COVID* was written to bring you into my personal experience. I am obviously not a medical professional, and the book was not written with a political agenda. I have changed the names of many, but those that I choose to keep their given names are not mentioned with their last names.

Acronyms

CDC: Centers for Disease Control and Prevention, the leading government agency charged with epidemic control, headquarters - Atlanta, Georgia.

COVID: Abbreviated name for COVID-19.

COVID-19: The clinical disease caused by SARS-2, involving a broad range of symptoms and severities, also used to refer to the pandemic itself.

FDA: Food and Drug Administration

PAPR: Powered Air Purification Respirator

PCR: Polymerase Chain Reaction - PCR assay tests are used to detect minute traces of genetic material associated with SARS-CoV-2.

PPE: Personal protective equipment, worn by health-care providers in order to protect against contracting an infection. Equipment includes by is not limited to: masks, gloves, face shields, goggles, powered air purification respirator, etc.

SARS-CoV-2: Virus known from the coronavirus family that emerged in 2019 spawning a worldwide pandemic.

WHO: World Health Organization

The Beginning

A kaleidoscope of butterflies flutters in my stomach as the plane takes off for my favorite annual ski trip to Vail, Colorado. My excited anticipation in joining friends from around the U.S. for the seventh consecutive year on the slopes engulfs me — nine days of extreme skiing and extreme fun! We will ski by day and dance by night. But this ski trip will be like none other, one forever burned into my memory.

History is in the making with a silent pandemic brewing on snow-covered mountains chock full of skiers and snowboarders from around the globe. The resort town of Vail has a cozy, quaint atmosphere — crowded with vacationers. An atmosphere ripe to spread the "novel" coronavirus at lightning speed — like a fire ripping through a dry brush-filled field with absolutely nothing in its path to slow it down. Who knew what "novel" really meant prior to this trip?

Friday, February 21st, 2020 begins the start of my journey you are about to embark upon. It opens with the reunion of friends from far and wide, all intent upon spending our days floating effortlessly down some of the most pristine ski runs Colorado has to offer. Each of us embracing vacation mode to the fullest while leaving our everyday cares back at home.

I love to ski. I especially love to ski with friends. About 40 of us end up skiing in Vail the same week each winter. My extroverted self is energized by spending this week with them! However, the number of people is not as important as the fact that it nourishes my soul to spend time with those who love an activity as much as I do!

When you find a group of friends who love the same activities you love and share your enthusiasm, you tend to hold on tightly; at least I do.

Middle age is a funny place to be when it comes to extreme sports. The number of friends willing to head down challenging black diamond ski runs becomes fewer and fewer as the years go by. So, when you discover this fearless enthusiasm in others, plans are made year after year, and the friendships deepen around your activity.

This takes me to why I was in Vail at the end of February. Skiers love good snow, and Vail is famous for copious amounts of it, especially at this time of year. This is consistently one of the best weeks of the year to ski, and it's also why the Burton US Open Snowboarding Championships are scheduled for this week each year. Coincidentally, it's also the place to be if you are a highly contagious virus — looking to infect the most people — in the shortest amount of time.

Picture the perfect setting for unwinding after a day of skiing: a bar or restaurant with cozy seating, excellent food, signature drinks, locally brewed beers, and a talented musician entertaining you with his craft. Yes... you get the visual... "cozy." In this instance, "cozy" equates to elbow-to-elbow bodies playing musical chairs to share a seat. "Sharing" is the key word here. Sharing chairs, sharing appetizers, and sharing sips of your drink as you help your friends decide which elixirs they should order. While all this sharing is happening — well, we are "shoulder-to-shoulder." Truly the picture-perfect scenario for the unstoppable rampage we now call "COVID-19," "coronavirus," or "SARS-CoV-2."

Thousands of people flock to Vail to experience the Burton US Open from around the globe. Combine the Burton participants with their spectators, add in ski enthusiasts from all corners of the globe, and "Voilà," you have a whole lot of bodies! A whole lot of "fit bodies" I might add. After years of trips to Vail during the week of the Burton US Open, it's become quite clear that scads of "shoulder-to-shoulder people" is the norm.

As you follow my journey with the novel coronavirus, keep in mind when I contracted it in late February, very little was known about the virus. Our government and the Centers for Disease Control and Prevention (CDC) shared little information about it. The World Health Organization (WHO) tweeted on January 21, 2020 that it was now very clear there was "at least some human-to-human transmission." Approximately four weeks later the virus began gaining a foothold inside my lungs. Scientists, doctors, epidemiologists, and health department officials were in a race to understand the novel coronavirus. At this time, very little was known about the symptoms of this deadly virus, so little was broadcast from our media.

As I relate my story, I will add a parallel chronology of what was being communicated to the public both nationally and globally. This is a textbook case of the old saying, "Hindsight is 20/20." So, put on a parka and join me as you experience an adventure like nothing else! After all, when do you get to read a true story about a historical pandemic in the middle of the actual pandemic? My recount will leave you shaking your head in disbelief while stirring up images of a human petri dish.

Chapter 1

Ride the gondola with me to the top of the mountain. A "bluebird day." A day of brilliant sunshine and blue skies. The magnificent view from the glass bubble gliding up the mountain tricks your eyes into thinking you are looking at a painting with soft, precise brushstrokes. Today is my first shot at the familiar runs that always bring a smile to my face and make me feel like a kid again. I am fortunate to be with good friends who share a love of skiing and who know this mountain like the back of their hands. Jill and Ellie take in the view with me as we talk about how we never tire of it. When we arrive at the landing pad midway up the mountain, the doors slide open, ushering in crisp mountain air that invigorates every bit of my being. We ski over to the pair of chairlifts and pause at the entrance to the ski queue — a maze of roped-off pathways. The three of us take turns offering our opinions about which ski run we should take for a top-to-bottom run as a warm-up. It doesn't take long for us to agree upon a plan, and we hop in line for the Mountain Top Express chairlift. During our ride up, we discuss which friends are arriving over the coming days. Chairlift rides are the perfect time to get caught up.

"Karley and Amanda are arriving this afternoon," I say with excitement. Jill lets us know Chris is here and has already been snowboarding for two days. Ellie updates us about a sizable group from Chicago that will arrive mid-week. "It's going to be another fun year," I say, smiling underneath my fuzzy neck gator pulled up over my nose. "Tomorrow we will have our core group together. The two of you, me and the Michigan girls." Karley and Amanda are always referred to as the

Michigan girls. We always refer to people we meet in Vail affectionately by their hometown states or cities.

All morning we feel like the three musketeers skiing the front side of the mountain together. I am just giddy to be here. The time and effort I put in throughout the year working out regularly and focusing on building leg strength has paid off. So far neither of my girlfriends have had to wait for me at the bottom. When you ski with people who are faster than you, it puts pressure on you to avoid holding them up. The morning disappears so fast that I am surprised when Jill recommends we stop for lunch at the Mid-Vail restaurant and meet up with her friend, Chris.

"It's noon?" I ask with raised eyebrows.

"Yup," Jill replies and suggests we eat. After a quick lunch, the three musketeers become a foursome when Chris appears with his snowboard under his arm. At ski resorts, there is never a limit on numbers of people due to space, availability, etiquette, etc. In fact, one of the best attributes of skiing is, "the more the merrier!" I love this about skiing because if there is one thing I try to be in life, it's inclusive.

We spend the afternoon carving our way across one ski run to the next, rarely stopping to catch our breath. All the runs are open due to the heavy snowfall this year. We feel fortunate to have so much snow because light snowfall inevitably results in sections of Vail becoming off-limits. We take advantage of the variety of terrain, exhausting our leg muscles. When the lifts close at 3:30 pm, Ellie and I ski off together down the last run towards our hotel. The typical cadence for a vacation day in Vail encompasses a full day of skiing, happy hour with friends, a quick shower to freshen up for the evening and a night out on the town (or in this case, "the Village"). From time to time, we take a dip in the hot tub and do a little souvenir shopping, but that's not on the agenda for today.

Evenings are massive social events! As you experience this trip with me, you will quickly be thrown into the middle of a melting pot of friends that come and go during my nine days in Vail. They arrive from cities that span the East Coast to the West Coast, the Mid-West to the Deep South. Regardless of our accents, we are all at home in the mountains.

The first order of business after freshening up is to connect with Karley and Amanda, the Michigan girls. Ellie and I receive a text from Karley, "Come over to our condo."

A brisk walk has us knocking on their door in less than five minutes. The moment the door opens, Karley is bubbling with excitement, arms outstretched.

"It's so good to see the two of you! Come in."

Ellie and I step in, take off our shoes, and I comment, "Nice find! This place looks like it's perfect for the two of you."

After we are given a tour, we settle into comfortable overstuffed furniture circled in front of the fireplace while we wait for Jill's arrival. Our conversation starts with our travels to Vail and moves quickly to how fast a year has gone by. With a knock on the door interrupting our trip down memory lane, we know Jill has arrived. Once our hello hugs are given, Jill picks up where we left off a year ago, not one of us skipping a beat. The five of us decide our first stop for this evening has to be Pepi's Bar and Restaurant. We grab our coats and begin the short walk down the charming village street.

I have a funny saying for vacation days in Vail. It goes like this, "Rinse and Repeat!" What does this mean, exactly, you might be wondering? Well, days begin with lots of texting. Mornings include gondola rides and skiing in back bowls. Afternoons include skiing the front side of the mountain. Evenings include hopping from bar to restaurant to bar, and sprinkled in, there is always dancing. So, there you have it — "Rinse and Repeat!"

Fast forward to day three. I have noticed on this Monday morning, February 24, 2020, that I have a little tightness in my chest when I try to take a deep breath. I think to myself: *This is odd as I didn't have a problem taking in a deep breath at the top yesterday or the day before. Oh well… I am going to keep pace with my friends, so I'm not going to focus on this right now and just push through it.* I have to remember — I am 50 years old skiing at 10,000 feet above sea level. Living in Minnesota does not prepare you for the altitude, and I never expect to feel 100% when I am in the mountains. So, I cut myself some slack. The hours fly by as we conquer the mountain, one ski run at a time. I do my best to keep up with my friends, working harder than usual to stay on their tails. When 3:30 p.m. approaches and the lifts close, all I can think about is slinking into the hot tub at the hotel to ease my aching muscles. It was a spectacular day of skiing but I realize I'm off my game.

Back at the hotel room, Ellie and I put on bathing suits and within minutes we tip toe slowly into the steaming outdoor pool. The muscles in my legs are screaming at me, so I'm praying the hot water will kick-start a quick recovery. I'm also in need of a pep talk from my girlfriend, hoping that will help get me in the mood for an evening out on the town. The fatigue from the day has set in, and I am a little low on energy. Luckily, time, hot bubbling water, and a convincing pep talk from Ellie combine to lift my spirits. We discuss happy hour, listing off our options one at a time, analyzing each establishment's pros and cons. She makes the pitch for the village watering hole, The Red Lion, and that eventually becomes the first stop of the evening.

The moment we walk into The Red Lion, a favorite cornerstone bar since 1963, we see Amanda and Karley. Ellie and I squeeze our way through the crowd to reach their table, while an old '70s song fills the bar, the music reverberating off the sea of bodies. Now that we have arrived, I notice we are only one table away from the edge of the stage. Karley introduces me to a few people she knows from her high school days, and I learn this is their last evening in Vail. As I make eye contact with as many of these new acquaintances as possible, I shout, "Are you flying back home to Michigan tomorrow? I hope you enjoyed the snow while you were here." A resounding yes and lots of nods come my way. (Seated this close to the stage means that communication depends upon reading lips and interpreting body language, so I do my best to pay attention and just smile a lot.) My friend, Jill, finds her way to our table in the middle of the next '70s song as our group of friends continues to grow.

Who knew as I was reunited with so many friends enjoying a glass of wine that my slight shortness of breath and aching leg muscles were more than fatigue from altitude and three consecutive days of extreme skiing? As I think back to this evening, I look at it through a new lens. The virus was setting up camp in my lungs. It was taking a toll on my energy level. How many people did I talk to? How many people were breathing the air around me as I socialized, laughed and sang? The entire bar was belting out, "Sweet Caroline!" How many people were closer than six feet as the coronavirus was replicating inside of me? This is one of those moments in time when looking back on it, I think to myself, "Wow!" I wonder…was I already spreading the virus? If I was contagious on this first day of slight symptoms, how many people inside The Red Lion became infected because of me? These are the questions I have been pondering for months which no one can answer.

Happy hour comes to a close, and the '70s music loses its allure to keep us singing. Jill takes off to meet Chris for a drink while the rest of us choose a charming little restaurant tucked into the center of the village, the Left Bank. This quaint French cuisine restaurant is known for having an extensive wine list, so as the saying goes, "When in Rome" or more aptly referred to here, "When in France." The four of us head straight to the bar to peruse the wine list as we wait for a table to become available. I make my selection quickly while the other ladies linger over the list and pepper the bartender with questions. (If ever I see a Syrah by the glass on a menu, I always order it.) The bartender presents the bottle of Syrah and pours a generous glass in front of me, showing off the label while giving me the history about the vineyard. I savor the first sip and then offer my glass to each of my friends for a taste, giving them the opportunity to make an educated decision with their selection.

Again, looking at this experience through the lens I mentioned earlier, I am thinking, this is exactly how this virus spread so silently. How many times have you been out with friends and offered a taste of something you were drinking or eating? These are the habits that so many of us have, and these are the habits that will soon be forced to change.

We enjoy a lovely dinner. Karley also orders the same glass of Syrah, thanks to my offer of a taste (One point for me!) We share a decadent chocolate soufflé, and the evening at the Left Bank was a successful saliva-swapping event. The night is still young, so we set off in search of some good music. We find what we're looking for at Bridge Street Bar, an underground watering hole. It has a casual vibe enticing us to get comfortable in the dark, windowless close quarters with live music performed by a duo of very talented musicians. For the next hour, we dance off some of our dinner and hopefully the soufflé. Each time I sit out a song, I massage the tops of my thighs, and Ellie takes notice.

"Hey, are your legs still feeling tired?"

"Yes, they are hurting a bit, but they are better thanks to the soak in the hot tub," I reply.

Remember, I am giving you an account of my very first noticeable symptoms with this virus. This is only the third full day of my vacation. On day three, I have been to three different establishments since 5:30 p.m., in tight quarters with countless numbers of patrons and restaurant servers. If I had been contagious at this moment, day one of the very first symptoms, with midnight approaching, how many people have I already infected? Let's look at the facts: I shared my wine, I sang arm-in-arm with friends at happy hour, I shook hands with people I met, and let's not forget, I shared an enclosed gondola with eight people traveling up the mountain.

This virus is stealthy, and literally on Monday, February 24th, the news reported the following information about COVID-19:

CNN reported:
https://www.google.com/amp/s/amp.cnn.com/cnn/asia /live-news/coronavirus-outbreak-02-24-20-hnk-intl/index.html

The number of deaths from the novel coronavirus has risen to more than 2,600

across the world. Europe's biggest outbreak is in Italy, where seven people have died and restrictions have been imposed on some municipalities.

South Korea announced 231 new cases today, with the nationwide total surging past 830. More than half of those are associated with a branch of a religious group.

How this affects US markets: US stocks plunged this morning on mounting worries about the spread of the coronavirus outside China to major economies, including South Korea and Italy.

Chinese President Xi Jinping has warned the novel coronavirus is the worst public health crisis facing the country since its founding, as new outbreaks continued to expand in South Korea and Italy, raising fears of a global pandemic.

Speaking Sunday, Xi said the "current epidemic situation is still severe and complex, and the prevention and control work is at the most critical stage." The crisis is "the most difficult to prevent and control in China" since the founding of the People's Republic in 1949, Xi said. He added the outbreak was likely to have a "great impact" on the country's economy, but that epidemic prevention and control methods were beginning to have an effect.

Following Xi's address, China announced it would delay the annual gathering of nearly 3,000 national legislators in Beijing, according to state media on Monday, underscoring the continuing impact and severity of the outbreak.

MPR News -Dan Gunderson - reported the following about Minnesota:
https://www.google.com/amp/s/www.mprnews.org/amp/story/2020/02/24/minnesota-experts-say-its-time-families-plan-for-covid19-outbreak

So far, there are a few dozen confirmed cases of COVID-19, the disease caused by the new coronavirus in the United States.

But Minnesota Department of Health infectious disease director Kris Ehresmann said it's very likely there will be outbreaks of the virus here. And Michael Osterholm, an expert in infectious disease at the University of Minnesota, said people should assume the virus will hit hard.
Ehresmann and Osterholm both said no one should panic, but everyone should prepare.

Now that you have read some news reported on the first day of my very first symptom, doesn't it make you wonder how many more people were harboring the virus? I am walking around Vail positive with the coronavirus, completely oblivious! The media are reporting there are a few dozen confirmed cases of COVID-19 in the United

13

States. How many thousands of people should be added to that number of a few dozen confirmed cases on February 24th? Are you scratching your head right now, wondering who else was beginning to show symptoms but did not understand they had symptoms connected to the coronavirus? How many others were spreading it unknowingly because there was no genuine alarm that this virus was in the U.S. on any mass scale at this point. There was no information being conveyed on February 24, 2020 by health experts and government officials to be mindful of symptoms connected to this virus. There was no one broadcasting to be on the lookout if you felt the same symptoms as the 77,658 Chinese citizens were experiencing. If there were more than 77,000 people experiencing symptoms with a new virus, why weren't those symptoms shared with the citizens of the U.S. using a Public Service Announcement?

Let's return to the Burton US Open. People traveled from all over Europe and Australia to compete in and watch this snowboarding competition. While reading the news reporting about Italy having large outbreaks, why wasn't someone at the CDC informing health departments at the state level to monitor large, organized gatherings in the U.S. that involved overseas travelers from known hotspot coronavirus outbreaks? This would have been the time and place to send in state health department officials to screen for symptoms and test at airports. Unfortunately, I do not believe there would have been enough COVID-19 tests available in February. At a future date, looking back at the month of February, Robert Redfield, Director of the CDC, said, "The introduction of the virus from Europe happened before we realized it was happening." This statement sums it up. The virus originated in China but probably

14

truly gained its foothold in the U.S. through infected travelers that came from Europe. I, along with many others in Vail, will become a cog in the wheel that ends up spiraling out of control.

Chapter 2

Tuesday, February 25th, I wake up in a pool of sweat and think, *Jeez, what's going on? Did Ellie crank up the heat to 80°?* I throw the comforter off and head to the bathroom for a cool shower. The moment I stand up, I notice my legs are extremely sore. I expect these old legs of mine to be a little sore after three full days of skiing, but this is more than a little sore. I massage my quadriceps ever so gently — it feels intensely painful! After a refreshing shower, I crawl back into bed, grab my phone, and begin looking at the mountain weather forecast for the day. The temperature is 4° below zero at the base. *Ugh! That would be miserable even for a Minnesotan,* is my immediate thought while an audible humph makes its way out of my mouth! Ellie begins stirring.

"Are you awake?" I ask.

A low grumble emerges from under the covers.

"It's four below zero at the base this morning, and it's not expected to get above zero before noon at the top," I whisper.

A few minutes go by as I scroll through future forecasts. "I'm thinking today might be a great day for rest and relaxation — I could use a massage."

"Yeah, I am not interested in skiing while it's subzero either, but I might ski for a couple of hours in the afternoon," Ellie responds as she rolls over to face me.

"After I get dressed and get us some coffee, we can figure out a game plan."

"OK, I'll hop in the shower in a minute," Ellie says as she stretches and inhales with the sound of a yawn.

This is the first moment I become fully conscious of the fact that fatigue and body aches are beginning to

16

take hold deep inside me. It takes an abnormal amount of effort to simply put on my pants this morning. I have been rationalizing these aches and pains as nothing more than three consecutive days of intense skiing at 10,000 feet above sea level combined with getting very little sleep for the last four nights.

The base of Vail Village is over 8,000 feet above sea level. Everyone reacts differently to high altitude. Luckily for me, I have never gotten altitude sickness, but high altitude definitely affects my sleep. Getting more than four hours of restful sleep when I am visiting the mountains rarely happens. In my six previous annual winter vacations to Vail, the excessive activity along with the shortage of sleep were not a problem. This year feels different.

Once I finish "trudging through mud" (what it felt like to get dressed), I grab a couple coffees in the hotel lounge and saunter back to the hotel room to formulate a game plan. I return to my earlier thoughts about getting a massage. After a few phone calls to several spas, I find an opening. A lovely woman at the Sonnenalp Spa informs me that a 1:00 p.m. appointment time is available. I ask her to hold for just a moment as I turn to Ellie, asking her if she wants a massage time as well.

She declines, shaking her head no and informing me, "I've already made plans to ski the front side. It gets plenty of sun and will be tolerable by noon."

I give her the OK sign and return to the phone call, snapping up the appointment. Sipping the last of my coffee, I am hopeful the caffeine will give me some energy. As soon as I hang up the phone, my thoughts move to the desire for a second cup.

"I really need this massage. I don't ever recall my legs feeling this sore after just three days of skiing, and I'm exhausted," I complain, stroking the top of my legs.

Ellie gives me a look of concern but then smiles and says, "I'm sure after your massage, you'll feel like a new woman!"

The two of us hang out for a few hours relaxing over a simple breakfast as we text with friends about their plans for this subzero day. Before I know it, it's 11:00 a.m., so I start my walk over to the Sonnenalp Spa. I want to have plenty of time to enjoy the hot tub and maybe order lunch prior to my massage. My lungs feel shocked at the first inhale of bitterly cold air. It makes the tightness in my chest even more pronounced than yesterday.

The virus is replicating itself by now, and my lungs let me know they are not happy.

Once I arrive at the spa, two cheerful receptionists check me in, and one gives me a tour of the facilities. I make myself at home in the locker room and put on a bathing suit because the hot tub is beckoning me. As the whirling hot water in the enormous tub envelopes me, I feel a little relief from the aching in my legs. I feel so fortunate to be on vacation. Having a day at the spa is a treat, but as I gaze out the large picture window, there is a little piece of me that also wishes I was on the mountain skiing. (The addiction to the adrenaline rush I get from skiing is nuts!) My daydreaming is interrupted briefly by a waiter.

"Good afternoon. Is there anything I can get for you? Are you interested in looking at a lunch menu?" he asks, holding a tray under his arm while peering down at me.

"Sure. I would love a cup of soup. What are my options?" I ask, looking up at him from my comfortable seat in the bubbling water.

The waiter rattles off the standard soup on the menu and then informs me about the "soup of the day." I place my order and promptly go back to gazing out the window, taking in the beautiful snow-dotted fir trees. When the waiter returns, he places a tray on a table next to a lounge chair. He gives me a wink while saying the proverbial, "Lunch is served."

"Thank you," I reply as I move toward the steps, grabbing the handrail to pull myself up one step at a time.

Plucking my towel from a nearby hook, I take my time drying off before wrapping myself in a heavy terry cloth robe. I plop down on the lounge chair and reach over to remove the lid from the bowl. Steam escapes, and from the scrumptious smells wafting towards me, I know I made the right choice with the "soup of the day."

My appointment time arrives before I know it. A tall, slender woman greets me, asking if I'm Laurel.

"Yes, that's me. Wow, it's one o'clock already?" I ask as I look up at her from my reclined position in the comfortable chaise.

"It is," the massage therapist replies.

"I sure am glad you had this appointment time available. I hope you can work out these aching kinks in my legs."

"I will do my best," she says with a smile.

The massage starts out relaxing as the therapist works on my shoulders and upper back. But when I flip over so she can focus on my legs, I practically jump off the table with the first strokes on my quadriceps. (Picture a cat ready to spring towards the ceiling with claws outstretched, poised to clutch onto a ceiling tile for dear life!)

"Wow, you are tender and tense. Hard days on the slopes, huh?"

I respond that I have skied for three consecutive days, but in the past, my legs never felt this sore. She explains I probably have some lactic acid that needs working out and massages my legs with a featherlight touch.

At this point, I am presumably highly contagious. How many people have I had contact with at the spa? Two receptionists that checked me in, the waiter that served my lunch, and now my massage therapist. Will they end up contracting the virus?

Once the therapist finishes with her magical hands, she leads me to the exercise studio and suggests I spend a little time using a foam roller on my thighs. I follow her instructions and have high hopes that this extra measure will give me the relief I am seeking. After twenty minutes with the foam roller, my body definitely starts to feel a little better; however, *it might be prudent for me to have one more soak in the luxurious hot tub.*

With 4:00 p.m. quickly approaching, I go back to the locker room, shower, dress, and pack up my belongings. I feel better than when I woke up this morning, but I am still plagued with the feeling of trudging through mud. I take my time walking through the village toward my hotel room. Out of the blue, I run into Jill's friend, Chris, making his way toward me with his snowboard in tow.

Surprised to see me, Chris greets me with a friendly smile. "Hey, where have you been all day?"

"Massage!"

He gives me a look expressing the sentiments, "nice" and "I completely understand," all wrapped up in one before letting me know where the group is going for happy hour.

I look at him with tired eyes as he speaks. As soon as he's filled me in, I collapse my body toward him, my head landing with a "thump" on the center of his chest. "The plans sound fun, but I'm just so exhausted. I'll do my best to rally," expressing my hopes, eyes closed, muffled voice, looking limp.

"Well, I'm counting you in, so I'll see you at The Red Lion shortly," Chris says as he pats my shoulder.

Once I arrive at the hotel and try to pull myself together, I realize the eyes staring back at me in the mirror are extremely bloodshot. (This is not uncommon when visiting the mountains. Dry mountain air coupled with a lack of sleep would cause anyone's eyeballs to resemble strawberries.) I squeeze a few drops of Visine into my eyes and try to make myself look presentable. As I get ready to walk out the door, I look at myself in the mirror one last time and think. *Darn! I can't believe my eyes are still red. Visine always works for me...Oh well, it is what it is...*

I later found out bloodshot eyes are a symptom of the novel coronavirus. One more symptom to add to the growing list.

I dash across the cobblestone street to The Red Lion bar without a jacket because I can easily pop back into the hotel to grab one later if I need it. Stepping into the bar, it's clear I am the first one of our group to arrive. I quickly zero in on the one and only available table, notably positioned directly under an air vent. I couldn't be happier with the heat flowing from the vent because right

21

now, I am freezing. My girlfriends arrive one by one, and I notice Jill is missing.

"Hey, where's Jill?" I ask.

"She took the day off. I spoke with her earlier today, and she said she had an upset stomach and was wiped out," Amanda said.

"What a bummer to feel under the weather on vacation. I hope after a full day of rest, she will meet up with us tomorrow," I say, concerned.

Everyone agrees, and I send a quick text to Jill, "Hope you feel better soon!"

The conversation ebbs and flows with each of us talking about our adventures for the day — the day that struggled to rise above zero. My chills continue as we chat. Even though I am sitting directly under the heat vent, I just can't warm up. Since I just finished a massage, I decide to start out drinking plenty of water this evening. After about thirty minutes, my chill becomes full-blown shivering. At this moment, Chris walks in wearing a spectacular, toasty-looking parka. My shivering brain says, *Wrap yourself in that jacket right now!*

"Can I borrow your jacket?" I ask desperately.

I am not sure I even said, "Hello," as my shivering brain keeps repeating, *Jacket, Jacket, Jacket!* The moment Chris generously offers his jacket to me, I am akin to an animal pouncing on its prey with the fraction of a second it takes to wrap it around me. It feels great to get it on, but it doesn't ease my uncontrollable shakes.

Karley looks at me with an odd expression and says, "I can't believe you're still cold sitting under the heat vent this entire time."

"I know, it's a weird feeling," I reply with my arms folded in front of me.

Reflecting on this evening, I now realize I had a fever. I should have been in bed! But, because I had just finished getting a massage, I chalked up all of this discomfort to the release of toxins post massage. (I have to admit, I have always been skeptical when massage therapists warn me to drink plenty of water to help with washing away toxins they claim to have released. But I thought at this moment it might be true.) The uncontrollable shakes lasted for a couple of hours.

My group of friends is becoming antsy and ready to move on to Pepi's Bar for some live music and more socializing. The evening has special meaning because today is Karley's birthday. For a brief instant, I consider going back to the hotel room and calling it a night.

We pay our tab, and I announce, "I will meet you at Pepi's. I have to run back to the hotel and grab my coat." I take off Chris' jacket and thank him effusively. "This definitely helped warm me up."

Walking into Pepi's, I find my group has met up with friends from New York and Kentucky. Before long, we have everyone in the bar singing happy birthday to Karley at the top of their lungs with accompaniment from Pepi's guitar player. It is memorable — it is fun — and it is packed. There is a huge group of people celebrating at the same time, and we delight in watching them dance in a conga line around the bar to the song, "When the Saints Go Marching In." Today is Fat Tuesday, and the spirit of New Orleans is with all of us thanks to this very festive atmosphere. As soon as the song ends, and the conga line has dissipated, the large group goes back to their tables.

Karley and I look at each other, and I suggest, "Let's go over and find out where they are from."

"Sure, fun idea," Karley says.

After a few seconds of conversation, we both have an inkling they are Australian with their delightful heavy accents. These are incredibly friendly people, full of energy and infectious enthusiasm. We quickly discover that they, too, have someone in their group celebrating a birthday. These Australians insist Karley partake in a "shotski" with them.

You may wonder to yourself, "What on earth is a 'shotski'?" Picture a wooden snow ski with perfectly spaced holes approximately a foot apart, securely holding shot glasses. The ski is long enough to hold four shot glasses. Participants willing to consume the liquor in this shotski line up, side by side, holding the ski with two hands as they tip it up simultaneously in order to quickly and efficiently consume their elixir. To enhance the experience, the entire bar starts clapping and shouting, "Shotski, shotski, shotski!" You can see how this would be kind of fun — unless you're someone that can't drink fast enough. Why, you ask? Because ultimately, your drink will run down the front of your shirt.

This was day two of my symptoms, and I was in bar number two shoulder-to-shoulder with friends and strangers from Australia shouting, "Shotski" and singing. I was presumably aerosolizing a virus I didn't know I had! How many other people in that bar had the virus and were spreading it alongside me? As the days progresss, you will be wondering how anyone will leave Vail healthy.

Chapter 3

Wednesday, February 26th arrives, and once again, I wake up in a pool of sweat. I throw the covers off and lie staring at the ceiling. My thoughts swirl around my discomfort as I let out an audible sigh. *Is this a cheap polyester comforter inside this luxurious duvet?* I wonder.

You might think... Laurel just turned 50. These night sweats are the onset of the "change of life." *(No, I do not think I am experiencing a typical symptom of menopause.)* I know some of you reading this right now are shaking your head, maybe even laughing — as you say to yourself... "Well... she is the perfect age to begin menopause." *(This train of thought should probably cross my mind, but it doesn't. Perhaps I live in a fantasy land, feeling like a teenager most of the time.)* I try to go back to sleep because it's only 5:30 a.m. After an hour of tossing and turning, I give up and hop in a lukewarm shower. When my feet hit the floor, I notice my leg muscles feel dramatically better than the day before. I give myself a mental "high five" and believe the massage worked its magic! Getting ready for the day feels more normal, and I am pleasantly surprised at my renewed energy.

Ellie and I eat breakfast together while mapping out our day. If you are curious about what mapping out a ski day entails, here it goes! Check in with everyone via text. Check the weather forecast. Check the grooming report. Lastly, coordinate a time and meet up location with friends who like to start their day early.

You would think we would turn on the TV and listen to the news while getting dressed. This never happens. Year after year, it never occurs to me to flick on the TV, and obviously Ellie feels the same. I take myself off the grid. I rarely check email. I don't surf the internet. I don't post on social media. The only thing of interest to me when I'm on a ski vacation is — when am I starting my day and — who is joining me? If the text popping up on my iPhone doesn't start with the words, "Gondola One, Golden Peak, or Blue Sky Basin," then that text goes on the back burner. A typical text response from me is, "What is your timeframe, because I want to hit the back bowls when they open at 10:00 a.m." Yes, I am a fanatic about skiing! Connecting with friends to maximize each day in a skier's paradise, skiing as many runs as possible, and searching for virgin powder — yes, those are my goals. At this point, you may think this sounds crazy! I realize we are a unique bunch of fanatics, and I take the cake. We eat, breathe, and sleep skiing! When we finish a day of skiing — well, we talk about our day of skiing. And, when we finish talking about our ski day — well, we talk about our ski plans for tomorrow. Crazy, but fun!

Ellie and I leave the hotel shortly after finishing breakfast. The first breath of cold air brings tightness back to my chest. A dry, annoying cough begins. *Oh well, my legs feel so much better, and I'm ready to ski. Taking yesterday off was a good decision. Hopefully, once I get moving, my lungs will open up and be just fine.* I think to myself.

Jill waves hello as she approaches the gondola.

"Good morning. I am so glad you made it today. How are you feeling? I hope whatever you had yesterday is gone," I say.

"Yes, I definitely feel better today than I did yesterday. But for some reason, my stomach is feeling off. I don't have much of an appetite. The full day of rest felt good, and I was able to get a good night's sleep, so hopefully my stomach will settle down and I'll work up an appetite by lunchtime," Jill replies.

The three of us join a few more friends, and all of us get in line for the gondola. The line is long, but it moves quickly. The gondola attendants efficiently herd us through the maze and into the cab, packing us in like sardines. As I sit looking out over the magnificent ridge of mountains, I try not to cough on anyone, keeping my neck gator pulled up over my mouth and nose as a shield.

Luckily, I'm not coughing much. But I wonder if the two strangers sharing the gondola with us ended up becoming infected by me. And what about Jill, who skipped a day of skiing because of her stomach issues? Are those symptoms the result of COVID-19? If so, could she be contagious? As the story continues to unfold, you will find the word "contagious" takes on a life of its own.

The skiing this morning feels great. Treating myself to a massage yesterday definitely helped to get me back in my groove. Skiing Blue Sky Basin with the group is fast and fun. My lungs don't quite feel normal, but the occasional cough doesn't slow me down.

The intermittent dry, tickling cough was annoying, but did I think this was strange? No, not really. I was skiing at 11,500 feet above sea level with people that push me to the brink physically on extremely steep terrain. Trying to keep up with friends who are expert skiers is always challenging for me every year. My situation could not be further from "normal" as I am utterly oblivious to my symptoms having any connection to a virus marching across the globe.

The lunch hour approaches and stomachs growl. We work our way out of the back bowls and over to Two Elk Restaurant at the top of the mountain. As we enter the grand Two Elk Lodge, several employees greet us,

27

offering tissues along with advice if we have questions. Vail resorts are known for their customer service, and this is a prime example of their outstanding hospitality. Each of us plucks a tissue for our cold, drippy noses. We offer our thanks before roaming through the sea of food stands in this cafeteria-style setting. We take our time perusing the options as we decide what will best fuel us for the second half of the day. When our trays are full, we begin the hunt for an available table. The restaurant is overflowing with skiers, and we end up sharing a table with a couple just finishing their lunch. It feels good to sit down and take a break with a steaming hot bowl of hearty soup and the best cornbread I've had since my days in high school. I have a brief conversation with this lovely couple who is kind enough to let us share their table. We talk about the runs they have been skiing this morning. (I appreciate this conversation because it gives me insight into what runs should be avoided this afternoon.) As the couple departs, we give them a resounding "Thank you!" for their kindness. As soon as we wave goodbye, our conversation turns to plans for the afternoon and wraps up with consensus that we will end our day at Los Amigos Restaurant.

There are two people sitting at this table in Two Elk with symptoms. Neither one of us has any idea we could be contagious with COVID-19, and neither one of us will ever know if we infected this couple who shared their table. You're beginning to experience the insidiousness of the "beginning." The silent bouncing of spherical, microscopic, spike-laden pathogens spewed from one person to the next. The beginning of the pandemic is taking a foothold. Soon the world will learn Vail, Colorado is a hotspot.

Our afternoon of skiing finishes with happy hour at Los Amigos, just as planned. We settle in with our beers at the table directly behind the gondola and enjoy watching the last few skiers take their last run of the day. A late afternoon sun warms us as we sit on the deck, noshing on chips and salsa. *(At this moment — I'm thinking all is right with the world! What a mistake that thought turned out to be.)*

Jill gets a text message about a group of friends arriving from Chicago. She lets them know where we are and encourages them to join us. Out of the blue, I remember our conversation from the morning and ask her how she's feeling.

"Hey, your stomach must be feeling better! It's good to see you eating and drinking again."

"Yes, lunch went down just fine, and this beer tastes good. I think whatever was bugging me is gone," Jill says with a jovial voice.

"Thank goodness! Nobody wants to be sick on vacation — that's for sure."

Jill's friends from Chicago arrive, hugs are plentiful, and we pull in a second table to accommodate seven more bodies. We quickly engage in conversations about the year that has flown by — reminiscing about last year's ski trip. We share plates of appetizers and order another round of beers.

Sharing a warm hug to greet a friend and offering to share appetizers is a "normal" part of life. It is worth considering whether this will be "normal" in the future. Are you thinking, "Oh no! People from another state are getting infected at happy hour — just hours after landing?" If you aren't thinking along these lines... well...you might want to be.

29

The dinner hour is upon us, so we go back to our hotel rooms to change out of our ski clothes and freshen up. As I am getting ready to go out for the evening, I notice my eyes are red again. I ask Ellie if she has eye drops because the Visine I used yesterday didn't work. She digs through her toiletry bag and finds some Clear Eyes.

"Here you go, give this a try," she says as she hands me the bottle.

Tilting my head back, I squeeze a few drops in each eye, hoping it will work. I finish getting ready for the evening, and as I am putting on lip gloss, I notice the redness in my eyes hasn't cleared.

"Darn it!" I cry out. "I just can't seem to clear up the redness in my eyes. The dry air must really be getting to me this year," I say, thoroughly exasperated.

"You might need to give the drops a little more time. Are you ready to meet up with Karley and Amanda?" Ellie says with a sweet and assuring tone.

"Almost. Just let me put on a spritz of perfume," I say hunting for my bottle of perfume.

I find the bottle in the bottom of my toiletry bag and spritz a little on each wrist. I immediately notice there is no scent. I unscrew the pump, thinking it might be slightly clogged. I bump my nose against the top of the bottle and quickly realize the fragrance is gone. *Why can't I smell my perfume?* I wonder. Holding the dark brown bottle up to the light, I observe it's only a quarter full. *Oh, I must have packed one of my older bottles by mistake — it must have turned.* I think to myself and don't give it any more thought as I walk out the door with Ellie.

Reflecting on this odoriferous oddity, I now know the sudden perceived lack of fragrance in my perfume was linked to COVID-19. In many people, the virus affects our olfactory senses. Researchers started putting two and two together when they released a survey on April 6th from the Virginia Commonwealth University (VCU) School of Medicine led by professor and physician Dr. Evan R. Reiter, M.D., F.A.C.S. Dr. Reiter asked people to complete a survey to help understand more about individuals that have experienced a change in their sense of smell or taste since January 2020. I remember hearing a report on the news when this was first touted as a common symptom of COVID-19 and recalling a hilarious story in connection with my perfume spritzing. More about that funny story later once I am back in Minnesota. In the meantime, get used to being asked if you have recently lost your sense of smell. Possibly more than half of everyone who contracts the virus experiences this bizarre symptom.

Ellie and I walk into The Red Lion restaurant. We spot Karley sitting at a high-top table against the window and worm our way through the crowd. When we finally make it, we are greeted with open arms from a group of Emergency Room doctors from Columbus, Ohio. This group of "Columbus doctors" skis at the end of February each year. The second we arrive at the table, we are offered stools, and the next hour is spent getting caught up with each of the eight doctors as we work our way around the table.

"How's your life been this past year," I ask over and over again.

By the time I have an opportunity to talk with Greg, I notice John is missing.

"Where's John?" I ask.

"He's here, but he's still back at the condo," Greg responds.

"Oh," I remark with a curious look, "Is he planning to meet up with you guys later?"

"No, John was feeling tired and a little run down, so he decided to stay in tonight."

"Bummer, I hope he will feel like skiing tomorrow. He won't want to miss the fresh powder we are going to get overnight. I think we are supposed to get several inches!" I announce with excitement.

"I'm sure he'll be fine, and he'll be out with us in the morning," Greg says with professional confidence accompanied with a wry smile.

The live music ends. Karley, Ellie, Amanda and I decide it's time to move on to Pepi's. Jill sent a text about a half hour ago saying she and Chris were having beers. When the four of us arrive at Pepi's, we see Jill and Chris sitting at a table with a few empty chairs. My girlfriends sit down and order some margaritas. Out of the corner of my eye, I see the group from Kentucky sitting at the long table against the wall, their usual spot. I skip over to say hello and ask them about their day of skiing. One of the Kentucky guys, Joe, shows me an app on his phone specifically designed for tracking your speed and distance. I freak the second I see the number on the screen! — "63!"

"Your top speed today was clocked at sixty-three miles per hour?" I ask in utter amazement. "Dude, thank goodness you didn't wipe out at that speed! Which run were you on?" I ask.

Joe flashes a cocky smile as he declares, "Blue Ox."

I look at Joe's phone one more time and then back at him, still shocked, and gush, "I am seriously impressed. I know I could never go that fast or have the guts to try. That speed is Lindsey Vonn territory!"

It is right about now that my toes start tapping as the sounds emanating from the one-man band become lively and energetic. I feel the urge to dance. "Single time swing" would fit the bill, so my search for a dance partner begins.

I get one "no" after another, but eventually one of the guys from Kentucky says, "I've always wanted to take dance lessons and learn how to partner dance. I don't know what I'm doing, but I'll give it a try."

Not wasting any time, I grab his hand and say, "I've been taking dance lessons for the past two years. I am no instructor, but I can show you a few 'single time swing' steps."

As the next two songs play, we do our best to stay on the beat. There is a lot of swaying back and forth along with stepping side to side, as I repeat the words, "Step, Step, Rock Step!" We have fun, but two songs are all we can manage. The crowded bar is difficult to navigate, giving us little space to move.

We end with a fist bump, a pair of smiles and agree, "That was a blast!"

Snaking our way through the sea of people, we briefly stop at the table with Jill, Chris, Amanda and Karley. We invite the four of them to move over to the "Kentucky Boys'" table against the wall. Eventually, everyone smashes into one big group and falls into the nightly ritual of socializing, imbibing, and nibbling. "Smashed in" is an understatement. The bars and restaurants in the heart of the village are always extra busy when the Burton snowboarders are in town.

As time goes on, you will learn the public health experts believe a large percentage of travelers who visited Vail in February and the first two weeks of March ended up contracting the novel coronavirus. We now hear so much information about exercising good hand hygiene — doesn't it make you cringe when you think about dancing hand in hand with someone, and then moments later your hand is full of tortilla chips as you sit happily munching away. Yeah, eating appetizers immediately after dancing is definitely not going to be something you will see people doing in the near future. I can safely make that prediction.

Chapter 4

Thursday, February 27th, I wake up once again drenched with sweat, so I toss the comforter off, allowing the volcanic level heat to escape. My body feels like it's on fire. "This is getting old," my brain laments. I stare at the ceiling, wondering why this has become a daily occurrence. "Maybe I should just skip the shower and jump into a snowbank?"

"Are you awake?" I whisper.

"Not really. What time is it?" Ellie mumbles with a froggy voice.

"I don't know, but I'm just roasting over here. Are you roasting?"

A few moments pass before Ellie responds. "No, I'm comfortable," she says, snuggling deeper into a cocoon of blankets.

"OK... Well, it must be me. I'm going to shower off this ridiculous amount of sweat."

"All right, wake me up when it's time for breakfast," she mumbles.

When I hop in the shower, a yawn comes over me. Breathing in the moist steam immediately plunges my lungs into a strange sensation. (Imagine — tiny fingers moving around at lightning speed creating an intense tickle, resulting in spastic, uncontrollable coughing.) Fortunately, the uncontrollable coughing subsides once I finish my shower.

I tiptoe over to Ellie, give her a gentle nudge on her shoulder, and let her know it's time for breakfast. "Meet me in the lounge when you are ready," I say, closing the door behind me.

The lounge of this charming hotel is as inviting as a friend's living room at their mountain cabin. The roaring fire, comfortable leather furniture and large picture windows overlooking snow-covered trees give you a warm fuzzy feeling, encouraging you to sit down and put your feet up. I choose one of the overstuffed chairs next to the fireplace, sip a cup of coffee, and check my text messages. I send Jill a message about her timing and ask her where she would like to meet this morning. Jill responds right away and says she may take the morning off and meet us at lunchtime. She says her stomach still doesn't feel well, and she needs to be close to a bathroom right now.

"Darn, I thought you were back to normal. I'm so sorry to hear you're not feeling well," I text back.

Jill assures me with some over-the-counter medicine, plenty of water and a little time for the medicine to kick in, she'll be just fine by lunch. I wish her luck and tell her to keep in touch so we can plan accordingly.

Approaching the breakfast buffet, I am met with a host of choices. I scoop a ladle full of oatmeal and load my bowl with walnuts, raisins, and berries. Just as I turn to walk back to my chair, Ellie arrives.

"Good morning again. I'm sitting by the fireplace," I say as I turn my head to cough.

"OK, I'll be right there. I'm going to grab a cup of coffee," Ellie responds.

Soon after, Ellie makes herself comfortable in a chair next to me. I tell her about Jill's text, and we get busy texting friends to see where they plan to start their day skiing. Ultimately, we make plans with Amanda to find some fresh powder in the trees from the overnight snowfall. Ellie knows the mountain like the back of her hand, so it's like skiing with a guide when you're with her. I feel fortunate to call her a friend, and I am thrilled she enjoys playing mountain tour guide.

We both eat a hearty breakfast as we relax in front of the fireplace. The food is delicious and healthy. I happily return to the buffet for a second helping of berries. As soon as we have satisfied our appetites, we walk over to Gondola One to meet Amanda.

Ellie's plan for finding virgin powder is successful. The pristine powder gives us a spectacular morning of skiing. The sensation of floating is joyous, and it's all captured on film thanks to Amanda's GoPro on top of her helmet. The noon hour approaches, and we learn from a string of text messages that a large group is meeting up in Blue Sky Basin at the Dawg Haus concession stand. Jill is included on the text string, so it appears she may have recovered. The moment she skis up to us, we inquire how she's feeling. Jill gives us the thumbs up and replies, "Much better, thanks."

At a much later date, research came out regarding digestive issues connected to the coronavirus. Medical experts determined a high viral load leads to digestive problems. If a person has a high viral load, does this makes them more contagious?

Data released on May 12, 2020:
The Lancet Gastroenterology & Hepatology **reported:**
https://www.thelancet.com/journals/langas/article/PII S2468-1253(20)30132-1/fulltext

Although respiratory tract manifestations are the most commonly reported symptoms in COVID-19, emerging data suggest that the gastrointestinal tract and liver might also be affected by SARS-CoV-2, on the basis that gastrointestinal epithelial cells and liver cells

express angiotensin-converting enzyme 2 (ACE2), the major receptor of SARS-CoV-2. We analyzed 204 patients with COVID-19 with full laboratory, imaging, and historical data and found that 103 patients (50%) reported digestive symptoms, such as lack of appetite (81 [79%] of 103), diarrhea (35 [34%]), vomiting (four [4%]), and abdominal pain (two [2%]). Although most patients presented with fever or respiratory symptoms, for six patients, only digestive symptoms were present during the whole course of disease.

Having read this research that was performed over the first few months during the outbreak of COVID-19 in the U.S. gives you an understanding about another symptom of which to be aware. Who would have thought Jill's stomach issues were caused by the same pathogen as my night sweats, chills, body aches, and dry cough? You can see how this virus may be spreading through different disguises.

Skiing in Blue Sky Basin all afternoon with a large group is a blast. One of the advantages of skiing with so many people is found on chairlift rides. Each time you head back up the mountain, you end up sitting next to someone different. Great conversations happen on these scenic rides, and this is where lasting friendships form. Each time I feel the dry tickling cough come on, I pull up my neck gator and try not to cough on my chairlift mate. During the brief time on a chairlift, noses get dabbed, Chapstick gets applied, and often a water bottle gets passed. The dry winter air gives many of us a parched feeling. It's usually my friends who carry water bottles in their backpacks or large jackets. I never fall into this category. However, I take a few swigs here and there when the bottle comes my way. Karley is one of those friends that always carries a backpack, and I remember sharing her water bottle more than once on the ski trip.

The lifts close early in Blue Sky Basin, so when 3:00 pm rolls around, our group begins skiing over to the front side of the mountain. I catch up to Jill while we slowly skate ski across flat terrain and ask how she's doing.

"Are you up for happy hour?" I ask.

"Absolutely, I'm looking forward to it, but I may just stick to water tonight to be on the safe side."

"Wise," I say.

The front side of Vail Mountain opens up into a maze of ski runs, some of which lead directly to the west end of the village, dumping you in front of a fun bar and restaurant by the name of Garfinkel's. This is a cornerstone bar in Lionshead at the furthest end of the ski resort. Garfinkel's large deck overlooking the ski runs is a lovely place to relax when you have a sunny day. The walls inside the restaurant are covered with photos of athletes and past events. A large cartoon moose greets you with a silly expression, and you instinctually know he is the mascot for this establishment which has been around since 1993. It's a popular place to end your ski day. Our large group filters in and bellies up to the bar, ordering pitchers of locally-brewed beer. Frosty glasses are filled to the brim, and we toast to a spectacular day.

Garfinkel's is one more establishment to add to the growing list where Jill and I are assisting the coronavirus in its inexorable march through this unsuspecting resort.

For me, happy hour ends after one beer and a lot of conversation about the morning's virgin powder. I am ready to make my way back to the hotel to get out of these ski clothes and into a hot shower. I catch Ellie's gaze and mouth the words, "Are you ready to go?" I get a nod back from her, we say our goodbyes, and we head out.

Back at the room, Ellie and I discuss dinner plans. We decide upon a restaurant in the basement of Vail's Mountain Haus Hotel, The George. I'm super excited about eating at The George this evening because for weeks after my return home from skiing, I dream about their shepherd's pie! Yes, it's true, I sometimes dream about food. You would, too, if you tasted this shepherd's pie. A hot steaming bowl of meat and vegetables blended with just the right amount of herbs and spices so as not to overwhelm the dish — all while bathing in au jus sauce and topped with a generous portion of creamy mashed potatoes. The food at The George is hearty and never disappoints. For me, it always hits the spot after a long day of skiing!

The hot shower is heavenly. I would prefer to take my time, but hunger pangs keep me moving at a swift pace. As we are about to leave, I reach for my perfume bottle out of habit. Spritzing a little on my wrists, I again realize I still cannot smell it. I am puzzled and disappointed, but tonight I decide to spray a couple of extra pumps onto my wrists. I think to myself. *Well, maybe I just need some extra since it's probably one of my older bottles?*

The George is an eclectic restaurant. It's known for having reasonable prices, a decent assortment of entrees, and a casual funky atmosphere. There are plenty of living room vignettes, booths, a few pool tables, and a long bar. As we walk in, we see Chris, Karley, and

Amanda in a booth. Our server greets us right away, takes our drink order and gives us menus with the "Everything is Half Price" spiel. (We already knew this fantastic fact! Everything is always half price at The George until 9:00 p.m.)

We begin our conversation about tomorrow — what do we want our day to look like? During a break in the conversation, I look at Chris seated next to me and say, "Hey, can I ask a favor?"

"It depends upon what it is," he quips.

"Cute!" I reply, smirking. Then immediately stick my wrist in his face. "Can you smell my perfume?"

If you could see Chris's face at this moment, you would think I just placed smelling salts under his nose to revive him. Poor guy, he can't pull his nose away from me fast enough!

"Yeah, I can definitely smell your perfume — there's no mistaking it. Why?" Chris asks as he lets out a slight cough through heavily exhaled words.

I look at him, head cocked to the side, puzzled, "This is just so strange; I can't smell my perfume! I wonder if I'm getting a sinus infection. The only time I can ever remember not being able to smell is when I've had a sinus infection."

During this weird exchange with Chis, the server arrives with our drinks. After a toast, we turn our attention to our first sips, and the perfume incident is quickly forgotten. The conversation at the table then moves to the precipitous drop of the stock market over the last several days.

Looking back, you have to wonder why Ellie said nothing to me about the pungent perfume fragrance. Getting ready in the room with me, she never said a word about my perfume smelling strong, spritz after spritz after

41

spritz! Most likely she didn't notice the strong fragrance because she was losing her sense of smell or had already lost it. The circle of friends is widening with infection, but none of us has a clue!

As we tried to make sense of the recent stock market plunge, look at what was being reported in the news on Monday February 25th:

Nasdaq.com:
https://www.nasdaq.com/articles/stock-market-news-for-feb-25-2020-2020-02-25

Wall Street routed on Monday following the severity of coronavirus outbreak across the globe. As much as 30 countries beside China are now affected by the COVID-19 illness and the number is growing day by day. Investors remained highly concerned about global economic growth. The three major stock indexes plunged as a result of the growing movement of funds from risky equities to safe-haven assets.

The Dow Jones Industrial Average (DJI) tumbled 3.6% or 1,031.61 points to close at 27,912.44. The S&P 500 tanked 3.4% or 111.86 points to close at 3,225.89. Meanwhile, the Nasdaq Composite Index closed at 9,221.28, plummeting 3.7% or 355.31 points.

The Dow closed in negative territory with all 30 components of the index closing in the red. Point wise, yesterday's drop was the third largest in its history and highest in more than two years.

42

For the first time since Dec 4, 2018, all three major stock indexes witnessed a single-day drop of 3% or more.

We finish our meals, and even though nothing I put in my mouth tastes right, my stomach is no longer begging me for nourishment. We have a great time at dinner, but we are all a little concerned about the abrupt drop in the stock market. We mention the fears surrounding a global pandemic, but again we believe this pandemic is happening everywhere except the U.S. No one at the table is following much in the news regarding what is being reported from South Korea, China, and Italy.

If only we understood what was happening in these other countries was also happening right here at this dinner table. If only we knew most everyone walking around Vail Village was infected.

Dinner draws to a close, and we move to the back of the restaurant, looking to snag a pool table. Amanda pulls me aside, informing me she has an upset stomach. I tell her I have some antacids in my purse and ask if she would like a few. She takes me up on my offer and excuses herself to the restroom. The rest of our group gets a pool table, and the balls are cued up.

"I'm going to head back to my condo and lay down for a bit. My stomach is cramping. Let me know where you end up later this evening, and maybe I'll join you," Amanda says.

"I'm sorry your stomach doesn't feel well. Is there anything I can do for you?"

"No, but thanks," she says.

Our group of seven plays pool for the next hour. We take turns and laugh each time I scratch. I like pool, but I've never been good at it — despite playing countless hours as a teenager. When everyone has enough turns with a pool cue, a unanimous decision is made to check out the music at Bridge Street Bar. Approaching the bar, we can see there is a line out the door. I look at Ellie and ask, "Do you want to wait in this line?"

Ellie shrugs her shoulders and gives me a "whatever" look. I take this, coupled with the shrug, as a yes!

The cold doesn't dissuade us thanks to the exit of a large group moments after we join the line. Once we get down the stairs and into the bar, we see a group of people we know from New York. The place is wall-to-wall people. It takes some maneuvering to work our way to the New Yorkers, but eventually we make it. Unfortunately, the music is so loud we all have to lean in and shout directly into someone's ear when having a conversation.

Bridge Street Bar has two sections. The first section you enter once down the stairs is the main section, which usually features live music. The second section, separated by soundproof doors, usually plays club music, hosted by a DJ. I enjoy both styles, so I break away from the group to check out the DJ. The music is great, and there is plenty of room – only a handful of "twenty-somethings" on the dance floor. I return to the group and let them know it's not crowded in the other bar.

"I'll go," Ellie says as she grabs a water to take with her.

A few moments later, Ellie and I are dancing freestyle in the middle of girls, half our age, having a great time. A couple of songs into dancing, I notice one of the girls leading her friend in a series of turns. It resembles a

44

cross between a "hustle" and a "single time swing" dance. (I am literally in heaven right now because if I can't ski down a mountain, then I love nothing more than to dance!) When the girls finish dancing together, I approach the one that appeared to be leading and compliment her. She says she knows a little swing, and that's what she was leading. I lean in close to her ear and tell her I have been taking partnership dance lessons for about two years and ask if she wants to try leading me. Before I can blink, the two of us are on the dance floor, and she's turning me, spinning me, and throwing me into a dip. It feels like I've just been on a merry-go-round by the end of the song! (At times like this, I feel like a kid again. Oh… to be that young and carefree!)

Breathing heavily from dancing, sharing pool cues, shouting into someone's ear, and dancing hand in hand. Each one is an excellent conduit for this stealthy virus. The numbers around the world are growing exponentially as each day passes on my vacation. I cannot say with certainty that I was spreading the coronavirus during this evening in the village, but I am symptomatic. We now know this virus spreads easily through respiratory droplets and manifests itself through many different symptoms. Sadly, we also know millennials can often be asymptomatic.

Chapter 5

I wake up to a picturesque ski day — sunshine, mild temperatures, and a dusting of snow. It's Friday, February 28th, and my vacation days are dwindling. Today, Amanda and I decide it will be fun to convince the Ohio ER doctors to ski the back side of the mountain in the late afternoon down to the Minturn Saloon. We plan to connect with the doctors after breakfast. Last year we skied to the saloon with these guys, and although it's extremely challenging, it was a blast. This is not something you want to try on your own. When skiing out of bounds (referred to as "off-piste"), one has to be mindful of what might lurk just under the surface of the snow. Skiing with people who "know the way" is essential! There are no signs, markers, or trails to guide you. If you are lucky, you will find ski tracks from previous skiers who have blazed a trail. At least… you hope there will be ski tracks once you get out there.

The Minturn Mile
www.minturnsaloon.com

> **The Minturn Mile is one of the most famous "off-piste" or "out-of-bounds" ski runs in the world. It is accessed from the top of chairs 3 or 7 on Vail Mountain and then by taking the out-of-bounds access gate at the top of the turn on the "Lost Boy" trail. An ability level of upper intermediate or better is suggested to enjoy the experience. The Minturn Mile is made up of varying terrain, beginning with**

46

bowl type terrain before proceeding into the trees. Midway down, one will get to the "beaver ponds" where many people enjoy a break before heading on. The lower portion is affectionately known as "the luge". It is essentially an old jeep road/game trail, so it is fairly narrow in spots.

It is important to know that if you come down the Minturn Mile that you have left Vail Mountain and are in terrain that is not patrolled. If you have an accident, you are on your own. Any safety rescue may result in financial charges for the person(s) being rescued. *__The Minturn Saloon does not encourage anyone to ski the Minturn Mile without full knowledge of the terrain and snow conditions as well as the responsibility and skills needed for "out-of-bounds" skiing.__* Anyone skiing or boarding the Minturn Mile should be prepared with the proper equipment, tools and accessories that one would take for backcountry skiing. You may unintentionally spend more time out there than you planned on! That being said, it is a great run and a wonderful experience best done with friends and ending at the Minturn Saloon for refreshments.

So, there you have it, a blurb about the Minturn Mile taken directly from the Minturn Saloon website. There is something very adventurous about leaving the boundaries of Vail property to ski through backcountry. The reward for your physically demanding effort is

47

bragging rights coupled with legendary margaritas and the best house made salsa and tortilla chips you will ever taste.

Ellie and I talk about the possibility of skiing the Minturn Mile over breakfast. I invite her to walk over to Amanda and Karley's condo with me after breakfast to help formulate a plan. Ellie makes no bones about her lack of interest in skiing out of bounds, but she is happy to tag along for a visit.

"Are you sure you don't want to ski the Minturn Mile?" I plead.

"Yes, it's not my thing," Ellie says with conviction.

"OK, well we aren't starting until late afternoon — so if you change your mind, let me know."

"Thanks, but I'm happy to ski with you and whoever else joins us today — in bounds!"

I start a texting chain with multiple friends, suggesting they consider skiing the Minturn Mile towards the end of the day. My suggestion gains traction, and before I know it, Ellie and I are walking over to the condo to plot our ski day with Karley and Amanda.

"Good morning, ladies! It's a beautiful day to ski Minturn!" I say, hands extended, knees bent, sounding out a swish and swoosh.

"Yes, it is!" Amanda laughs at my antics.

"Karley, are you in?" I ask.

"No, Ellie and I talked yesterday about going shopping together in the afternoon," Karley answers.

"Oh, yeah. I forgot about that. We talked about going to Gorsuch to look at ski sweaters," Ellie chimes in.

I spend the next few minutes trying to convince Karley to join us and entice Ellie to do the same. My persuasive skills are obviously rusty because Karley and Ellie are sticking to their plan.

Amanda and I move forward with our own plan. A few text messages are sent, and when the gondola starts running at 8:30 a.m., we meet up with four of the ER doctors. As we gather, ideas fly! We talk about the best time to start our adventure and the most convenient place to meet.

"OK, it's a game plan! Three o'clock at the top of Game Creek Bowl chairlift," I announce with a hand up ready for someone to high five me.

Amanda and I join the long, orderly gondola line to be escorted into a cab for a glorious start to our day. The ER doctors stay behind, waiting for several friends to join them.

My dry cough continues to annoy me. Fortunately, it is most troublesome when I wake up. Once I get moving and breathe in the steam from a shower, the tightness lessens. Besides, I have accepted the reality that deep breaths are not at my disposal for "whatever reason." I put it out of my mind and resolve to have fun skiing.

"I'm so excited the ER doctors are game to ski the Minturn Mile again this year! We need to eat a hearty lunch because we're going to need fuel. Today is going to be *beyond* challenging," I posit.

Amanda nods in agreement, and I'm thinking to myself, *I sure hope my lungs can keep up.*

"By the way, how is your stomach feeling this morning? It's too bad you had to call it a night right after dinner," I say with concern.

"Whatever was bugging me last night is gone. I feel fine today," she says.

"Thank goodness you're feeling better. I wonder if you had the same thing that Jill has been dealing with?"

"I don't know, but I'm glad I stayed in for the rest of the night. I needed a good night's sleep. I haven't felt that exhausted since my days in medical school," she responds.

A few texts scroll across my phone, giving me the time and place to meet up with Karley and Ellie. A text from Chris chimes in simultaneously, asking about the plans for the day. Responding back, I tell Chris to find us at Mid-Vail Restaurant at ten o'clock.

"We need to meet them at Mid-Vail Restaurant at ten o'clock for a cup of hot cocoa," I say, while reading the text.

"All right. Hot cocoa sounds good — about now — actually. But I can wait," Amanda says with a chuckle.

The gondola doors slide open, and we promptly ski over to the Mountain Top Express chairlift for the next ride up. (Getting to the top of the mountain in the morning takes a while.) Once at the top, we are met with a host of options for runs funneling down to Mid-Vail Restaurant. We take advantage of the time we have, carving across perfectly packed runs and promptly arrive at the restaurant at 10:00 a.m. Karley and Ellie walk in just moments later, ready for a cup of hot cocoa, and I tell them to be on the lookout for Chris; he's joining us today.

"Great! Is Jill coming too?" Karley asks while taking off her jacket.

"No, Jill is skiing with the Chicago group today."

Ellie offers to get drinks while the three of us shed our coats. I keep an eye out for Chris, glancing periodically at the entrance. Ellie soon returns with four cups of steaming hot cocoa topped with whip cream.

While we sip and chat, I spot Chris walking in, swiveling his head looking for us. Standing up, I wave to catch Chris' attention.

"Hey, you found us!" I say when Chris reaches the table.

"Yes, thanks for the speedy reply this morning about your plans. The timing was perfect," Chris replies.

"Pull up a seat. Do you have any ideas about where you want to ski this morning?"

"Nope, I'm along for the ride," Chris says with a boyish grin.

The five of us hang out tossing ideas around. No one seems to have an agenda as the conversation flows, diverting occasionally to the upcoming Minturn Mile run later today.

"We have so many options. Which chairlift do you want to take to the top? I personally wouldn't mind skiing over to Northwoods. There are several runs over there that would be good this morning," I say, hoping they like my suggestion.

All four of them agree Northwoods sounds terrific. We sip the last of our hot cocoa, pull ourselves together and leave the restaurant bound for the Mountain Top Express chairlift.

The five of us ski nonstop for the remainder of the morning, eat lunch at Two Elk Restaurant, and run into friends. The "New York guys" join our table, and we talk about tackling the Minturn Mile. These guys ski Vail every year and rarely let a year pass without skiing to the Minturn Saloon. We ask them if they would like to join us this afternoon, but they decline. They are connecting with family who arrive later today. I make a joke about Pat's attire, telling him he would be easy to follow down the mountain if we had a snowstorm. The neon colors in his outfit (resembling a combination of peas and carrots) would act as a beacon. The green pants evoke peas and the orange jacket evokes carrots. I decide to give Pat a new nickname: "Peas and Carrots." As I make the announcement, we all start laughing. My laughs bring on a coughing fit, so I turn my head and use my elbow as a shield.

After lunch, we have a couple of hours to ski, so we head out with the New York guys. We take it easy skiing a few groomed intermediate (blue) runs before the guys take off to meet up with family. The rendezvous time with the ER doctors is fast approaching, so we finish up our last run in Game Creek Bowl and say goodbye to Karley and Ellie.

"Have fun skiing to the saloon you guys," Ellie says as she adjusts the strap on her helmet.

"Yes, have fun, but don't get hurt!" Karley scolds, sounding like a quintessential mom.

The three of us give Karley a reassuring gesture and acknowledgement while preparing to make our way to the meeting spot. Our sizeable group converges, and we do a headcount to make sure we know exactly how many people to keep track of as we head "out of bounds." We ski to the fence plastered with signs warning us about exiting this area. There is a passageway in the fence, but it clearly states the fence is the Vail property line. The official sign bearing a "skull and crossbones" screams: "YOU ARE LEAVING THE SKI AREA BOUNDARY. NOT PATROLLED OR MAINTAINED BEYOND THIS POINT. AVALANCHE DANGER! YOU ARE RESPONSIBLE FOR YOUR OWN SAFETY AND SURVIVAL."

It's a little intimidating to be face-to-face with a red stop sign adorned with a skull and crossbones! But there is safety in numbers! That's my rationale — and I am sticking with it! We take a few pictures with the signage and ski past the warning signs. The snow has been good this year, giving us a thick base to ski on as we tackle the first section. Without a good base and plenty of fresh snow, trying to ski this terrain would be impossible.

I take a tumble not long after we finish the first section. While trying to make a sharp turn, I pop a ski sending me "ass over teakettle," my loose ski shooting down the mountain at full speed. Thank goodness John caught sight of my fall out of the corner of his eye. He happened to be in the right place at the right time, grabbing my ski as it zipped by him. His quick thinking saves me from the chore of figuring out how to ski down on one ski. (Not that I could have figured that out!) I start laughing and coughing at the same time while I lay submerged in the deep snow. *What am I going to do now?* I think to myself. There is no way I can attempt one-legged skiing over to John! I will have to slide down to him. I struggle in the deep snow to release my boot from the binding. After several attempts, I finally pop the ski off. Cradling the lone ski in the crook of my arm, I slide down the mountain on my derrière towards John. Digging myself out of the snow, releasing the ski, and righting myself takes an enormous amount of effort. I am huffing, puffing, and coughing as if I were a chain smoker. The inability to inhale fully is taking its toll.

I finally make it down to John. He offers his shoulder to me for balance while I attempt to get my skis on. For the next five minutes, the process to snap on skis looks like this: balancing while pressing on John's shoulder, scraping snow off the bottom of the boot, aligning the ski with the boot, slipping — plunging my boot back into the snow, and starting over again. Repeated tries eventually are met with success. I feel a sense of victory when I hear the snap of the second boot clicking into the binding. *Jeez, this is exhausting! I need to make sure I don't fall again!* I think to myself. The group is scattered nearby taking a breather as they wait for me, and I couldn't be more thankful.

"Thanks everyone, I'm back in business. I'm ready when you are!" I holler.

As we continue down the mountain, most of us are thrilled when we get to the skinny section of the run — the "luge." However, there are a few in the group who would prefer the steep bowl over the luge. Amanda narrates as her GoPro captures the craziness of skiing single file on the well-worn trail. At one point, I come down around a bend and run right into her! I straddle my skis to the outside of hers and wrap my arms around her waist, making sure not to poke her with my poles. We both let out a shriek and then break into a huge belly laugh. Luckily, I am not going very fast, so we don't tip over.

I think most of us in this group are definitely pushing the "outer limits" of our endurance. Each of us has already skied a full day. I can tell you I am definitely pushing my outer limits.

At one point, I realize I am going a little too fast on this winding, undulating, skinny trail. There is nothing to prevent me from slipping off the edge into the cavernous ravine littered with trees below. I quickly surmise if I don't get my speed under control, I am going over the edge. Fortunately, I make a split-second decision to force a hockey stop and turn myself sideways, screeching my skis to an abrupt halt. With my skis hanging off the lip, I stare down into the ravine. Chris is close behind watching this unfold, and he quickly springs into action with a calm, controlled voice guiding me to safety.

"Take a breath and take your time backing yourself off the ledge," he says, calm as a cucumber.

Another example of a friend — in the right place — at the right time. — I was right about there being "safety in numbers!"

Remembering the Minturn Mile and reflecting upon the amount of effort it took, I can't believe I could ski so many hours that day. When I think about how difficult it was to catch my breath and regain my composure, I have to believe the virus inside my lungs was multiplying at a frantic pace.

The entire trip down the back side of Vail Mountain to the Minturn Saloon takes us about an hour and a half. It's a sunny, warm, beautiful day, just above freezing. The snow is soft and forgiving. All of us have unzipped our jackets and removed our fuzzy gators by the time we arrive at the halfway point. Sweat drips down our backs, forcing us to untuck our base layers. When a residential neighborhood is in sight, the end is near. The last portion of the adventure ends with skiing behind a few homes onto a flat road. At this point, flat ground is a welcome sight. We all take our skis off, perch them on our shoulders, and begin the half-mile walk. The arrival at the Minturn Saloon has us wondering if we have arrived at a ski shop instead of a bar. There are skis everywhere! Rows and rows of skis wrap the building.

I look at Amanda and declare, "We made it, thank the Lord! Is your stomach still feeling OK?"

"Yes, I'm definitely ready for a Margarita!"

Entering the Minturn Saloon is like walking into a time warp. It's been around since 1876 as the Minturn Saloon and as a restaurant establishment since 1901. Taking in all the memorabilia on the walls is like strolling through a museum, as you see the famous, near famous, and local heroes who have frequented the saloon over the decades. The perusing could eat up hours of your time if you so choose. Past Presidents have dined here, and ski enthusiasts take the advice of popular magazines to experience the saloon. The restaurant has been named by *Men's Journal* as one of the "Best Après-ski Bars in the World" and *Esquire Magazine* has included the Minturn Saloon in their "Best Bars in America" list every year since 2007. When *Outside Magazine* created their "Ultimate Winter Bucket List," they listed coming down the Minturn Mile to the Minturn Saloon as one of their

56

"32 must do items." Surely you can understand its attraction when you have perfect conditions — like today's blue skies, warm temperatures, and fresh snow.

We make our way into the bar and stake out a corner near the fireplace. I immediately find John and thank him for helping me with my skis after my epic ass over teakettle, cartwheel, yardsale wipeout. I told him he was missed the other night for happy hour.

"I heard you weren't feeling well?" I inquired.

"Yeah, I was feeling run down. I didn't think I should push it since I was just getting started with my vacation."

"I don't blame you."

The carafes of infamous margaritas complete with salt-rimmed glasses and freshly-cut lime wedges arrive along with baskets of chips and bowls of the famous house-made salsa. I make a concerted effort to finish a big glass of water before I partake in my libation. The nine of us are milling and having a great time in the cozy corner while the crackling fire warms us. It feels good to sit. Taking in the simple pleasure of a bar stool after a long day of skiing is glorious.

I strike up a conversation with Dave about his day-to-day in the ER. He describes a strange situation that took place in the hospital the week prior. Pulling up a picture on his phone, he hands it to me for a closer look.

"Look at this hazmat outfit — 'a spacesuit' I was required to wear in order to treat one patient. The hospital was concerned about my patient having this new COVID-19 virus," he explains with a big smile, raised eyebrows and his free hand waving through the air as if it was a puppet putting on a show.

He educates me about the extra time it took him and the nurse to get suited up in the special gowns and headgear or Personal Protective Equipment (PPE). He explains the strict protocols enforced before entering or exiting an examination room and ends the conversation with, "After all that — the patient ends up having strep throat!" he chuckles, shaking his head. "I sure hope this is not my new normal."

If only we knew what was happening right then, right there, while sipping margaritas. Clearly from this event just a week earlier, some, if not all, hospitals in the U.S. were beginning to pay attention to the information about COVID-19. If you are doing some mental tracking about who in this group at the Minturn Saloon is showing symptoms and could be infectious, I can confirm that it is at least me, Amanda, and John.

When the carafes are empty, we consume the last few sips of our margaritas and say goodbye to the famous saloon. We all slip on our jackets and wait outside for the town bus to drive us back to Vail Village. The bus is empty when it shows up, so we spread out with each of us taking a bench. Along the way, we pick up a few riders and, wouldn't you know, one of them sits next to me! I make small talk during the bumpy ride back to the village and find out this pleasant young man works at one of the restaurants in Vail. I comment about his shift starting late, and he explains they called him in last minute to fill in for another employee who went home sick.

Well, what do you think? Did the employee who went home sick at this restaurant have the virus? Will this young man end up contracting the virus from me? As I sit next to him and chat, periodically I turn my head and cough into my elbow.

The bus pulls into the transportation center in Vail. We grab our skis and start making our way through the village back to our respective hotels and condos. A few people in the group recognize friends through the large picture windows at Pepi's and decide to pop in. Determined to take a hot shower, I decline when asked to make this pit stop. My extreme exhaustion becomes apparent once I enter the warm, quiet hotel room. My tired, overtaxed body urges me to lie down, and I immediately acquiesce, flopping onto the bed. Lying quietly for a few minutes... I suddenly remember a yoga pose on your back with legs up the wall. *The pose (actually referred to as legs up the wall) will rejuvenate me!* I think to myself. A yoga instructor once told me that relaxing into this pose for fifteen minutes is like giving your body a two-hour power nap. *Boy, if this yoga instructor is right that will be great! I desperately need a two-hour nap!* My mind tells me.

I crawl down onto the carpet, scooting my butt up to the base of the wall. I straighten my legs upward with my feet stretching for the ceiling. The feeling of relaxation is immediate. Staring at the ceiling, my thoughts float towards sleep. *Sleep could ensue at any moment, but I also feel like devouring a hamburger — or any red meat, for that matter.* I keep my legs up for at least fifteen minutes, but I don't fall asleep. My stomach is churning — I am starving. I slowly stand up, taking my time to regain my balance and step into a steaming shower. While getting ready for the evening, I text with friends and my roommate Ellie to see what has been planned. They suggest the bar at The George Restaurant for our starting point. Once again, I spray some perfume on my wrists, befuddled that I still can't smell it. The good news is my eyes are no longer bloodshot, so I walk out the door on that positive note.

Entering the restaurant, I scan the bar for my friends. It's busy tonight. I spot Ellie and a few others from our group standing at the end of the bar. When I walk up, they are talking about the day and discussing where we should go for dinner.

"Hey, you made it! How are you? Do you want a beer?" Ellie says in rapid succession.

"Sure, thanks," I reply.

We try to be unobtrusive and polite as we reach in between people seated at the bar to grab our beers from the bartender, but there are a lot of, "excuse me, pardon me, and excuse my reach" comments. I strike up a conversation with one couple about their delicious looking appetizer. We have a back-and-forth comparison about our favorite dishes. We share a little about where we live and talk a bit about the Minturn Mile. Friendly and social is what you will always find with people you encounter in Vail.

Unfortunately, for this couple, my friendly conversation with them may have been more than just friendly conversation. It may have been another infection waiting to blossom.

While I am having a side conversation, my friends decide upon the restaurant, Sweet Basil.

"Wow! Did somebody get a reservation?" I question.

The resounding answer is "No!"

"We are going to take our chances and try to get seats at the bar and punt if that doesn't work out," Ellie says optimistically.

"OK, I'm game for this gamble," I say with a smirk, skeptical this will not end in a punt!

It's a short walk over to the restaurant. The hostess greets us with an inviting smile and an encouraging prediction.

"If you are willing to wait, I think enough bar stools may open up for all of you in the next thirty minutes. I would be happy to take a drink order for you," she says as she looks over at the bartender.

We decide to wait and take advantage of the hostess' hospitality. We enjoy a glass of wine standing off to the side of the bar, and within fifteen minutes, the prediction comes true. I am thrilled to be proven wrong. By now all of us are famished, and we waste no time deciding which appetizers to order. When the first appetizer arrives, I take a bite and notice it is surprisingly bland. I am studying the ingredients in the dish and spot a few green olives. I look over at Ellie to see if she has tried it.

"Do these green olives taste funny to you?" I ask.

"I don't think so, but I'm happy to take another bite for inspection," Ellie says just before the fork enters her mouth.

I heap another generous portion onto my plate as I study Ellie's face looking for a clue to answer my question.

"Nope, these green olives taste just fine to me," Ellie says as she finishes chewing.

"OK," I respond, feeling tired and strange.

I stab an olive and pop it into my mouth. Focused on chewing, I realize I can't taste it. What I am really experiencing on my tongue is a metallic taste. Imagine sucking on a penny — that's what this olive tastes like.

My stomach takes over for my brain as my voracious appetite enjoys the next helping, regardless of what my tastebuds are saying at this moment.

A month later, at home in Minnesota, reading about this pandemic, I learn about anosmia. Losing one's sense of smell may cause a perceived lack of taste.

Further reports indicated a link between COVID-19 and a metallic taste. The article conjures up memories from my ski trip. Specifically, "sucking on a penny" while eating at Sweet Basil. I always thought the inability to taste green olives was so strange because green olives have such a pungent flavor. Who knew this would become a key indicator symptom to help determine the likelihood that someone is positive with the coronavirus?

Reported by The New York Times on March 22, 2020:
https://www.nytimes.com/2020/03/22/health/coronavirus-symptoms-smell-taste.html

Lost Sense of Smell May Be Peculiar Clue to Coronavirus Infection
The American Academy of Otolaryngology on Sunday posted information on its website saying that mounting anecdotal evidence indicates that lost or reduced sense of smell and loss of taste are significant symptoms associated with COVID-19, and that they have been seen in patients who ultimately tested positive with no other symptoms.

Dr. Rachel Kaye, an assistant professor of otolaryngology at Rutgers, said colleagues in New Rochelle, N.Y., which has been the center of an outbreak, first alerted her to the smell loss associated with the coronavirus, sharing that patients who had first complained of anosmia later tested positive for the coronavirus. "This raised a lot of alarms for me personally," Dr. Kaye said,

because those patients "won't know to self quarantine."

Did the Chinese know about anosmia having a connection to COVID-19? Who was the first person to make this connection? Did the Chinese know about the myriad of different symptoms in January, February or possibly earlier? Did our government work with the Chinese to understand everything they knew about symptoms? During these early days in 2020, how many people at the Centers for Disease Control and Prevention (CDC) were working with health experts around the globe gathering data on COVID-19 symptoms? In hindsight, if they had released public service announcements the moment symptoms were understood, could the spread of the virus have taken a different path? Was this a possibility? I can't answer that question. I can only ponder it after the fact.

When our appetites are satiated, my friends are ready to go dancing at the Shakedown Bar. I never have to be coerced into going dancing, so at the first mention, I am raring to go.

"Friday night — it's going to be packed, so be prepared," I announce, warning my friends.

"Who cares! This is my last night in Vail, and I'm ready to dance!" Karley exclaims.

"I second that!" Amanda says.

When bending the corner — we see 20 people standing at the entrance.

Thankfully, the line is moving, so we are hopeful it won't take too long to get in. Everyone is excited to hear Scott Rednor, Shakedown's co-owner, a very talented singer, songwriter, and guitarist. Scott has toured with the Dave Matthews Band, Blues Traveler and Lenny Kravitz, among others. The Shakedown is an intimate underground space with rustic wood finishes, a large dance floor, and a world class sound system. When we finally make it to the bottom of the staircase, we know we got lucky. It looks like it's close to capacity. A sea of bodies bobbing and swaying, completely mesmerized by the sounds of a guitar solo. Scott is in his zone jamming with his eyes closed and his fingers flying along the neck of the guitar. The brief wait and $20 cover charge are worth it. We squeeze our way through the crowd and onto the dance floor, working our way as close to the stage as possible. The four of us dance and fall in sync with the crowd. What a way to end an epic ski day! After a while, I break away from my girlfriends and look for a place to sit down. I make out a few barstools along the wall near the stage, and I am hopeful with some hovering in the vicinity, eventually someone will vacate a stool. It only takes a few minutes, and my hovering pays off. A kind gentleman with a ten-gallon hat stands up and motions for me to take his stool. This guy is quite the character. No one else is wearing a cowboy hat, much less one adorned with feathers running along the side. I thank him as I stare at his hat. The moment I sit, I offer my thanks again, telling him my "derrière" thanks him more. He laughs with a huge smile and glowing white teeth, courtesy of the black lights shining down. He asks me if I am alone, and I answer him, "My girlfriends are dancing, but I need a break. I'm exhausted. These old legs of mine are aching," I tell him, rubbing the tops of my thighs.

"Long ski day," he replies with those distracting glowing teeth.

"Yes, a full day plus the Minturn Mile," I brag, practically screaming over the decibels pulsing through the bar.

"Well, I can see why your legs are aching," he says with wide eyes.

Sitting on this stool gives me a bird's-eye view of the musicians in action. Every bit of me is grateful to be sitting. I take in the jam fest on stage for a few more songs before Scott announces the band is going to take a short break. Within moments, my girlfriends find me, and the four of us chat about the fantastic music and the crazy number of people packed into this place.

We are enjoying our last night out together to the fullest; however, none of us is grasping what we will be taking home with us from Vail. A souvenir not available for purchase in any of the gift shops.

Chapter 6

Dry pajamas! *Whatever was causing my night sweats and chills is finally gone!* At least, I think so, reaching for my iPhone to silence the alarm on Saturday morning, February 29th. If I am waking up to an alarm, it means I slept "hard." I quickly and quietly get dressed to avoid waking Ellie, slipping out the door to walk over to Karley and Amanda's condo. They have a long day of travel ahead, and I want to say goodbye. The moment I leave the hotel, my lungs now have their typical response to my first breath of the cold mountain air — constriction. Imagine someone cranking down on a vice grip. This is what it feels like in the depths of my lungs. "The depths" of my lungs should expand with air — but instead my breath is cut short with spastic coughs. I expect it. It's now a normal part of my daily routine. At this point in my vacation, I believe it's just a chest cold, and I hope each day is the last day it's with me. *The night sweats and chills are now gone, so isn't it reasonable to think the cough will soon disappear?*

It's a short walk over to the condo. Amanda answers the door at the first rap.

"Come on in. I'm eating what's left over in the refrigerator for breakfast."

I sit down on a stool at the bar in the kitchen and watch Amanda pull out fruit and cold pizza. Karley walks in — looking as if she didn't sleep a wink, donning "scary raccoon eyes" — (obviously because she didn't remove her eye makeup before bed.) Karley reaches for the coffeepot as she mumbles good morning.

When she turns toward me and offers a mug filled to the brim, sarcastically I poke, "I'm not sure I should drink your coffee."

"Why not?" Karley asks, holding the mug with lips pursed and a furrowed brow.

"The way you are looking this morning — honey — I believe you might need the entire pot for yourself," I quip with a wry smirk.

"Thanks a lot!" Karley retaliates, placing a hand on her hip.

The three of us roar with laughter! Soon we're recounting the entire week of vacation — wishing it wasn't over.

"We had another year of terrific skiing, wonderful weather, plenty of snow, no injuries, and all the same fun people as last year. I'm going to miss the two of you."

Both of them chime in, "Awwww, we're going to miss you too."

Karley offers the last of the raspberries with a smile, and I try to focus on her smile and not her raccoon eyes.

"We have to put a date on the calendar for a summer rendezvous this year," Karley says with certainty.

The three of us happily spend a few minutes munching on the raspberries as we talk about our possibilities. Amanda chimes in and asks me if I would help her carry the leftover food and bottles of wine to the ER doctor's condo across the street.

"Absolutely! Happy to help," I reply.

Karley thanks me profusely and tells me the last thing she wants to do right now is change out of her pajamas and carry food up a flight of stairs. She is definitely not feeling well and needs to be close to a bathroom.

"Oh, I remember Jill had this bug a couple of days ago. I thought for sure I escaped getting it, but at least I won't lose a ski day over it," Karley responds with a raspy, froggy voice.

"True, but traveling in a shuttle van to the airport may be challenging if you need to have a bathroom nearby," I reply.

Karley grimaces, lets out a sigh, and excuses herself. Amanda and I finish packing up the food and wine as we continue our conversation about the fun we had all week. With grocery bags in our arms, we walk across the street. Our delivery timing is good. We catch the guys just as they are about to walk out the door to start their ski day. They give many thanks along with farewell hugs to Amanda.

"Until next year," the guys say.

Amanda and I walk back to her condo, and I ask if she needs help with any last-minute packing.

"No, I'm almost finished, and then I'll probably help Karley with what she needs. I appreciate it though."

I say my goodbyes, give her a big hug, and tell her I'm going to knock on the bedroom door to say farewell to Karley.

With a tap on the door, I ask, "May I come in?"

"I'm in the tub, but come on in."

I crack open the door and tell her, "I just wanted to say goodbye and tell you that I hope you feel better soon. I'm headed out to ski with Jill and Ellie."

"Thanks. Wish me luck on the shuttle ride to Denver. I'll be in touch."

The tentacles of this virus just got longer. Most likely already contagious, Karley and Amanda are getting ready to take a two-hour shuttle van ride to the airport and then board a two-and-a-half-hour flight to Detroit. The ten people who share the shuttle ride with the two of them may end up unwittingly getting more than just a ride to the airport.

I am leaving for home tomorrow afternoon, so before I hit the slopes today, I want to figure out how to get in a little more skiing tomorrow. I am curious about storing my luggage so I can squeeze in a half day of skiing prior to my shuttle van ride to the airport. Every day the same woman is sitting at the front desk of the hotel, taking care of anything and everything that pertains to customer service. This is my first time staying at the Christiania Lodge, and it has proven to be a superb choice. I have loved the convenient location, excellent customer service, and delicious, healthy breakfast served daily. I inquire about storing my luggage for a few hours tomorrow morning. The kind, helpful employee gets up from behind the desk, opens a door to a nearby office, and shows me the space. The two of us end up having a delightful conversation for a few minutes about how happy I am that I could book a room here this year. Always in high demand, this hotel rarely has a vacancy for nine nights in a row. I compliment her for all she has done over the past eight days to make my stay feel so welcoming. I remind her about an earlier debacle with locking my key in the room, and a sweet smile flashes across her face as she explains, "That's what I'm here for."

I stop by the breakfast lounge to pick up coffees before going back to the room. I am hoping to find Ellie awake and ready to attack the mountain since it will be our last full day of skiing. Entering the room, I am pleasantly surprised to see Ellie dressed and almost ready for the day.

"Hey, good morning! It's another beautiful day out there!" I exclaim.

"Oh, good to hear! Did you say goodbye to Karley and Amanda this morning?" Ellie inquires.

"I did, and it was sad to see them go. I must say, I'm thrilled we have another day to ski together. Oh, and, by the way, Jill and her friends from Chicago are going to hook up with us."

"Awesome," Ellie says with a smile.

"I'll be ready to go in a few minutes, but first I need to get organized and obviously put on some ski pants," I say, laughing at the idea of walking out the door in my leggings.

"No problem, I will wait in front of the gondola, so just look for me when you get out there," she says as she closes the door behind her.

"Sounds good," I reply.

Ten of us meet in front of Gondola One. We create a plan for which chairlifts we will take to the top of the mountain and then move to which runs are best this morning. As soon as we decide upon the runs that will grace our skis first, we break up into two groups for the gondola ride. Jill, Ellie and I sit next to each other on the ride up, chatting about Blue Sky Basin and whether it's in the cards later today. I update them about Karley not feeling well this morning and how she is experiencing the same stomach issues Jill had a few days ago.

"Well, I hope she can make it through the two-and-a-half hour shuttle ride and gets over it quickly like I did," Jill says

"Oh, so you're back to feeling 100% now?" I inquire.

"I think so," she says with a shrug.

What none of us understands right now is that nobody is 100%! None of us, I tell you! None of the employees operating the gondolas and chairlifts, none of the waitstaff in the bars and restaurants, none of the staff at the hotel and spa, and certainly not me or any of my friends. As this story progresses, you will see a game of dominoes. We are nothing more than a line of those black and white tiles poised to topple over in succession. Once it begins, the dominoes fall so fast and with such efficiency, they create an energy that emanates. This leads to the complete shutdown of Vail Village, the complete shutdown of Colorado ski resorts, and the complete shutdown of all the resorts Vail owns, the largest ski resort operator on the continent. The chain reaction that occurs in the U.S. doesn't stop here. Rather, the dominoes continue to topple across the Atlantic to bring the entire worldwide ski industry to a screeching halt.

Reported by the Colorado Sun:
https://coloradosun.com/2020/04/15/colorado-ski-resorts-shutdown-backstory/

On the morning of March 14, Gov. Jared Polis studied data on coronavirus infection rates in Colorado's ski towns, which were 20 to 30 times higher than the rates on the Front Range.

It was Saturday and the busiest day of the season for ski areas — the day when Colorado's $5 billion resort industry welcomed the largest wave of big-spending, spring-breaking vacationers, pouring in largely from New York, Florida and Texas.

The Governor had concerns that social distancing strategies deployed by the crowded resorts weren't adequate. Cleaning gondolas and limiting ridership to just families wasn't enough. Limiting access to mountain facilities wasn't going to stop the spread of COVID-19. Ultimately, the Governor of Colorado was right and his decisive action proved to be the best decision and here is what the Governor had to say,

"There were many, many mountain communities that said, 'This is our livelihood. This is our business. We need the tourists.' But I'm making the decisions based on the science and the data. Eagle County has one of the highest infection rates in the country," he said in a recent interview. "If we had not acted early... not only would those numbers in those mountain communities be higher, but more people would have brought the virus back to the Denver metro area."

Phone calls were flying back and forth within the ski industry and here is what was discussed between the resort at Telluride and the resort at Vail:

"I got a premonition," Bill Jensen said. So he texted Rob Katz, the head of Vail Resorts, asking what was up. They hadn't connected in months. Katz called him immediately and told him he was shutting down his company's resorts for eight days.

"All the Colorado resorts?" Jensen asked. "He told me, 'No. All of North America.'"

Minutes later, at 4:09 p.m., Vail Resorts, the largest resort operator in the continent, began the chain reaction that would see all of Colorado's ski areas closed by nightfall and resorts across the world closed within days. Katz suspended operations at 34 resorts in 15 states and Canada. Minutes later, Polis issued a statement praising Vail Resorts "for taking this difficult, responsible step," and urged other resort operators to follow suit.

Aspen Ski Co. Chief, Mike Kaplan, said the following, "It was a crazy several hours. But when the governor said shutting down would save hundreds of lives, we said 'OK, we are done.' And really, him saying that made the decision easier for us."

The shutdown you have just read about happened exactly 14 days after I departed Vail, but for now, I will enjoy an extra day of skiing in February thanks to leap year. The 29th of February gives all of us another picture-perfect day on the mountain. We skiers count the days — the number of powder days, the number of bluebird days, the number of days we have skied and the number of days we have left to ski… that is… until next year.

The doors to the gondola open swiftly. We file out one by one, grabbing our skis, making our way through the crowd, and looking for an open spot to put on our skis. We ski over to the Wildwood Express lift to continue the journey up to the top. I sit next to Mike on the chairlift and ask him how the vacation is treating him. Mike pulls down his neck gator and lets out a long sigh.

"I have been exhausted for days. I think I may be getting too old to do this," he complains with tired eyes peering through his goggles.

"Oh, I am so sorry to hear that. You're definitely not too old! I just think everybody has a touch of something. Several people have had stomach problems and complaints about feeling tired, I have a dry cough and sometimes achy legs, and Karley just went home not feeling well, too," I assure him.

"Well, we have to make the best of it and enjoy what we can while we are here because this is an epic year for snow," Mike says with a childlike grin.

Skiers live by the motto, "Carpe diem!" Every day on the mountain is a gift, and you have to make the best of it. There are days that are just too cold — days where the blowing snow makes it too difficult to see — days that are so warm the snow is painfully slushy. Some years there is too little snow and some years "life" makes scheduling a ski trip impossible. Therefore, when you make it to the mountains — with ample snow and great weather — regardless of how your body is feeling — a skier must "seize the day!" Because, as we will soon find out — one never knows when the season will come to an abrupt halt.

We begin on Avanti, a blue run that today sports a perfect silky-smooth corduroy groomed surface for our warm-up. What a way to start the day! This type of run takes no effort. Normally, you can float down such a soft groomed run except when the coronavirus is multiplying rapidly inside you. My legs burn with lactic acid immediately after I carve the first turn. *I may have to take a minute or two to stretch when I get to the bottom. This will definitely help my aching legs. Right?* I think to myself. The stretching feels therapeutic as I watch a few of my friends finish the last portion of the run, coming in hot toward the chairlift line. I continue to stretch my legs as everyone gathers.

Jill challenges us, "Avanti one more time?"

Everyone agrees with nods, "uh-huhs" and a few "sures" as we all ski into the roped-maze for the lift line. I am sandwiched on the chairlift between Jill and Chris. Jill and I gab about the jam-packed fun evening at the Shakedown Bar last night. I look over at Chris and tell him he missed a hell of a night.

Chris laughs saying, "I needed my beauty rest!"

The three of us laugh in unison before Jill switches the topic to several more friends flying in from Chicago today.

"Jules, Debbie, and JD will join us this evening. The three of them are arriving at the Eagle airport late this afternoon."

"This circle of ski friends gets bigger every year. I just love it!" I exclaim.

For the remainder of the morning, our huge ski group stays together. We get lucky with short lift lines, skiing one run after the next. When lunchtime rolls around, we make our way over to Two Elk Restaurant and search for a table large enough for all of us. Again, we get lucky and find a table big enough to share. With trays filled with lunch favorites, we relax for an hour, sharing our selections along with stimulating conversation.

Lunch is shared, literally and figuratively. French fries get shared, desserts get shared, and the coronavirus gets shared. With all of this sharing, we are giving the coronavirus reason to smile from ear to ear.

Yes, I picture this virus having a devious smile, similar to the emoji sporting a scary face and devil horns.

I begin the afternoon feeling sluggish, but soon I find my groove in China Bowl. Skiing directly behind Ellie — mimicking her every turn — not only helps me to focus on form but also elicits pure joy. Over the years, I have found shadowing better skiers to be extremely helpful as I continue to seek improvements with my technique. The afternoon evaporates as quickly as a snowflake landing on the heated streets of Vail. (Yes, you will never see snow piled up along the streets of Vail thanks to the engineering marvel of underground pipes delivering a heated water-glycol mix, consistently keeping them just over 32°).

Happy Hour is calling to me through a telepathic channel I cannot ignore. I live by the famous song, "It's 5 O'Clock Somewhere" while I am on vacation. So, I pay attention to the sound of the Jimmy Buffet song playing in my head and tell Ellie I will see her at Pepi's later. I work my way down the mountain, ignoring the aching in my thighs.

I make a quick detour at the hotel to shed my ski clothes and freshen up before walking over to Pepi's. My aching body encourages me to pop an Advil, and my tired eyes stare back at me in the mirror. I put my hair up in a topknot and think to myself, *I may look tired, but at least my eyes don't need Visine.* This is my last après-ski (happy hour), my last evening with friends, and (as I will soon find out), my last evening with this metallic taste on my tongue.

Friends trickle into Pepi's while the Advil works wonders, giving my legs life again. As the live music plays, we huddle in closer to hear one another speak. After taking a sip of my drink, I realize it's not what I ordered. Looking down at the glass in my hand, I immediately notice it is not my drink. It only takes a moment for me to register that this drink belongs to Jay, seated next to me. With an apologetic smile, I place the drink down in front of him and admit to accidentally taking a swig.

"No big deal. It's a good cocktail don't you think?" Jay says, shrugging.

"Thanks. Yes, it's tasty," I reply, sheepishly.

Under normal circumstances, accidentally taking a swig from someone's glass is "no big deal!" But these aren't "normal circumstances." Jay doesn't know it yet, but eventually he's the first domino to drop. As February bleeds into March, life gets more interesting by the day. Keep this scene involving an accidental swig at Pepi's in the back of your mind as you continue on this journey.

The one-man band at Pepi's ends his set. The din of conversation with no music is the cue for our large group to leave in search of dinner. The majority of us are ravenous! The easiest choice presents itself with Jill's suggestion — Vendetta's. The family-owned Italian restaurant and pizza bar is in the heart of Vail Village just a few steps away. Thanks to the casual nature of this restaurant — walking in as a large group won't be a stretch for the staff. The moment we enter Vendetta's, our senses take in the heady aroma of hot, oven-fired pizza. If you weren't already ravenous — you are now! We wait at the end of the bar for someone to ask us if we need a table. A couple of employees assume we do and begin re-arranging a large booth and table to accommodate us. A server walks over holding up her index finger with a "just a minute" look. The wait is brief, and we waste no time ordering appetizers, pizza and salads all at once.

This is my last night in Vail to share stories, meals, and, of course, "the virus" with anyone in my vicinity. It's always a bittersweet evening year after year, because on the one hand, I will miss being on vacation, but on the other hand I am ready to go home to alleviate the exhaustion and reconnect with my family and friends.

The hearty Italian fare satisfies our ravenous appetites, so we are off to the next stop — 10th Mountain Whiskey & Spirits. As we enter the bar, we are greeted by Jill's friends from Chicago — Jules, Debbie, and JD. I am thrilled to see the three of them because I wasn't sure if our paths would cross this year due to crazy work schedules. I don't get to ski with the three of them this year, but at least I get to socialize with them on my last evening. A few of us become engrossed in a conversation with Jules about her latest travel destinations.

"My job sent me to Europe this year," Jules says with excitement.

"Where have you been? Did you have time to sightsee and play tourist when you weren't working?" I ask her.

Jules lists off all the countries she has visited in the past year and then drops the bombshell on us, except we don't take it as a bombshell at this moment.

"I just returned from Milan on Monday."

"That was just five days ago? Wow! Quick turnaround! Are you jet lagged at all?" I ask her, curiously surprised.

"No, I don't have any jet lag, but I will tell you many people are getting sick in Italy with this novel coronavirus, and it's really taking a toll on the country."

Jules talks about her time in Milan, ending with, "I think I got out just in time because in the last week a lot of cases have been reported, and several people have died."

Listening intently, I confess, "I feel so out of the loop right now with what is going on around the world."

Time passes at 10th Mountain Whiskey & Spirits with our golden elixirs poured over the rocks, setting up the atmosphere for clinking glasses with friends — friends who embrace the mountain with their passion for skiing and who make time in their hectic lives to escape with others cut from the same cloth. This is exactly why I look forward to this annual trip, and this is why in the coming weeks — my life becomes consumed with reaching out to check in and check up with so many from this trip.

The walk back to the hotel room, arm-in-arm with Ellie, is full of chatter about the fun we have had this week and promises to stay in touch throughout the coming year. We vow to bunk up with one another again next year, and she cajoles me to commit to multiple ski trips in 2021.

I enjoy planning and looking forward to future events. If someone had told me that would not be possible in the year 2021, I would have told them they were crazy.

Chapter 7

An annoying phone alarm invades my slumber at an ungodly hour on my last day in Vail, March 1st. I look over at the clock on the nightstand, squinting to focus on the bright red "5:30 a.m." I feel like letting out a groan, too, but I don't.

"What time is your shuttle arriving?"

"Seven," Ellie says, yawning.

"OK, I'll try to doze while you shower and then get some coffee for us when you start packing," I say while adjusting the comforter.

"That's so nice of you. I'm going to need some caffeine."

The ambient sound of the shower should lull me into a short restful sleep, but no such luck.

It's a cloudy Sunday morning, and the forecast shows snow will roll in by midafternoon. Luckily, my late departure time of 1:00 p.m. allows me to squeeze in one final half day of skiing.

I walk alongside Ellie to the lobby, pulling her carry-on bag behind me. The shuttle arrives right on time, and we hug goodbye. She tells me she will text me later, as I see her off, watching the bags get loaded. The sight of the luggage being heaved reminds me that I still face the daunting task of packing. Instead of starting the inevitable, I stop in the lounge for breakfast. I text Jill while eating to find out when she and her friends plan to ski. No response. I am not surprised since it's barely light out. I take my time eating breakfast, enjoy the warmth of the fireplace, and relish the solitude.

With my second cup of coffee in hand, I head back to my room to take on the dreaded chore. Glancing at the red digits "7:45 a.m." upon entering the room, my thoughts shift to the gondola starting up in 45 minutes. *If I am efficient with my packing, I will check out of the hotel and arrive on the slopes before 9:00 a.m.*

Packing to return home is dispiriting. It's the undeniable sign that my sojourn in this winter wonderland is over. I give little care to organization which results in a messy suitcase, but it makes the process quick! I keep a watchful eye on the time, rushing around the room. While packing to leave really is a downer, I don't dwell on it but rather focus on getting a few more hours on the mountain. Zipping the suitcase at 8:30 a.m. makes me feel victorious! I double check for any random items I may have overlooked and proceed to roll my monster suitcase to the lobby. There is an art to packing light, and right now, I wish I had mastered it. Struggling to manage a suitcase, a carry-on, and a backpack — I wonder why I do this to myself year after year.

The same hotel employee, who seems to live at the front desk, greets me with a smile. "Good morning. Checking out?"

"Yes. Also, I would like to store my suitcases this morning since my shuttle isn't picking me up until one o'clock."

"Sure, I showed you the office yesterday where they will be kept. Right?" she says with a look of understanding — another tourist taking full advantage of her time on the slopes.

"Yes. I appreciate the hospitality here," I reply.

Within minutes I am checked out and walking toward the gondola with my skis perched over my shoulder. Having only a few hours at my disposal, I waste no time getting in line. Sitting quietly during the ride up, I listen to strangers' conversations around me, feeling as if I am invisible. I am on my own this morning. When the gondola reaches the landing pad, I pop in my ear buds, crank up some good tunes, and ready myself for a top-to-bottom run. I take it slowly this morning, stopping periodically to catch my breath. The pounding of my heart unnerves me, so during my breaks, I pause long enough for my heart rate to slow before continuing. My lungs feel tight and tired. It takes double the time to ski to the base today compared to my first day on the slopes. As I get close to the base, my phone chimes, alerting me to a text from Jill. She is on her way, so I pop my skis off and take a seat on a nearby bench. At times like this, I wonder how we ever skied without this amazing technology. Texting has become invaluable.

I love people watching when I have time to kill — especially watching skiers gather to start their day. I can always pick out the person in a group that has an agenda. Sometimes it's the person with a splayed map pointing and encouraging confirmation from their ski buddies, or sometimes it's the person peppering a ski patrol with a barrage of questions. This morning, an animated display involving a splayed map catches my gaze.

I know my body is telling me to slow down — as a coughing fit erupts. *When Jill arrives, I will ask her if we can ski some easier runs.*

My body feels beat up. Akin to a boxer in the 12th round holding on for dear life. The combination of the altitude, lack of sleep, daily exertion, non-stop socializing, (maybe the whiskey sampling last night), and my age seem to have conspired to "take me down" this year. All of these secretly coupled with — an invisible force. A force throwing jabs and punches at me, causing me to exert massive amounts of effort, making me bob, weave, and duck. This invisible force on the verge of knocking me out of the ring. The aforementioned combination definitely contributes to the "beat up" feeling, but ultimately, it's the invisible force with its spike covered protein invading my cells, wreaking havoc on my lungs day after day that is taking me down. My dry cough has worsened.

Jill approaches, walking toward me down the cobblestone street, but it takes a minute for me to recognize her.

"Hey, good morning!" she calls out, raising her arm, ski poles in hand.

"Oh... hey. Good morning. I didn't recognize you. You're wearing a different jacket today," I say, surprised.

"Yes, I chose this jacket because of the forecast for snow this afternoon."

"Oh. Do you know how much is expected?" I ask.

"Several inches. It's supposed to snow at one or two this afternoon."

"Well, this could make my drive to the airport interesting," I reply with raised eyebrows and mild concern.

"Let's hope not. Are you ready to get in line?"

"Yes, let's go! But can we ski some green runs?" I inquire.

"Sure."

Weekends in Vail are extremely busy, and this particular Sunday morning is no exception. After waiting in line for what seems like a half hour, we pack into a gondola with a family of four.

One of the children blurts out, "My cousin was supposed to ski with us this morning but couldn't because he was sick last night."

"Oh, that's such a bummer," I commiserate. "I hope you'll be able to ski with him tomorrow."

I don't give the comment from this cute little girl much thought. Why would I? Kids get sick all the time, and they usually bounce back quickly. Was this a typical stomach bug, head cold, or altitude sickness, or was it the novel coronavirus? I will never know.

Jill and I ski a few green runs for an hour when suddenly, multitudes of text messages bombard our screens.

"My friends from Chicago are up and moving this morning!" she announces, amazed.

"I see that. The text chain is blowing up."

Each message gives us a play-by-play surrounding their morning and their timing. While the two of us ride the chairlift together, sifting through the texts, we talk about our adventurous week together. I tell her I am glad her stomach bug didn't last too long and comment about most of us having — "a touch of something this year." The chairlift dumps us at the top, regretfully my last time this year.

"Sadly, I need to start skiing towards the base. I wish I could meet up with the others, but my shuttle will be here before I know it," I say, pausing between sentences to cough.

"I understand. So glad we got to ski a few runs together this morning. Take care of that cough," Jill says, inching and shuffling her skis toward me for a hug.

We vow to stay in touch throughout the year, and I leisurely ski down on easier runs. Knowing this will be my last opportunity to enjoy "visual eye candy," I take breaks to soak in the breathtaking views.

The shuttle van picks me up at exactly one o'clock. I choose a seat in the back row where I quickly become smashed between a cute couple and a woman traveling to India. During my pleasant conversation with all three of them, I try my best to cough into my elbow. The drive to the airport is bumper to bumper, and just as predicted, the snow starts to fall. Big fluffy flakes come down at a pace that forces the driver to turn his wiper blades on high speed while slowing the vehicle. Since the van is full, each of us is forced to sit thigh to thigh. The slow pace gives us ample time to converse, and I end up learning all about life in India, asking one question after the next. My "smashed in" seat mate is more than happy to oblige my curiosity.

Does anyone on this shuttle van become infected because of me? How many people already have the novel coronavirus and don't know it? Did the woman sitting next to me enter the van with the virus? If she didn't, it seems likely that she left the van with mine! Did she end up feeling sick during her stay in India?

Is the Denver Airport another petri dish — incubating the virus? Immediately after the full plane takes off, I nestle up against the window and fall asleep. Looking back, this was definitely the best scenario for the strangers sitting in my row since sleeping kept me from conversing with and possibly infecting them.

Touchdown in Minnesota. Ten o'clock Sunday night, March 1st. This is the date when the tide turns in my journey. A virus that flew out of Colorado possibly contributes to "community spread" as it lands in Minnesota. New terminology will soon work its way into my lexicon: quarantine, convalescent plasma, serology tests, and antibodies. Very soon — life as we know it — will be no more.

My husband picks me up at the airport, asks about my trip and fills me in about his daily happenings while in charge of our 16-year-old.

"Never a dull moment," he remarks.

"Well, I am glad she kept you on your toes," I mumble, bending over to pull a tissue from my backpack and covering my mouth as I cough.

"Sounds like you picked up a cold while you were skiing."

"Yeah, this dry cough has been bugging me the entire trip."

The drive from the airport to home is short. The second I lay eyes on my daughter, my arms stretch toward her, inviting a hug.

"I missed you! Someday we will have to make a mother-daughter trip out to Vail," I propose, embracing the child who no longer looks like a child.

My daughter nods in agreement.

"Anything interesting happening this week?" I ask.

"Not that I can think of."

"OK. Well, I am exhausted, so let's catch up tomorrow."

"Sure. You look tired, Mom. I don't think you will have any problem falling asleep."

I agree with her wholeheartedly. Thirty minutes later, I am snuggled up under the covers — dead to the world.

Chapter 8

I wake to the irritating vibration of a text message jarring my phone on the nightstand. "Karley" and "urgent care" jump off the screen, so I immediately unlock my phone to read the text in its entirety.

"I'm sitting in urgent care. I don't know what's wrong with me? I am exhausted, my entire body aches, and I feel like I have the flu! The nurse is testing me for influenza A and B."

It takes a moment for the message to sink in. My groggy brain begins to wake up, and the thought crosses my mind… *I wonder if all of us have been fighting the flu this past week. Could the flu be the reason this dry cough continues to linger?* I send a return text to Karley, sharing my concern and asking her to update me with her results.

I walk downstairs, taking each step with care, gripping the handrail. I am feeling lightheaded. But it isn't just my head; my entire body feels beat up. Re-entry into "everyday life" after my ski vacation is not going smoothly this morning. I push the discomfort aside and start brewing a pot of coffee. Shortly after pouring my first cup, my daughter and husband come downstairs for breakfast. The three of us briefly discuss the upcoming week, and within a matter of minutes, the two of them are out the door. Listening to the garage door close, I consider going back to bed. A reminder pops onto my screen, prompting me to open my calendar. I see a dance lesson scheduled at Cinema Ballroom at one o'clock with my dance partner, Bob. I scrap the idea of going back to bed and start in on my housework and unpacking. I am definitely not listening to what my body is telling me — *Rest — Rest — Rest!*

I feel fortunate to have found ballroom dancing almost three years ago. Attending social dances and lessons around the Twin Cities gives me exposure to people who share a love for learning partner dancing. Over the last couple of years, invitations to attend private lessons have come my way. It's a treat to learn with a partner, and I never want to take the gift of a private lesson for granted. However, today I am struggling. One side of my brain is telling me to stay home and rest, and the other side is saying don't cancel as it would disappoint Bob. "Pull it together, Laurel — show up for the lesson." I heed the "don't disappoint" message, rationalizing that it would be rude to cancel on such short notice. Also, with several weeks without a lesson, I miss it terribly.

I walk into Cinema Ballroom with all of its grandeur — high ceilings, fabric-laden chandeliers, soft lighting, beautiful music, and enthusiastic instructors. At this moment, it's clear I made the right choice to show up; stepping into the ballroom reminds me of how much I enjoy weekly dance lessons. Slightly early for the lesson, I take my time putting on my dance shoes as I watch an instructor demonstrate spiral turns to his student. It's so easy to get lost in the moment watching the instructor's graceful movements. While waiting for Bob and the instructor, Grace, I pull up a video of my previous lesson, pop a cough drop, and sip some water. Hopefully this combination will keep my dry cough at bay. When Bob and Grace arrive, the three of us catch up, and I share a few highlights from my ski trip. We only have an hour, so the conversation quickly turns to which dance figures Bob would like to focus on this afternoon. We work diligently on very specific steps in the "foxtrot," gliding across the floor from one end of the ballroom to the other. Midway through the lesson, my strategy of sipping some water periodically and sucking on a cough drop seems to work. As always, Grace's instruction is extremely helpful. Each week, Bob and I seem to make subtle improvements in our frame, technique, and connection. Dancing with Grace, assimilating her instruction, and then dancing with Bob proves a successful strategy for our learning styles. The hour passes quickly, and I am ecstatic that my elbow is only occasionally needed as a shield. Bob and I say farewell to Grace and then spend a few minutes looking at the Cinema Ballroom calendar. We pencil in several group dance lessons and social dance parties for March. Browsing the ballroom calendar jogs Bob's memory — he takes a look at his personal calendar where he discovers a dance lesson scheduled this Wednesday at Dancers Studio. He wants to refine some very specific patterns in "East Coast swing" and asks me to attend this lesson with him. I check my calendar, and since I don't have anything pressing, I commit. Putting the calendars aside, we decide to spend a few minutes working on what we just learned. We sashay onto the dance floor and take advantage of the song currently playing.

The dance lesson and practice felt good. Driving back to the Twin Cities suburb, Edina, I have a renewed energy level. This is important because I nanny boy and girl twins on school day afternoons. Looking after two 5-year-olds is extremely rewarding but also a bit taxing. When the kids hop off the bus and see me standing in their driveway, they greet me with squeals of delight and big hugs. Calling it a warm reception would be an understatement. I have missed these two sweethearts, and they have clearly missed me. They burst into stories about all the happenings in their "kindergarten worlds" while I have been away. Our time together comprises an elaborate demonstration of their newly-acquired snack-making skills, playful wrestling with their puppy, Ruby, and snuggles on the sofa as we read a book together. It isn't long before my energy wanes, so I am thrilled when they ask me to read to them. When the twins' father arrives home with his 2-year-old daughter in his arms, he explains having his parents fill in for me while I was gone worked well.

However, the kids constantly reminded Grandma and Grandpa, "That's not the way Laurel does it!" I laugh!

We talk for a few minutes about my ski trip before I say my goodbyes to the twins, always ending with, "I'll see you tomorrow, same time, same place."

On my drive home, I stop at the grocery store, pick up a few essentials for dinner, and pull into the garage minutes before my daughter.

I hear the door open and call out, "Hi honey, how was dance class?"

She enters the kitchen with a smile, sits down at a stool, and rests her arms on the counter as she replies, "It was fine."

While I chop vegetables for dinner, the two of us get caught up about her day, and she surprises me with details about what she did while I was away. Each time I feel the urge to cough, I turn my head and back away from the counter. Our conversation turns to school, and she remembers an assignment she needs to complete.

Before she heads upstairs to her room, she looks at me with a troubled expression and asks," Do you have a cold, Mom? You still look tired, and that cough doesn't sound good."

"Yeah — I think you might be right, Sweetheart."

March of 2020 is here, and this becomes a pivotal month — not only for me — but also for the nation. On this day, March 2nd, half of my ski buddies are back home, but half are still skiing, drinking, and dancing in Vail. This virus can be compared to a "hurricane." It starts out as a small disturbance in the ocean. As it gains momentum, it turns into a "tropical storm." When the tropical storm develops substantial strength, ultimately a deadly hurricane is born. At this point, in the United States, COVID-19 looks like nothing more than a "disturbance" with very few cases reported by the CDC and the media. This virus is actually equivalent to a tropical storm on this second day of March. We just don't know it yet. The hurricane hunter hasn't arrived inside the eye to measure the barometric pressure. In other words — the symptoms felt by many haven't caused alarm. Our hospitals don't yet have testing capability, and our government isn't providing the public with much information.

Reported by CBS News – March 2, 2020:
   https://www.google.com/amp/s/www.cbsnew
   s.com/amp/live-updates/coronavirus-
   outbreak-death-toll-us-infections-latest-
   news-updates-2020-03-02/

Health officials in Washington state said Monday that four more people have died of the new coronavirus, bringing the state's death toll, and the nation's death toll to six. Georgia reported its first two cases Monday, bringing the number of states with confirmed cases to 15.

The potential for mild or even asymptomatic cases to go undetected but still spread COVD-19 has been noted repeatedly by health officials as one of the biggest challenges in fighting the disease. It makes the virus a deceptive enemy and, in spite of assurances from officials that the risk to the general public is low, the stockpiling and last week's stock market losses show that, like the disease itself, fear is still spreading.

Mild symptoms, flu-like symptoms, cold-like symptoms, coupled with asymptomatic carriers — these are the attributes contributing to the stealthy spread of this deceptive enemy. Vail, Colorado was certainly a hot bed for this virus. But are you starting to feel like it's in your backyard?

March 3rd, I wake to a quiet, empty house. Looking at the clock, I rub my eyes in disbelief: *9:30 a.m. What on earth — I slept for 11 hours —* I think to myself! *I must have needed it.* I get up and start the day with my usual cup of joe while sifting through the mail. Nothing interesting so I check email, read a few text messages, and look at my calendar. I see a message from my husband about his flight to North Carolina this morning and wonder... *Did I know he had a trip to North Carolina today? Why can't I remember the conversation about this business trip? This is odd and unlike me not to remember he had an upcoming business trip.* I file the thought away and get to work cleaning out my refrigerator. Suddenly I remember the need to get in touch with Karley. *I should find out how she is doing after her trip to Urgent Care. I think I'll send a text.*

"Hey, how did things turn out after your visit to Urgent Care?"

"Give me a call."

I barely recognize her voice when she answers.

"You sound rough, my dear," I remark, in a concerning manner.

She fills me in about how sick she has been since she left Vail on Saturday.

"Getting out of bed to shower and going to Urgent Care is the only thing I've done since I arrived home. I have no energy and no appetite."

She is on day four since her first noticeable symptom with the coronavirus. But the staff at Urgent Care doesn't mention COVID-19 or the novel coronavirus during the examination. Serious illnesses are ruled out right away. Strep throat and flu tests both come back negative. With no positive test results and no red flags for a serious health problem, Karley is sent home.

"The doctor just told me to go home, rest and hydrate," she says with a raspy voice.

"I am sorry you are so sick. I hope your family is cooking for you."

We only talk for about five minutes, but I get a rundown of her symptoms: extreme exhaustion, inability to think clearly (foggy brain), severe body aches, splitting headaches, and a low-grade fever.

Karley experienced all of these symptoms for a week before they slowly dissipated over days seven to ten. Luckily, she never developed a cough or had to be hospitalized. Ultimately, she only discovered she had the coronavirus when she received a positive antibody test through a plasma donation several months later.

This day in my timeline is punctuated by fluctuating energy levels, an unshakeable, persistent cough, and a funny discovery I make as my toiletries are organized. While unpacking, I pull out the perfume which notably had no fragrance on the trip. On a lark, I decide to spray some on my wrists before putting the bottle away. Removing the cap, I instantly catch a whiff of the aromatic citrus fragrance — without spritzing! I immediately burst out laughing remembering Chris' expression when I shoved my perfume drenched wrist under his nose, asking him if he could smell my perfume. I ponder all possible explanations: *Maybe the perfume "turned" and then "turned back," perhaps the high altitude dampened my olfactory function, or conceivably the dry mountain air affected my sinuses, distorting my ability to smell.* Ironically, I burst out laughing again for an entirely different reason. Because I tend to be thrifty, I was disappointed that a quarter of a bottle of my perfume may have gone to waste, but now I am no longer disappointed. —Now— you are probably laughing.

On March 4th, I finally return to my morning routine at the gym. I make a point to attend at least four exercise classes every week, so getting back to my routine is essential. Entering Studio 1 for a total conditioning class, I decide this cough will not slow me down. I say hello to several "regulars" and grab exercise equipment to set up my space. The instructor takes her place at the front of the room, the music begins, and my heart rate quickens during the warm-up. Within minutes, my breath becomes shallow and strained, igniting a coughing attack, requiring me to slow myself down and modify some of the exercises. I take it in stride knowing the exercise is good for me. At the end of class, I return the equipment and exit Studio 1, all while engaging in a conversation with several ladies. We gather outside of the studio and chat about what everyone has been up to for the past two weeks.

They ask about my ski trip, and I offer a few highlights. After a few minutes, I take off, allowing enough time to shower and make it to Dancers Studio for a noon lesson.

Where could this virus be lurking now — thanks to me? The exercise equipment I just used in Studio 1? The nasal passages of the ladies I conversed with after class? The door handles I touched entering and exiting the building? I could continue on with more hypothetical examples of where this invisible, underreported, undetected virus could be lurking, but I have no doubt your imagination will fill in the rest.

I zip home from the gym on this cold, dreary day, taking notice how brown the landscape became during my absence. Scattered lumps of dirty brown snow are all that's left of old man winter at the moment. It's a depressing look, especially after spending nine days in a winter wonderland, one that would rival any fairytale illustration in your favorite childhood storybook. I remind myself that winter is not over. March is often an "unpredictable" month, and a whopper of a snowstorm could bring Minnesota into "winter wonderland" status at a moment's notice. The good news about a lack of snow is — dry, safe roads. Roads allowing for a speedy drive home, giving me ample time to ensure an early arrival at Dancers Studio. Today's dance lesson will focus on "East Coast swing." Thrilled to be attending a second lesson just days after my return, I am hoping I can get through this lesson without coughing.

Bob and I agree to arrive fifteen minutes early to warm up and practice. The exercise and steamy shower this morning have collectively given me a burst of energy — as well as amnesia about my need to modify physical activity. As soon as Bob and I lace up our dance shoes, we each pop in an AirPod, choose a song from his "East

95

Coast swing" playlist, and start practicing. The dance patterns are full of turns, spins, and syncopations. After only two songs, my heart rate is soaring, my breathing is heavy, and beads of sweat dot my brow. A feeling of euphoria overtakes me! I am delighted to be back in the studio learning dance. Our fifteen minutes of practice slips by in the blink of an eye.

Our instructor, Gordon, walks into the ballroom right on time with a welcoming twinkle in his eyes and a smile from ear to ear. "Good afternoon, I'm glad to see the two of you back on the dance floor."

The three of us enjoy a quick conversation and dive into the agenda Bob has for the lesson. Gordon constantly switches between us — dancing the follower's role with Bob and the leader's role with me. It's very "hands-on." We learn a lot and have a few breakthrough moments. Both of us walk away at the end of the lesson with inspiration to practice what we just learned. For the next 30 minutes, we take advantage of a separate studio and get to work.

As always, Gordon is a master at giving us the motivation to continue practicing and attending more lessons. Unfortunately, this will be my last dance lesson at this studio forever — I just don't know it yet.

Taking things for granted is a normal human trait. We all do it. I learn that a deep breath should not be taken for granted. The freedom to have "normal" human interaction should not be taken for granted. And certainly, what is considered a "normal day" should definitely not be taken for granted. These epiphanies will all surface in due time.

I go directly from the dance lesson to the twins' house. The three of us start with our daily routine, but today I insert a trip to the library. Breaking up the monotony of routine is often a good thing — especially with five-year-olds. The announcement of a trip to the library is met with screams! As soon as the snack is scarfed, we hop in the car and make the short drive over to the library. Greeting us in the children's area is the weekly rotating hands-on exhibit. This week it's all about science. The kids begin experimenting with the props and I take a seat, waiting for their questions.

Could this be any more ironic? Visiting a science display for kids, role playing as a scientist and pretending to study tiny creatures with a toy microscope. You can't make this up! A worldwide pandemic is about to explode within a week, I am unknowingly harboring the novel coronavirus, and no one is the wiser.

According to the news on March 4th:
Reported by The Guardian –
https://www.google.com/amp/s/amp.theguardian.com /world/2020/mar/04/coronavirus-latest-at-a-glance-4-march

Coronavirus at a glance: Number of global case nears 93,000, WHO reports 3,160 deaths caused by the virus, 81 countries and territories around the world have reported the virus, South Korea, Iran and Italy are emerging hotspots outside of China, Italy closes all schools and universities, Lufthansa airlines grounds 150 planes, Japan cancels a national ceremony, residents of Washington state struggle to get tested, all nine US deaths from COVID-19 have occurred in Washington state.

Reading these global excerpts about the world shifting on its axis highlights the serendipitous nature of role playing as a scientist with kindergartners. I could have been infecting these darling children. Writing these words sends shivers down my spine.

Pulling into the garage after a full day of exercise, dance, housework, and an afternoon at the library with the twins leaves me wanting an early dinner and bedtime. By the time I start folding a basket of laundry and flip on the ten o'clock news, I can hardly keep my eyes open. I abandon the laundry basket and crawl into bed. Drifting off quickly, I am soon awakened by nagging coughs which ultimately give me a fitful night's sleep.

Chapter 9

The sun pushes around the edges of my curtains, illuminating the room, acting like an alarm clock. I roll over to check the time. The red numbers glare at me, showing, once again that I have stayed in bed for double digits — 10 hours to be exact! This is not typical. I sit up, stretch, and wonder what it's going to take to get over the hump with this chest cold. As soon as my feet hit the floor, a yawn comes over me — spawning a spastic fit of coughing.

Today is Thursday, March 5th, and for the third time this week, I have a dance lesson. Every Thursday for the past two years, I've been attending an hour-long lunchtime lesson with Dave Tsang. I am grateful to be invited into Dave's weekly private lesson with Char Torkelson (Howard), a seasoned instructor who teaches out of her home.

I distinctly recall several things about this dance lesson: sharing hugs with friends who later tested positive for COVID-19, difficulty remembering dance patterns, and working hard to stymie my cough.

When I entered the studio, a small group class had just finished. I knew several of the dancers. Candy and Larry's presence sticks in my mind because they both eventually contracted COVID-19. I chatted with them in the parlor as they changed into street shoes and I into dance shoes. When they got up to leave, I gave each of them a hug goodbye.

A second clear memory from this lesson is the difficulty I had in remembering patterns just moments after demonstration. I don't claim to be Julianne Hough, but my passion for dance "normally" elicits easy recollection of patterns and specific steps, so this struggle caught me off guard.

Lastly, I remember my desire to stifle my persistent cough. Just as I had experienced while skiing, I could not take a deep breath while dancing. Each time I tried, my lungs would immediately spasm. I avoided inhaling fully, but this was not very easy while dancing a "cha-cha!" Stifling a cough is similar to stifling a sneeze — sometimes it works, and sometimes it doesn't. I don't recall whether my attempts were successful but do remember the terribly uncomfortable feeling. My best efforts held back the cough temporarily. Whenever Char focused her attention on Dave, I stepped to the side, turned my head, and coughed as unobtrusively as possible into my sleeve.

That afternoon, I again drive to the twins' house and meet them as they bound off the school bus.

As they run toward me, Perrie yells, "What are we doing today?" And her brother, Myles, immediately repeats the same question.

I love their enthusiasm, and I don't mind stoking it. I throw my hands up in the air and shout, "Today is cookie day!"

They launch into their "happy dance" — jumping and screaming. The three of us dance up the driveway toward the house, laughing, while I wave my "jazz" hands as if I am performing on stage! The second we enter the house, we hastily discard our boots and coats and race each other up the stairs to the kitchen. I gather the ingredients, set out the bowls, and find the hand mixer. The kitchen becomes our playground as mixing and measuring rapidly turns messy and sticky! For the next hour, flour flies, batter is beaten, and fingers are frequently licked.

I am recounting my daily activities in some detail this first week after returning from Vail because it illustrates something we never used to think about — that is — how many people and how many things we touch every day. Who knew that "hands" were going to become an obsessive focal point in our society? "Hand hygiene" takes center stage as we navigate the "new normal" of frequent hand washing and constant sanitizing.

In partnership dancing, one's hands are constantly in contact with others' hands. Four days after arriving back in Minnesota, I have already danced with three professional instructors and two partners. How many students does a dance instructor touch in a typical day?

What about cooking at home? How often do you wash your hands while you prepare food? No doubt, adults are more circumspect than kindergarteners. Nevertheless, how many pots, pans, bowls, spatulas, knives, forks, spoons, salt & pepper shakers, and other utensils get touched while preparing a meal or baking cookies?

The baking adventure was fun, but will it end up being a catalyst for the coronavirus? (And, by the way, when the cookies emerged from the oven, they were ooey gooey goodness!)

On a typical Thursday evening, I would race home, make a quick dinner, and hustle to arrive at Dancers Studio by 7:00 p.m. for a group class. This Thursday is an exception. Walking into my house, I am met with the warmth of the living room fireplace. My daughter, Avery, must have turned it on when she arrived home from school. I don't know whether the effect on me is physical or just psychological? Regardless, it is just too inviting to consider going back out on this frigid Minnesota winter evening. Suddenly both relaxed and exhausted, my body is rebelling against my brain — the latter has ignored the former long enough! As much as I would love to be dancing this evening, I just can't. I need to stay home and give my body a chance to get over this chest cold.

My Thursday evening schedule change from dance class and a practice party to a light dinner, hot tea, and a soothing bath is just what the doctor ordered. I open the refrigerator, scan its contents, and contemplate what to make. Pulling open the vegetable keeper, I concoct an idea for dinner salads. Chopping veggies on the counter I do my best not to cough on them. With Avery at ballet class, I cozy up to the fireplace with my salad, find a *60*

Minutes episode on the DVR, and happily lose myself in the stories. Done with my salad and the episode, I bend over to place my dishes in the dishwasher. As I stand back up, a lightheaded feeling overtakes me, forcing me to steady myself. Regaining my balance, I again muse about tea and a bath and reach for the tea kettle. Choosing a soothing herbal chamomile tea seems like a wise idea as I coat the bottom of my mug with honey. Waiting for the kettle to boil, I read a text from Karley.

"A nurse came to the house today to administer a bag of IV fluid because I'm massively dehydrated. It's moments like this I am happy my husband is a doctor."

My mind roils with concern. What is happening? I can't believe she is still so terribly sick! Do I have what she has? Are any of the other skiers feeling crummy?

"Your husband ordered a bag of IV fluid?" I ask with a bolt of shock running through me.

"Yes! It really helped!" Karley exclaimed.

"I'm available if you want to talk."

She replies right away and suggests we talk in the morning.

"Sounds good. I hope you sleep well tonight," I text back.

I immediately start a texting chain with our core ski group.

"How is everyone feeling? I'm still coughing and feel crappy. Heading for a soak in the tub now. Karley was given IV fluids at home today!"

The whistle slowly begins to blow, so I reach to turn off the flame. When the boiling water hits the bottom of my mug, the honey melts, and I add the tea while squeezing a wedge of lemon for good measure. I hope sipping this old-fashioned remedy will help me feel better as I soak my worn-out body. Maybe it will act as a sleeping pill — I desperately need to sleep through the night.

Minutes after sliding into a steaming tub, I hear the familiar chimes of text messages. My mind is racing with questions.

How is it that Karley has been sick since I said goodbye to her in Vail on Saturday — it's been "five flipping days!" Why can't I shake this cough? Is my cough somehow related to Karley's dehydration? It doesn't sound like we have the same thing. Is this what happens when you turn 50? Are we all just falling apart? Are we all too old for extreme skiing and dancing the night away?

I sip my tea, close my eyes, and focus on my breathing, consciously pushing the questions and worries out of my mind. The long soak with my version of meditation is necessary right now, but I find it hard to keep the worries at bay.

Just as the water cools, my daughter knocks on the door and announces she is home from dance. *Perfect timing!* I tell myself. *I can get myself ready for bed, talk with her about her plans for the upcoming weekend, and then slip under the covers.*

After crawling into bed, I check my texts one last time. The group text chain I started over an hour ago overflows with replies. Every one of my girlfriends who skied in Vail last week is sick! The array of symptoms they are complaining about is vast. I want to reply but don't have the energy tonight. Bleary-eyed and barely able to think, I place my phone on silent, set it down on the nightstand, and attempt to drift off to dreamland.

Chapter 10

The sandman visited overnight and sprinkled magic granules over my eyes, bestowing upon me a restful night's sleep.

Finally, a good night's sleep! I think the tea worked! This is the first morning I wake with energy. My daughter and I eat breakfast while she talks about her upcoming tests next week. She is eager for the tests to be over and the start of spring break.

When she leaves for school, I check the text chain I started last night. Ellie, Amanda, and Jill each complain they are feeling under the weather. Instead of replying, I call Karley.

"Good morning. How are you feeling?"

"I'm better than I was yesterday," Karley replies confidently.

"Well, that's encouraging news! The IV fluid must have helped you!"

"Yes, I had enough energy this morning to get dressed, and I'm going to do some much-needed grocery shopping after we hang up."

"Wow, Karley, this is terrific news! It sounds like you have turned the corner!"

Sitting at my kitchen counter, I listen intently as Karley recounts the myriad of symptoms she has experienced the past six days. I ask if she has read the texts from Ellie, Amanda, and Jill.

"Yes, I glanced at them last night before going to bed."

"Oh. I just read them this morning. Do you mind if I place you on speaker so I can pull them up while we talk?" I ask.

"No, go ahead!"

We spend a few minutes reading through the texts, discussing the symptoms the three are experiencing. There are similarities and obvious differences. Ellie mentions extreme fatigue and achiness. Amanda complains of a drippy nose and feeling run down. Jill's upset stomach has returned, now accompanied by extreme exhaustion. No one mentions the loss of smell or taste.

"With how sick you've been and your response to IV fluids, I'm shocked you tested negative for the flu!" I blurt out.

"Me, too!"

"I hope you stay on this road to recovery."

"I'm sure I will," Karley assures me.

"OK. I will let you get to the grocery store. Take care, and we'll talk soon."

Hanging up the phone, I feel relieved knowing Karley has made improvement.

My girlfriends and I are unknowingly battling the coronavirus, each with varying symptoms. However, we all share "one" consistent symptom: fluctuating fatigue. Still, none of us considers a possible connection to COVID-19 — even though Ellie and Amanda are doctors, and Karley is married to one!

By lunchtime, fatigue sets in once again. But alas, ignoring aches and pains has become my modus operandi. I have things to do, places to be, and kindergarteners to entertain. Since I have no time for fatigue, chest colds, and body aches, I forge ahead. This Friday afternoon, the usual ritual of greeting the kids and making a snack happens without fanfare, but the energy needed to come up with creative entertainment is missing. I just don't have it in me. So, bloody exhausted by four o'clock, I can't even muster the effort to read to the kids. I reluctantly turn on the TV. Sadly, cartoons will bail me out today.

My Friday night looks a lot like last night: hot tea, hot bath, early bedtime. When my husband arrives home from North Carolina, he is surprised to find me in my pajamas.

"No dancing tonight?" he asks with raised eyebrows.

"Not tonight. I'm fighting a chest cold," I reply through a coughing jag.

"Wow! It seems like you've been fighting this cold for a while."

"Yes, this dry cough is really frustrating. If I can't shake it by Monday, maybe I should call my doctor."

My husband agrees with me, encouraging me to rest.

Aroused by my own spastic coughing on Saturday, March 7th, I peer at the clock. The bright red digits cut through the room's darkness: 4:30 a.m. — way — way too early! Lying in bed, willing my lungs to calm the cough, I resolve to get up and find a cough drop. Crawling back into bed, I tell myself, *go back to sleep. You will never get over this cold if you don't sleep.* Gradually, with persistence and a second cough drop, I drift off for a few more hours. When I wake for the second time today, my body feels like a lead weight. Staring at the ceiling, I wonder what to do. *Get up or just lie here? This feeling of lethargy is so foreign to me! It just feels wrong. Unacceptable!* An antsy inclination arises and drags my body out of bed. The morning cup of joe does little for my spirits. *How odd — no caffeinated jolt today?*

107

I succumb — spending the remainder of the morning listlessly lounging in my pajamas, watching TV, and skimming emails. Facebook Messenger dings with notifications from dance friends inviting me to dance tonight. I'd love to go. I'm tempted for an instant, but I know I shouldn't and sadly decline. (This proves to have been a fortuitous decision!)

My typical weekend usually involves "social dancing" — swing, ballroom, or country western. On the first Saturday of March, I normally would attend the "First Saturday Swing," a fun, energetic "East Coast swing" dance featuring a live band at 301 Main on the edge of downtown Minneapolis. But the way my body felt on this particular first Saturday in March was not normal — fortunately, I took heed.

As I watch *Dancing with the Stars* on the DVR, my coughing intensifies. Luckily, my husband has no interest in dancing or dance shows, so he is safely sitting in another room watching golf. My daughter also easily avoids my mist of respiratory aerosol during these coughing fits. She recently got her driver's license, so she is out with friends.

After a lazy day, I find it hard to comprehend why I am exhausted at 9:00 p.m. I don't fight it but instead, make my way upstairs. Getting ready for bed is quick, and falling into a deep sleep is effortless.

Sunday morning, March 8th, brings an enormous improvement over Saturday. I slept well, waking without the nagging urge to cough. Half of the morning has disappeared, but rising at 10:00 a.m. gives me renewed energy. *Maybe I have finally turned the corner!* I think to myself.

Thoughts about the monthly ballroom dance at Cinema Ballroom trickle in as I dress. *The Jerry O' Hagen*

Orchestra is playing tonight. I haven't attended one of these dances in quite a while. It would be a treat to dance for a few hours because many excellent dancers always show up. I wonder if Bob will be there? I should text him. Last night, I resigned myself to staying home all weekend — but now... maybe I could go?

The internal debate is in full swing. My rational, logical, and "slow-thinking" self suggests I probably should not trust this renewed energy after a solid night's sleep. My emotional, "fast-thinking" self is optimistic — confident the chest cold is behind me! (If you haven't read Nobel Prize winner Daniel Kahneman's best-selling book about human psychology and decision-making, *Thinking, Fast and Slow,* it's one to place on your list.) My "deliberative self" points out that caution is necessary — fluctuating energy levels have plagued me, rankling coughing fits have racked me, lingering ailments have dogged my ski buddies, predicting the effect after exertion is difficult, and spreading something to others is always possible. It would certainly be prudent to stay home tonight. My "intuitive self" is simply optimistic — I slept great, I am not coughing, exercise always helps, and sharing the joy of dance with a group of enthusiastic dancers is always energizing and uplifting!

This internal debate results in a comprise. My deliberative self argues that if I go dancing, I will stay for the entire three hours, even if I don't feel very well. A cocktail of neurochemicals — adrenaline, dopamine, oxytocin, etc. — will keep me jazzed regardless of what my body experiences. My intuitive self suggests I test myself with an afternoon barre exercise class at the gym. It's only forty-five minutes, but it's more intense than ballroom dancing, so it will be a good indicator. If muscles ache or coughing returns, I can leave the class early. Alternatively, if I can handle the class, then I can be confident about my recovery and dance the night away at Cinema Ballroom.

The barre class feels great! In fact, it feels so good that I stay after class to stretch and exercise my legs on the barre a bit more. Upon arriving home, I dig into some housework that's been neglected and continue to feel energized. I take my good fortune as a sign and prepare for my evening out. An early dinner, a shower, and some good music get me in the mood to dance. I start a playlist of newly added "favorites" while applying makeup. I am not a singer, but for some strange reason, I have an irresistible urge to sing tonight! A harebrained idea pops into my mind! *If I can sing without coughing, then I can dance without coughing.* The song of choice is, "Fall for You" by Leela James. I stand in front of my mirror applying blush, belting out the lyrics with verve, "So catch me, I'm falling for you, I'm falling, I'm falling, I'm falling…" Can you hear my off-pitch, out-of-tune voice singing at the top of my virus-infected lungs? (I think Leela James would have been horrified to hear my rendition.) This beautiful song with simple, meaningful lyrics along with its perfectly-timed bridge takes me on a journey — daydreaming about choreographing a lyrical dance. Ultimately, so pleased with myself, (because I didn't cough) I restart the song and sing it again.

Coming down the stairs, I hear John call out from the TV room, "Was that you singing upstairs?"

"Yup! And I didn't cough once, so I'm off to Cinema Ballroom!"

He laughs and responds, "Well, have fun. You may want to focus on the dancing tonight and pass on singing to your dance partners!" I laugh in agreement.

110

For an amateur ballroom dancer, attending the Sunday Cinema Ballroom dance is a lovely way to end a weekend. Walking into the elegant ballroom and hearing the sound of the orchestra starting always gives me a feeling of belonging. I am thrilled to be at a social dance tonight. I haven't attended a ballroom dance for almost a month, and I have missed it. As if on cue, the moment I secure the buckle on my dance shoes, the sounds of a waltz fill the room. A gentleman approaches me with his hand outstretched and invites me for a dance. Graciously accepting his invitation, we clasp our hands in dance hold, and I float down the floor, our steps keeping time with the exquisite vocals of Charmin Michelle.

Social ballroom dances give amateur dancers an opportunity to practice what they learn in lessons. Mixers encourage people to rotate partners. The gentlemen line up on one side of the floor while the ladies line up on the other side. As the lines converge, partners are paired. Each couple dances one pass down the floor before parting ways to re-enter the line for a new dance partner. Connecting and dancing hand in hand for a portion of the song are the goals of "the mixer." Dancers find this to be an excellent way to dance with as many different people as possible, typically for three songs.

The ballroom community largely comprises people in their retirement years, and this becomes an important factor when a global pandemic is on the horizon. Almost everyone I danced with that evening was over the age of 65.

The orchestra plays their last song at 9:30 p.m. The dance floor is still half full, but as the evening wraps up, and the last musical note lingers to a soft end... I relish the gentle dip from my dance partner. I say goodbye to a few people, thank Bob for the many dances, and tell him

I will see him back here tomorrow for his noon lesson. As I change out of my dance shoes and slip into my winter boots, my friend Patti sits down next to me. I mention the terrific turnout, and she agrees.

"There weren't enough hours to dance with everyone," Patti says, dropping her dance shoes into her bag.

"I agree. It's rare that I ever want a night of dancing to end."

I give her a hug, tell her I'm happy to be back on the dancing scene, and say goodnight.

During this unusual time, both dancing and skiing give me physical exhaustion merged with euphoria. So when my head hits the pillow, sleep comes easily. Sadly, this will be one of my last peaceful night's sleep for a long time.

Chapter 11

Today, we are one day closer to hearing a declaration from the WHO. Soon the words "global pandemic" will be spoken, and our lives will start down a path we never saw coming.

I slept like a rock last night and wholeheartedly believe the exercise yesterday was good for me. Unfortunately, my sore muscles don't agree with my well-rested brain. My cough is noticeably better, but my muscles are aching. Only my need for an Advil forces me to drag myself out of this warm, toasty bed.

My Monday morning falls into a familiar routine: coffee to caffeinate the brain, breakfast to break the fast, exercise to entertain the metabolism, and sweet goodbyes to my family. Thirty minutes after a cup of joe, an Advil, and a hearty homemade breakfast sandwich, I am ready to take on the day. I look at my calendar and organize a list of errands. Suddenly, a text message about the twins pops up.

"Kids are sick with a stomach bug. Staying home from school today."

Instead of texting, I call the twins' father to find out how they are doing. Regrettably, a stomach virus swept through their house over the weekend, and everyone except Dad was "praying to the porcelain God."

"Oh, I am so sorry to hear this," I expressed my concern.

"Have you had any stomach problems this weekend?" he asked.

"No... not yet anyway."

I ask if there is anything I can do to help, offering to run errands or bring over a meal.

"We are doing OK right now. I appreciate your offer though."

"OK. Please don't hesitate to call me if you need something," I reiterate.

"Thanks. I'll let you know how we are doing tomorrow. Hopefully, the vomiting has run its course. Stay healthy, and don't get this stomach bug — it's a doozy."

The moment the call ends, my thoughts shift to Jill. "I wonder if this is the same stomach bug Jill's been fighting with off and on?" Feeling grateful my weekend didn't include vomiting, I return to organizing my day, which now looks quite different. Sadly, the twins' miserable bout with a bug gives me an unexpected block of time.

As I move through — exercise, errands, housework — my chest once again feels constricted as the dry cough creeps up. I consider cancelling the 12:30 p.m. dance lesson with Bob at Cinema Ballroom. I ponder my rollercoaster symptoms — the dry cough, aching muscles, and fluctuating fatigue — and wonder why, a full week after returning from Vail, I am still not feeling 100%. *This is maddening!* I push the thoughts away, turning the shower lever toward the hottest setting. The steam will ease the tightness in my chest, I convince myself, watching the vapor billow over the shower door.

Driving to the ballroom, I listen to Frank Sinatra. His melodic voice transports me to the Sands Hotel and Casino in 1950s Las Vegas, getting me in the mood to "foxtrot."

"Good afternoon," I say, with a cheerful lilt.

"Good afternoon. Who is your instructor today?" the receptionist asks, smiling back at me.

"I'm here for Bob Sondag's lesson with Grace."

114

"No problem. You've been here before, so just sign in."

"Yes. Thank you," I say with a nod, scribbling my name.

I take a seat on the nearest bench, change from snow boots into practice shoes, and find an empty table while waving at a few familiar faces. The pre-dance lesson routine begins with reviewing last week's video, reading a memo regarding today's lesson, and stretching my aching legs. Grace walks in first with Bob close behind. As soon as Bob finishes showing Grace his agenda, the plan for the lesson takes shape. The three of us move to face the mirror and begin the warm-up routine. Grace's instruction to stretch through the rib cage provokes a cough, so I am forced to turn my head, shielding it with my sleeve. I do my best to focus on Grace's directions, but unfortunately my cough becomes more frequent. Moreover, the Advil I took this morning is wearing off, so the body aches return, and it's a struggle for me to focus. Working hard to hide my discomfort, I am hopeful Bob will get through all the bullet points on his agenda despite my lack of energy. When the lesson ends, I tell Bob I am not feeling up to practicing this afternoon and thank him for including me — week after week.

"Glad you could make it! I learn so much more when Grace tells me what she sees while I'm dancing with a partner."

"Well, I certainly learn a lot at your lessons. So — thank you Bob! I'll talk to you soon. Have a good rest of your day."

The moment I sit down in my car, the need to call my doctor's office is apparent. *Could this unshakable cough and awful chest cold really be pneumonia?* I contemplate reaching back into my memory bank for what the last bout with pneumonia felt like as I dial T.C. Family Physicians. The scheduling nurse tells me a 5:00 p.m. appointment just opened up for Dr. Gamren if that will work for me.

"Yes, please. I'll be there at five."

Once I am checked in, the nurse asks routine questions and takes my blood pressure. As Dr. Gamren pulls her stethoscope from her pocket, she warns me it's going to feel cold. It only takes two deep breaths with strained exhales for her to make a diagnosis.

"You definitely have bronchitis. I can hear it. I can't diagnose pneumonia without a chest X-ray so that will have to be next."

The myriad of symptoms plaguing me for two weeks is explained in detail as I give her a timeline, starting with tightness in my chest on February 24th in Vail. I describe the rollercoaster symptoms and my experiences with pneumonia in the past, pointing out the similarities. She sends me down the hallway to the radiology room. The X-ray technician greets me at the door and takes the time to make me feel comfortable in the dimly lit room. He positions me multiple times, making sure to capture a sharp picture, and sends me back to the examination room. While I wait for my doctor to return, I sit wondering. *Will she prescribe an antibiotic?*

When Dr. Gamren returns, she cautions, "First, your bronchitis is contagious, so stay home for the next couple of days and rest. Second, I am prescribing a Z-Pak, so start taking that right away. And, as soon as I get the results from the radiologist, I will call you. If the X-ray shows pneumonia, I will change your prescription."

"Thank you. I'll look forward to your call."

"OK — feel better," she responds, exiting the room.

I head straight home, follow the doctor's orders, and call my husband, John. I catch him while he is driving home from work and ask if he will swing by the pharmacy to pick up my prescription.

"Oh, so you went to the doctor today?" John questioned, soberly.

"Yes, I knew it was time to see my doctor. She confirmed bronchitis and possibly pneumonia. We will see what my X-ray shows in a day or two."

"Ok, I'll swing by the pharmacy, and hopefully your prescription will be ready," he replies.

A half hour later, John walks into the TV room to find me in my pajamas, snuggled under a heap of blankets, sipping a hot cup of tea.

"Drug delivery," he says as he hands the Z-Pak to me.

"Thanks, this should do the trick. It always has when I've felt like this."

This would be an excellent time to look at what was reported globally about the coronavirus on Monday, March 9th:

Fox News, Tucker Carlson, Reported:

https://www.google.com/amp/s/www.foxnews.com/opinion/tucker-carlson-the-coronavirus-will-get-worse-our-leaders-need-to-stop-lying-about-that.amp

"The Chinese coronavirus is a major event. It will affect your life. And by the way, it's definitely not just the flu."

He also cited statistics, noting that the flu has a mortality rate of about 1 in 1,000 in a typical year.

"The overall death rate for this virus, by contrast, is as high as 3.4%. That is 34 times deadlier."

CNN Reported:

https://www.cnn.com/2020/03/09/health/us-coronavirus-monday/index.html

717 people in the United States are confirmed positive with the coronavirus

36 states have reported coronavirus cases

26 people have died from the virus in the United States

All except four coronavirus deaths were in Washington State

The Dow had the worst day since 2008, falling more than 2,000 points (7.8%)
There was the biggest oil prices crash in nearly 30 years.
Boston cancelled its St. Patrick's Day parade

There are also more than 100 cases in New York, where officials announced 16 new cases Sunday. Officials have urged more than 2,500 people to self-quarantine, and Gov. Andrew Cuomo declared a state of emergency Saturday.

The Grand Princess, a cruise ship carrying at least 21 people who have tested positive for the coronavirus, arrived in the port of Oakland and some passengers began to disembark.
Sen. Mitch McConnell opened his remarks on the floor of the Senate by reiterating health officials remarks that the risk of US citizens catching the virus is low.

"This is not a time for fear," the majority leader said. "It is a time to continue calmly scaling up the serious and smart preparations that have already been under way so the United States can continue working to blunt, slow and mitigate the spread within our borders."

US Surgeon General Jerome Adams gave the following information:
The US response to coronavirus has shifted from containment to mitigation, Adams, the Surgeon General, said Sunday.

"Initially, we had a posture of containment so that we could give people time to prepare for where we are right now. We're shifting into a mitigation phase, which means that we're helping communities understand you're going to see more cases," Adams said.

"Unfortunately, you're going to see more deaths, but that doesn't mean that we should panic."

Adams said those who aren't sick should not wear face masks as they often cause more harm than good. Instead, people should wash their hands with soap and water frequently for at least 20 seconds and stop touching their faces, health officials advise.

As I lay on my sofa, believing I may have pneumonia, the thought of harboring the coronavirus still hasn't dawned on me. My doctor didn't mention the coronavirus at all; nor did she link my symptoms to any virus. Additionally, Ellie and Amanda, both doctors, never suggested the possibility that any of us could have this virus. And as you just read — Senate Majority Leader Mitch McConnell reiterated health officials' remarks stating the risk of U.S. citizens catching the virus is low. Why would I suspect that I should be a positive COVID-19 case to be added to the 717 reported cases in the U.S. today?

What has crossed my mind is clarity that I overdid it yesterday. Going to the gym combined with several hours of dancing may have set me back just as I was beginning to make progress. In fact, the only thing making progress is — the coronavirus. If you try to add up the number of people with whom I have been in contact from February 24th to March 9th, across two states and a variety of cities, you quickly realize you may need a calculator.

Becoming one with the sofa this evening, I peruse my recent photos, deleting duplicates. Looking at my girlfriends' smiling faces reminds me to update the four of them. I send a text on the group chat, giving them the bronchitis diagnosis. All four of them respond quickly with well wishes and a few questions. Before I answer their questions, I throw out one of my own questions.

"Do any of you think you might have bronchitis too?" I text.

A resounding, "No!"

I answer their questions regarding my doctor's comments, and Ellie gives us the good news about her extreme fatigue finally disappearing. I don't know if it's the power of suggestion, but as soon as I see the word fatigue, I yawn. I sign off the group chat and move from the sofa to the bed. As I am walking up the stairs toward my bedroom, my husband reminds me he is flying out tomorrow morning.

"I'm going to New York City in the morning. Don't be alarmed if you hear me bumping around at 4:00 a.m."

"An o'dark thirty flight, huh? When are you coming back?" I ask with a tired voice.

"Thursday night — late — sometime after ten. I'll let you know because I may go standby on an earlier flight," he replies, reaching into the cookie jar.

"Ok, thanks. I'm dying right now, trying to keep my eyes open, so I'm going to bed."

My body melts into the mattress the moment I pull up the heavy down blanket. Exhaustion takes over, and I pass into slumber within minutes. Staying in this "slumber" becomes the challenge. Waking to the tickle of a cough that never feels productive interrupts my sleep over and over again. Sips of water, sucking on cough drops, and propping pillows to elevate my head help a little. I tell myself, *be patient, have faith in the antibiotic. The Z-Pak will do its job over the next few days.*

Soon I will learn antibiotics render themselves useless against this novel foreign enemy as my lungs rage a battle — fighting for air.

Chapter 12

Lying in bed after a fitful night of coughing, sucking on lozenges, and sipping water — punctuated with periodic episodes of sleep — I wasn't in any rush to get out of bed. I was hoping the Z-Pak had worked its magic, but the way I feel this morning, there is no evidence that it had. Reaching for the phone, my first thought is the need to message the twins' parents. They have to know I am not available today.

"I'm sorry to tell you I have bronchitis. Can you call me?"

A few minutes later, the phone rings.

"Good morning, Craig."

"Hi Laurel. We're sorry to hear you're sick."

"Thanks. My doctor put me on antibiotics last night. It will likely take a few days for them to kick in. In the meantime, I was told to stay home and rest because I'm contagious. I may have had this bronchitis for a while. I sure hope the kids don't end up getting it from me. Is their stomach bug gone?"

"Yes. The kids went back to school this morning."

"Oh, good. How's Michelle doing?"

"She's Ok. Actually, she is waving at me now to tell you hello."

"Well, hello back to her. I'm glad to hear the stomach bug didn't linger for her. As soon as I turn the corner and calm this cough, I will let you know."

"All right, thanks for calling. Take care and get better soon."

"Thanks Craig, I'll be in touch."

I stay home, following the doctor's orders. I try to nap, but when that doesn't work, I move to the sofa, turning on a morning talk show. Eventually the drone of the TV lulls me to sleep. Waking to the sound of dishes clanging, I know Avery is home from school. I have paid no attention to the time, so with Avery in the kitchen making an afternoon snack, I realize I've gone all day without eating. I think to myself. *I'm not sure if I'm hungry or not but a little food certainly wouldn't hurt. Besides, I could use the company!* I drag myself off the sofa and greet Avery with a cough as I try to say hi.

We sit at the kitchen counter, picking grapes off a gnarly stem. I ask about her day at school. She shares a few details, but like most teens, she isn't particularly anxious to get too in-depth, so I shift the conversation to dinner plans. Would she prefer to eat before or after tonight's ballet class? I keep some distance from her while we talk, but if she's going to catch my bronchitis, she most likely already has! When the conversation fades, and Avery requests we eat dinner after ballet class, I excuse myself.

"The bathtub is calling my name!" I announce.

As I undress, I hear the distinctive text message chime from downstairs. I pause to listen, hearing one text after another hitting my inbox. I pull on my robe and head downstairs. Picking up my phone, I quickly swipe through messages from several girlfriends. The alerts continue one after the next as the alarming texts pop onto the screen.

Text #1: "Jay's in the hospital on oxygen!"

Text #2: "Jay was admitted to the hospital 2 days ago."

Text #3: "Mark sent this text to me:"

"Jay went to the doctor the day after returning home. His asthma was acting up. Doctor was concerned symptoms align with the novel coronavirus. Sent him to a private lab for a test. He's positive! His breathing became labored, checked himself in at the ER. The lab that tested him was not approved by the CDC. Hospital is re-testing him. He's on oxygen! Staying overnight for observation."

Text #4: "Jay's positive with COVID-19!"

I can't believe what I am reading. I don't know how to respond. My brain is in a fog, and the exhaustion is debilitating. Heading back upstairs with my phone, I grab the handrail to help put one foot in front of the next. *What do I do with this shocking news? I have to think. I need to get a grip.* I draw a hot bath, add some lavender Epsom salts, and grab my half-finished book, *Suggestible You* by Erik Vance. By coincidence, I have just read a chapter about the power of the mind to "cure" illness. It occurs to me — *perhaps I need to have more of a positive attitude toward the Z-Pak I started last night! Placebos are scientifically proven to work on many people — maybe I can "will" or "wish" this bronchitis away? Yes, that would be nice.*

Slipping into the tub, the water immerses me up to my neck, giving my chest comfort and constriction simultaneously. I try to relax and find my place in the book, but soon I begin to cough. So much for the power of positive thinking! The coughing episode has aroused me. I try my best to get engrossed in the book, but I repeatedly lose track of my place. I can't concentrate. Once again, my mind returns to Jay in the hospital on oxygen.

This is distressing! I had heard people were dying in China and Italy from this virus. I hope Jay is doing OK. I hope this doesn't become serious for him! How serious is his asthma? How does this new virus affect someone with asthma?

The ring of the home phone startles me. I hear Avery answer it from my adjoining bedroom and quickly surmise she is talking with my doctor.

"If that's my doctor, please bring the phone to me!" I holler.

Avery enters the bathroom, hands the phone to me, and mouths the words, "I'm leaving for dance."

I wave and mouth back, "Thank you!"

"Hello Dr. Gamren," I say with a cough.

"Laurel, I'm calling you with the results from the radiologist about your chest X-ray. You have a small spot of pneumonia, an infiltrate, in the lower lobe of your right lung. I want you to stop taking the Z-Pak because I'm prescribing a stronger antibiotic. I will be sending over the prescription in the next few minutes for Doxycycline Hyclate."

I am unfazed. "I figured I had walking pneumonia. My lungs felt just like this the last time I had it."

Dr. Gamren goes on to explain in a reassuring voice, "The stronger antibiotic should help you get over it."

I thank her for the after-hours phone call. "Oh, one more thing, Dr. Gamren. I found out tonight that someone I skied with in Vail tested positive for this coronavirus thing. He lives in Atlanta. Apparently, he went to the hospital for oxygen because his asthma was acting up."

"Well, that changes things! I am going to have to call the hospital and find out their protocol. We don't have those tests here in our office. Because you've had contact with a confirmed positive case of COVID-19, I need the hospital's advice. I will call you back."

"OK."

I hang up the phone and set it on the floor next to the tub. My mind is racing. Jay's health problems suddenly seem personally relevant! *How long has Jay been sick? Did I ride in a gondola with him? Did we sit next to one another on a chairlift? Which nights did I socialize with him? Was he having trouble breathing in Vail? What about the other guys in his group? Are any of them feeling sick? Was he coughing at après ski? O — M — G, was it his drink I accidentally sipped at Pepi's? I think it was...*

There is a maelstrom in my head! I try to replay the week's skiing, eating, and drinking with a focus on Jay and his ski buddies. It's frustrating that I can't instantly recall it all clearly! This frantic conversation in my head explodes into a full-blown — FREAK OUT!

I try talking to myself — or at least calm my rational side as it tries talking to my emotional side. *Let's not panic. Remember Laurel, there is a wise old saying: "There is nothing to worry about until there is something to worry about."* My emotional side is unconvinced — *Are you kidding? Of course, there is something to worry about! Our doctor thinks we might be sick with this "new" novel coronavirus that is killing people! She is calling the hospital for advice right now!*

Fortunately, the return phone call from the doctor arrives within five minutes of this obsessive rumination. The moment I say hello to Dr. Gamren, she launches into a series of instructions.

"Laurel, you need to drive to Fairview Southdale Hospital right now! The receptionist in the emergency department is expecting a call from you. I'm going to give you the phone number so you can call her from your car when you pull up. She will give you instructions about where to park. Be prepared to be escorted in. A mask will

127

be given to you, and you'll need to follow their directions. Do you have a pen and paper to write down the phone number?"

I ask the doctor to hold for a minute to grab something to write on as I get out of the tub. With my phone up to my ear, while wrapping a towel around me, I begin with an embarrassingly childish complaint.

"Uhhh…Dr. Gamren, I don't want to go to the hospital — that's where all the germs are."

At this moment, I am not thinking — I might be the germ!

The good doctor ignores my grousing and responds with, "I understand, Laurel, but now that we know you were exposed to the coronavirus, we must test you. Pneumonia can become serious, and we need to know if it's connected to this new virus."

"OK. I understand. I'm ready for the number."

Composing myself, I scratch out the receptionist's name and number and thank Dr. Gamren for working so late.

The hospital is only five minutes from my home. I call the receptionist as soon as I pull up. She tells me to wait in my car until someone comes out to greet me. Ten minutes pass, and I become antsy, so I call her back. As soon as she realizes it's me, she apologizes.

"I'm so sorry no one has come out to your vehicle yet."

"Well, I was just wondering how long I should stay in this temporary parking space. Do you want me to park somewhere specific?"

"Yes, if you don't mind finding a space in the parking garage, that would be best."

"OK. After I park, should I wait outside the emergency room door to be greeted?"

"Yes, that may be a good plan. There is a bench outside the door. You could wait there."

"All right."

"I'm sorry, we have never had anyone come in for one of these tests, so this is all new to us," she says apologetically.

It only takes a minute to park the car and walk over to the bench outside the emergency room. There I sit. While waiting, a man wanders around the drive-up to the ER entrance. He has a plastic Fairview Southdale Hospital bag in one hand (most likely containing personal items from an overnight stay), and he is dressed in tattered clothing. He appears to be talking to himself as he shuffles around randomly. I watch him with his odd behavior for several minutes, wondering if he's waiting for a ride. Suddenly, he extends his arm, points his finger, and shoots something — or someone! His imaginary gun emits fierce explosive sounds — he is now vocalizing gunshots!

I don't know if this is a normal occurrence on a Tuesday night at the local emergency room, but I do not like my spot on this bench! The fight or flight syndrome kicks in as my mind shouts at me. *That's it! You're out of here!* I bolt from the bench, heading straight for the vestibule. Immediately upon entering my new location behind a plate of glass, a security guard sprints for the door. I watch him try to guide this disturbed man toward the nearby bus stop. Frazzled nerves keep me on high alert as I continue to watch this scene unfold. Soon the two of them disappear around the corner, and my attention returns to the matter at hand.

Why is it taking so long for someone to get me? Hmmm...the receptionist did say they have never had anyone come in for a COVID-19 test. That is a little disconcerting!

The security guard returns alone, re-entering the vestibule. Before he can pass me, I grab his attention.

"Excuse me. Could you let someone know I'm the patient waiting for an escort? I'm here for the COVID-19 test."

He responds with, "Sure," completely unfazed by my request.

But, as he leaves, a woman passes him with a mask in hand. I assume this mask is for me, and my escort has finally arrived.

"Are you Laurel Fischbach?" the woman asks, keeping her distance.

"Yes."

"Please put on this mask and follow me, but stay 6 feet behind. Don't touch anything on our way to the examination room. I will be opening all doors for you," she instructs, reaching her gloved hand toward me with the mask dangling by its strap.

I follow her, walking briskly down one corridor after the next. When she slows her pace and pauses at a door, I surmise we've arrived at the examination room.

She places her hand on the door handle and looks at me with steely serious eyes before she says, "You are about to enter a negative pressure room. It's specifically for airborne infections, so it's important that once you are inside, you don't open either of the two doors."

If my eyes could speak at that moment, they would have said, "Are you freaking kidding me? This new virus is so contagious it warrants a special examination room?" My doctor thinks I'm walking around with a deadly infectious virus?

130

The door opens. The nurse stands to the side as she motions her hand to enter and says, "Someone will be in shortly." Just as soon as I clear the door, she promptly closes it, creating a whoosh sound as the air moves to equalize.

I take a seat in a chair, choosing not to jump up on the examination table. After several minutes of staring at my surroundings, and taking in this very strange experience, I pull out my phone and begin texting my girlfriends. I pull up the Vail ski group text, take a photo of the room and add the caption "COVID-19 test happening now!" My textees are mostly available, so the responses are quick. The first is, "What the F#&?%!"

Moments after the text messages begin to fly, a doctor and nurse enter the room together, looking as if they are prepared for a spacewalk. I remember the picture Dr. Dave showed me on his phone at the Minturn Saloon. They are suited up just as he had been to examine the patient who merely had strep throat. We had a good laugh about all that gear he had on while sitting in the saloon sipping margaritas — now this doesn't seem quite so funny!

With the door open, hand sanitizer is applied over the double-gloved hands. Once their gloves are thoroughly coated, the door is closed, and the top pair of gloves is discarded. They each grab a fresh pair of gloves, stretching them over the initial pair protecting their hands. After the glove routine is completed, plastic face shields are adjusted. Only now — do they look up and acknowledge me.

Their gear reminds me of the HBO mini-series "Chernobyl!" My Lord, I think, is this the equivalent to a nuclear disaster? This is becoming creepier by the minute!

131

The doctor introduces himself and the nurse as she reaches for the blood pressure cuff. The doctor explains what is going to happen during this exam and asks if I have any questions.

I'm so distracted with the spacesuits, the goggles, and the face shields all I can manage to sheepishly say is, "No...um, I really...um don't think I have this coronavirus."

The doctor pauses, his eyes crinkle from behind his goggles, and he says, "Well. We are going to find out because we will swab you and test for it. You know, everyone is eventually going to get this virus."

With my eyes like saucers, I think to myself, WHOA! — Is that supposed to be reassuring? Is he serious? Is he smiling under that mask? "Everyone is eventually going to get this virus?" What! Seriously? Really?

The nurse takes my temperature and my blood pressure while the doctor looks into my ears. It's all rather typical. During the examination, the doctor takes the opportunity to run through a slew of questions. He is focused on where "exactly" I thought I was exposed to the coronavirus. I describe my annual ski trip to Vail a little over a week ago with various people from around the country. I elaborate on the evenings which were consumed with socializing; sharing appetizers, meals, and drinks; and of course — topped off with dancing. I go on to explain one of the skiers recently tested positive for COVID-19.

"Where does this person live?" the doctor asks.

"Atlanta."

"I'm making a note in your chart. This information could be helpful down the road."

132

When the nurse finishes, the doctor asks for my left index finger. He explains he is placing a pulse oximeter on me to measure the oxygen in my blood.

The readout is quick, and the doctor says with apparent surprise, "Your oxygen level is 99%. That's very good!"

"Oh," I reply, not really understanding what this means exactly.

"All right, I need to listen to your lungs. Take a deep breath for me," he says, placing the cold metal stethoscope on my chest.

I try to take a deep breath, but inhaling fully is impossible. My lungs are tight, a coughing fit begins, and answering the doctors upcoming questions are a struggle.

"I can hear the rattling in your lungs. You're taking an antibiotic, right?"

"Yes, my primary doctor prescribed one."

"All right, the nurse is going to take over from here, she'll be swabbing you. Do you have any questions before I leave?"

"No. I don't think so," I reply, feeling like a deer in the headlights.

"You should have your test result in a few days. Expect a phone call from the hospital. Stay home and keep yourself isolated from your family as best you can until we know the results."

"OK, I will. Thank you," I eek out with one more cough before the fit finally calms.

The nurse steps forward with an extra-long Q-tip looking swab.

"You'll need to remove your mask. I'm going to start with swabbing your throat."

She rubs the long swab from side to side along the back of my throat, eliciting a gag which turns into another series of spastic coughs. As soon as she removes the swab, I apologize that I coughed in her face.

"That's why we wear face shields, so don't you worry about it. Take your time to catch your breath."

Once the swab is secured in its vial, she places it in a red biohazard bag.

Next, a second long swab is pulled from the test kit, and I'm asked to tilt my head back. I don't remember if swabbing took place in one nostril or two, but I do remember her advice.

"Wiggle your toes — it will help with the discomfort."

My toes begin their calisthenics, and I keep them moving for the entire slow count down from ten to one. I do think the toe-wiggling helps to keep my head from pulling away. (Certainly, it is an excellent distraction from the burning sensation that causes your eyes to water.) When the nasal swab is securely placed in its vial, the nurse asks me to put my mask back on.

"I'll be back shortly with your discharge papers."

Of course, she couldn't just walk out the door. The exit from the negative pressure examination room had to be followed as methodically as the entrance. The carefully choreographed routine related to infectious diseases outlined by the CDC looked like this: hand sanitizer, removal of extra overlay gown, more hand sanitizer, opening of door, removal of top layer gloves, more hand sanitizer, closure of door, more hand sanitizer.

Wow! Is this what hospitals will be doing for everyone who is potentially infected with COVID-19? It's so time-consuming, and the amount of wasted medical supplies is mind-boggling! If the doctor is correct, "Everyone is eventually going to get this virus," how is this going to be sustainable?

Waiting for the nurse to return with my discharge papers, I browse through a few text messages. The firestorm of texts that began earlier multiplied quicker than a hutch full of rabbits. I was soon included on multiple text chains with ski buddies from all over the U.S. Everyone wonders if they need to be concerned or if this virus problem is being blown out of proportion.

The nurse returns within 15 minutes, leaving paperwork on the counter for me to take home. She asks if I have any further questions and tells me to return to the emergency room if my breathing becomes difficult or labored.

"Someone will call you with your results just as soon as they are available."

"Thank you. I appreciate it," I reply, holding back a cough.

"Wait until I have left the room and secured the door before you open the other door to exit. Also, please keep your mask on until you are in your vehicle, and be sure to drink plenty of fluids; bronchitis and pneumonia can dehydrate you. Take care."

I walk in the door to an empty house and plop down on the sofa. I am physically exhausted and mentally overwhelmed. I call John, and his voicemail immediately picks up, informing me he is most likely out to dinner with clients. It's 9:30 p.m. in New York City, and I'm hoping he will call me back within an hour or so. I turn on the TV and flip from channel to channel. My attention vacillates between the TV and my text messages. The texting chains are expanding exponentially, and I've been asked to please update everyone when I get my result.

Avery walks into the mudroom a little after nine o'clock announcing she is home. Entering the living

135

room, she sees me lying on the sofa and asks, "How are you feeling Mom? What did the doctor say?"

I explain the pneumonia and the trip to the hospital. More importantly, I tell Avery she'll get no forehead kiss from me tonight when I turn in.

She laughs and says, "Yeah Mom, that's probably a good idea."

I give her a few details about the emergency room visit, and she stands there staring at me intently.

"Do you think you have this coronavirus thing?" she asks, concerned.

I reply to her with feigned confidence, "No, I think my doctor is just overly cautious. I've had walking pneumonia before. It feels the same. I'm just run down from the ski trip. I'll be fine just like the other two times."

The evening drags on, pushing into the ten o'clock hour. My daughter has gone to her bedroom for the night. I am still sprawled out on the sofa, anxiously awaiting a call from John — half watching the local news. A segment about a critically ill patient with COVID-19 airs:

Minneapolis (WCCO):

https://www.google.com/amp/s/minnesota.cbslocal.com/2020/03/10/coronavirus-in-minnesota-mdh-confirms-3rd-presumptive-case-of-covid-19-patient-in-critical-condition/amp/

A third person in Minnesota has tested positive for coronavirus (COVID-19) and is in critical condition, state health officials announced Tuesday.

The Minnesota Department of Health (MDH) says the infected person is an Anoka County resident in their 30s who was likely exposed to COVID-19 through contact with international travelers outside of Minnesota. According to MDH, the patient had no apparent prior health conditions.

The patient developed symptoms on Feb. 28 and was evaluated and released on March 3 based on symptoms at the time. Officials say the patient sought care again on March 9. Samples were sent to the MHD Public Health Laboratory and the test was found positive earlier Tuesday.

"MDH is awaiting confirmatory testing from CDC, but health officials consider the presumptive results actionable," MDH said in a release.
MDH says the patient is currently hospitalized in critical condition.

According to MDH, the department is working with Anoka County Public Health and health care partners to identify and contact all those who may have come into contact with the infected person. Officials say the patient took "great care" to isolate themselves and minimize contact.

This comes four days after the first confirmed presumptive case of coronavirus

(COVID-19) in the state of Minnesota was announced Friday.

This is quite a coincidence! Paying close attention, my initial reaction is to scour my mind for distinctions. *This person probably got it from international travelers outside of Minnesota. My ski friends are from the U.S. No has been to China recently — or on a cruise ship to Japan! Remember, Dr. Dave tested his patient in Ohio, and it turned out to be just strep throat! I'm sure it's just walking pneumonia, and the test I just took will prove it!* Nevertheless, I'm not able to completely ignore some obvious facts as my mind continues to analyze. *Vail is always full of international travelers. When I was there, it was teeming with hundreds of snowboard competitors and their fans from Europe. Plus, I had just read a text claiming Jay had been in the state of Washington, near the COVID stricken town of Kirkland, on a business trip just before arriving in Vail. He could have picked up the virus there.*

Finally, it was impossible to ignore the fact that the young Anoka patient had not been overly ill initially. The patient was seen by a doctor and sent home. Six days passed before the patient returned for more medical care. *Hmmm… ten days later, this patient is making the news and in critical condition!*

Hoping my bedtime routine will snap me out of thinking obsessively about my health, I get up and start my nightly ritual of setting up my coffee maker. Scooping fresh beans, filling the carafe with filtered water, and setting out my favorite mug combine to press the "mental" pause button. Before my thoughts can circle back to the woman fighting for her life in the hospital, the phone rings. I know from the ringtone it's John.

138

I answer with a sigh, "Hey, I have some news to share about what's going on here at home."

"Sorry I couldn't call back sooner. I just got back to the hotel room after a very long dinner with my sales rep and a client," John explains.

"I understand. Let me fill you in. Dr. Gamren sent me to the emergency room to be tested for the coronavirus tonight. Anyway, I don't think I have this new virus. I believe the doctor is covering her bases because I told her one of the people I skied with in Vail just tested positive."

"Wow, you've had quite the evening! When will you know your test result?"

"The doctor said the hospital would call me within twenty-four to forty-eight hours."

"OK, did you find out if your chest X-ray showed pneumonia?"

"Yes, a small spot in the lower right lung," I replied as my left hand moved to my right ribcage.

"Well, keep me up to date and get some sleep so you can get over the pneumonia. It's not like you've never had it before. You know what to do to get over it," John said as he yawned.

I woke up this morning believing I caught a cold in Vail. I accepted the chest cold turned into walking pneumonia. I definitely over-exerted myself on the slopes and socialized through the night, resulting in very little sleep for seven days after getting it. After all, this was the third time that I can remember getting a chest cold, which later turned into walking pneumonia. Antibiotics have always provided a relatively quick cure.

I had clung optimistically to this plausible explanation — even in the face of Jay's positive diagnosis. Time and time again, I was able to hold the tide of growing angst out to sea. However, the trip to the ER, the hazmat suits, the critically ill local woman, and my pneumonia were gnawing at me. No longer could I hold back the tide — the angst was growing within me! I collapse into bed as the "soon to be confirmed" coronavirus brewing inside my lungs consumed what little energy I had left. I could no longer think ... I could no longer keep my eyes open.

Chapter 13

March 11, 2020 – Pandemic

Life can only be understood backwards; but it must be lived forwards.

-Soren Kierkegaard

I am one of those lucky people whose circadian rhythm includes a built-in alarm clock. Sadly, with my recent unusual daytime fatigue and protracted nighttime sleep, I felt it necessary to set a "real" alarm before bed last night. Capturing a sliver of time with Avery before she rushes out the door to start her day is important to me, and now, with the alarm blaring, I know it was the right choice. Mustering the energy to pull back the covers takes extraordinary will power. My body wants to lie here, and my brain wants to go back to sleep. Coughing and fatigue take center stage once again. When I do finally pull back the covers, I remember the need to pick up my newly prescribed antibiotic, giving me the only reason to change out of my pajamas.

Standing in the kitchen, I greet Avery as she opens the fridge door.

"Can I make an egg sandwich for you?" I ask.

"No thanks. I'm just going to have cereal this morning," Avery mumbles.

"So, what do you have going on after school today?"

"I'm not sure. There might be a theater meeting. I'll text you."

"All right. It's just you and me for dinner tonight because Dad is still in New York. If you have a special request, let me know."

"OK. Thanks, Mom."

As I write this today, I reflect on how much has changed with COVID-19 testing and the protocol surrounding it. When I left the hospital, neither the doctor nor the nurse mentioned the need for my family to quarantine while waiting for my test results. This is just one example of many changes that will be made over time to the official recommendations for efforts to stop the virus' spread.

Pulling up to Walgreens, I decide to go inside instead of using the drive-thru. Making my way to the pharmacy counter, I join the back of the line and wait. Standing there, zoning out, a text chime invades my consciousness. It takes a minute before I realize it's my phone, but when I do, my eyes focus on "MUST READ!" Tapping on the text, the first line grips me: "Group of ladies celebrating birthdays in Vail same dates as us – Extremely Sick!"

"What on earth!" My mind roils while taking in this announcement.

This group of women mostly hails from Chicago. Jill shares a long letter from one of them, describing her experience over the past week. I start to read it, but soon the pharmacy assistant motions to me, so this worrisome news is tabled. It only takes a few minutes to get back into my vehicle where I urgently revisit the letter.

I am a healthy 50-year-old living with my husband and four children outside Chicago. I celebrated a neighborhood friend's 50th birthday with a ski weekend in Vail at the

142

end of February. The ten of us returned through O'Hare on March 1st and I am nearly certain I got COVID-19. I say this with as much medical certainty as I can obtain because I do not qualify for testing, but here is what I know:

1. My roommate in Vail, "A" and I became sick by Tuesday after flying home Sunday. We were both in bed with painful aches and just feeling awful. Several others had similar ailments, with less severity.

2. There was a second group of neighborhood moms who also spent that weekend in Vail. Four of those moms have confirmed positive tests for COVID-19, along with at least one of their children. Like us, that group was very sick by Tuesday.

3. Compared to my roommate "A", I had mild symptoms. The virus was astonishingly painful. My mild symptoms were still so awful that for the first time in 25 years and four pregnancies, I asked my husband to stay by my side because I was scared of how much discomfort every muscle in my body felt.

4. Aches and lethargy were the most immediate symptoms. In addition, I had no appetite, and when I did, nothing tasted right. I had a 101-degree fever and barely enough energy to get downstairs to my desk. Ibuprofen did nothing for the pain in my muscles the first

few days but eventually it started to work. (Note the WHO says NOT to take ibuprofen as it is making coronavirus worse). I slept nearly round the clock the first day or two and then napped daily for the next 10 days or so. My roommate "A" was sicker. She could not get out of bed at all for ten days. She could not lift her head. She took a shower on day 6 for an important family event and fell back asleep in her robe and didn't wake the entire day. We both had a bit of a cough, but it seems neither of us got full blown pneumonia. I have been told that the pain experienced amidst Vail - Mom Group 2 - was so severe they thought their lungs would explode from their bodies.

5. We did not believe that first week that we had COVID-19 because we were largely asymptomatic of the cough prevalent in severe cases. At that time (March 3-4), Chicago/the US really weren't communicating much about the virus and certainly not testing at that time. "A" went to the doctor and was put on an antibiotic, but it didn't do anything for her. She was twice rejected from getting the COVID-19 test because her symptoms on day 8 didn't qualify her. Still, neither of us can obtain the test. From what I understand about Vail - Mom Group 2, - they also were initially rejected from the COVID-19 test and then finally got tested after infecting others and suffering

6. I exposed my kids and husband daily and unfortunately, my 80-year old mom on Day 7. No one in my family is showing signs of the virus, so I am extremely thankful it appears I did not pass it along. My roommate's family is the same. No signs. Unfortunately, the other mom group that had worse respiratory symptoms and have confirmed cases amidst their kids.

7.

On day 8 and 9, I ran a few errands because I started to feel better. This set me back and I stayed home this time worried I might have the coronavirus. I have strictly quarantined since that one day out.

With additional information, it is just today that "A" and I have near certainty that we had the COVID-19. I share our story in hopes that it helps others by raising awareness. COVID-19 is all over our community now and just because my family dodged a bullet not getting it from me last week, they can from others.

The grip on my phone gives way. I fumble to grasp it as it plops onto my lap. There are so many snippets of things flashing through my mind. A coherent thought can't be mustered. My brain feels like a TV with a picture turned to snow — the signal lost. I have been steadfast in dismissing the possibility of COVID. My mind strains to grasp what I have just read. Grappling with the striking similarities presented with: "erratic energy levels," "severe fatigue," "body aches," "lethargy," "nothing tasted right," "full blown pneumonia," "lungs would explode". . . "She felt better — ran errands — got sick again." "They didn't believe."

These women were in Vail at the exact same time I was. We are all sick. Jay is in the hospital. Karley needs an IV. One of these moms gave it to her kids!

I have no idea how I got home from Walgreens. The five-minute drive was performed on autopilot. My first priority when I walk in the door is to take my medication for the pneumonia. Feeling depleted and ready to lie down, I change into comfortable sweatpants and curl up on the sofa with my phone. Desperate for understanding, I immerse myself in researching COVID-19. When I reach a dead end with my research, I send texts to my ski buddies, asking about this grave letter. Only Amanda replies — "super busy with patients." Exhaustion overtakes my body as I continually push away my pressing panic. *I am back to the feeling of holding the tide of swelling angst out to sea.* I put down the phone and turn on the TV, hoping to distract myself. Luckily, I find the perfect sedative — a sweet, slow, romance on the Hallmark channel. My slumber continues through the afternoon, interrupted only by a slamming door.

"Hi, I'm home," Avery belts out with a sing-song ring in her voice.

Sitting up, the ratsnest on top of my head becomes visible from across the room.

"Were you sleeping, Mom?"

"Just dozing," I say, with a quiet voice, trying to squelch a cough.

"Sorry to wake you. I've got a lot of homework to do before ballet, so I'm going upstairs."

"OK, honey."

146

I look at the clock on the wall, stretch out my arms, and draw in air for a yawn. My "nap" added up to a whopping five hours of sleep, but it was far from restful. The yawn sparks the need to cough, giving me the familiar feeling of constricted breath.

The late afternoon turns into evening, and I am pleased to find enough leftovers in the refrigerator to assemble two plates for dinner. The last thing I feel like doing right now is cooking. When the timer on the microwave goes off, I text Avery, "Dinner is ready." Keeping a close eye on the clock, I nudge her to finish so she won't be late for ballet. I offer to clean the dishes, and she hurries out the door. As soon as the kitchen is clean, I flop onto the sofa and begin flipping through the channels. I stumble upon breaking news on CNBC. A tweet was just released from actor Tom Hanks informing the world he and his wife tested positive for COVID-19:

Twitter:
March 11, 2020 - 8:14pm

https://mobile.twitter.com/tomhanks/status/12379098970 20207104

> **Hello, folks. Rita and I are down here in Australia. We felt a bit tired, like we had colds, and some body aches. Rita had some chills that came and went. Slight fevers too. To play things right, as is needed in the world right now, we were tested for the Coronavirus, and were found to be positive. Well, now. What to do next? The Medical Officials have protocols that must be followed. We Hanks' will be tested, observed,**

**and isolated for as long as public health and
safety requires. Not much more to it than a
one-day-at-a-time approach, no?
We'll keep the world posted and updated.
Take care of yourselves!
Hanx!**

Hello, folks. Rita and I are down here in Australia. We felt a bit tired, like we had colds, and some body aches. Rita had some chills that came and went. Slight fevers too. To play things right, as is needed in the world right now, we were tested for the Coronavirus, and were found to be positive.

Well, now. What to do next? The Medical Officials have protocols that must be followed. We Hanks' will be tested, observed, and isolated for as long as public health and safety requires. Not much more to it than a one-day-at-a-time approach, no?

We'll keep the world posted and updated.

Take care of yourselves!

Hanx!

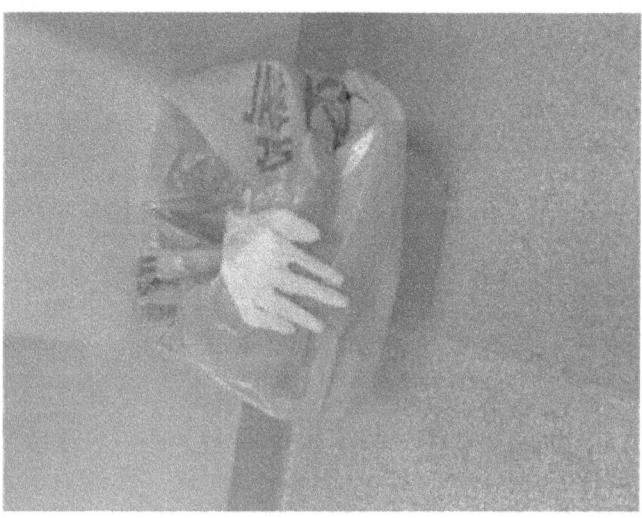

In severe cases, an infection from coronavirus can lead to pneumonia, severe acute respiratory syndrome, kidney failure and death.

<u>Most people who become ill won't develop serious symptoms</u>, but 15% to 20% of the people who are exposed to the virus get severely sick. The odds of developing COVID-19 increase with age, starting at age 60. It's especially lethal for people over 80.

Around the same time that Hanks and Wilson disclosed their diagnosis, the National Basketball Association suspended its season indefinitely after learning that a <u>Utah Jazz player tested positive for coronavirus</u>. The NBA canceled Wednesday night's game between the Jazz and Oklahoma City Thunder.

Since my ski trip, I frequently find myself unable to take a deep breath without coughing. Tonight, I am alone — Avery is at ballet, John is in New York City — and I'm thinking, *I can't take a deep breath without coughing!* Absorbing the breaking news and listening to the reporters talk about the coronavirus strike an uncomfortable chord with me, especially when I learn about Rick Cotton. He is the executive director of the Port Authority of New York and New Jersey, and medical experts believe the reason he tested positive is possibly a result of his frequent visits to airports and train stations. *John just flew into New York City. At this point, I have to tell myself — again — not to worry.*

My mind runs through a list distinguishing my case from those in the news: Tom and Rita Hanks are in their 60s, and they are doing just fine. I most likely just have walking pneumonia. The ER doctor wasn't alarmed, and my exam didn't reveal anything unusual. I wasn't kept overnight for observation. My blood oxygen level was 99%. All of these rationalizations ease my troubled mind but only for a few minutes. The letter creeps back into the forefront of my mind, consuming me, and a horribly miserable evening lying on the sofa alone would soon become the start of a journey I never imagined possible.

Chapter 14

Thursday, March 12th, is the last school day for Avery this week. A teacher workday is scheduled for Friday the 13th, and spring break starts next week. We plan to escape still-chilly Minnesota with a quick trip to South Florida. We talk briefly during breakfast about this warm, beachy respite while her bowl of cereal disappears at record speed. We are excited to spend some days on a balmy, breezy beach, and Avery has been making a list of places she wants to visit. As quickly as the cereal disappears this morning, so does Avery, grabbing her lunch, slinging her backpack, snatching her key, and sprinting out the door.

Tackling housework doesn't excite me, but at least I got a decent night's sleep. The caffeine in my morning coffee should give me the jolt I need to get something done. Most importantly, I need a distraction. Despite my chipper conversation with Avery about Florida, I fear the vacation is hanging in the balance. The evidence points to COVID. But isn't it possible that I am on the tail end of it? Couldn't my lingering cough relate to a pneumonia virus or bacteria that infected me when I was weakened by the coronavirus? I remember having pneumonia as a secondary infection in the past. None of the articles I found on COVID-19 talked about this possibility.

Around 9:30 a.m., the phone rings. It's Angie, a neighbor and friend.

"Hey, I heard you weren't feeling well. We missed you at the parent meeting for the summer science trip Tuesday evening. Avery mentioned to me that you're sick with bronchitis. I hope it's not too serious. Do you have a little time to talk? I want to ask you a few questions and go over a few of the trip details."

"Sure, happy to," I respond, pouring another cup of coffee.

"Did your doctor talk to you about this coronavirus?" Angie asked, sounding worried.

"No, but I brought it up on the follow-up call about my chest X-ray. I had just heard that one of the people I skied with tested positive and is in the hospital. With that news, she said she had to call Fairview for guidance. I ended up in the ER Tuesday night getting tested."

"Oh my gosh, when will you know?"

"I'm not sure. I hope the hospital calls soon. The waiting is a little nerve-racking," I say, coughing into the phone.

"I'm sure it is, Laurel. This virus has me a little freaked out, and I'm thinking of keeping the girls home from school after spring break if I hear the virus is spreading."

"I completely understand how you feel. Watching Tom and Rita Hanks share their positive test results with a tweet on the news last night was surprising."

"I saw that tweet too. Kind of puts it in perspective for me. Well, let me fill you in about the summer science field trip."

Angie goes through her notes, sharing the highlights while occasionally making funny comments with her dry, witty sense of humor. Her hilarious delivery thankfully diverts my attention, but each time I laugh, another coughing fit commences. (I will say, though, it's worth every annoying cough because she is just so darn funny.) I jot a few notes, set a reminder to research the company in charge of the science trip, and enter important dates into my phone. As soon as we hang up, I create a folder and file it in my desk drawer.

"That sure was nice," I think to myself. Thank goodness for kind friends. Little did I know how much my friends would be doing for me in the coming weeks.

The coffee isn't working. I feel like crawling back into bed. But the idea is to stay busy and not dwell on my coronavirus test. If the caffeine isn't going to do the trick, I need music and movement to do the job. I tap on the playlist icon, turn on the portable speaker, and fill the house with the sounds of the Riverside Swing Band. The horns mixed with Kyle Tennis' voice transports me to the dance floor, giving my broom rhythm. Sweeping, swiffering, and stovetop scouring all become much more enjoyable with the happy sounds of "East Coast swing." So far, so good...

Lunchtime approaches, and I must eat something. Taking my new antibiotic for the pneumonia on an empty stomach wouldn't be wise. Opening the refrigerator, I start pulling out vegetables one-by-one, lining them up on the kitchen counter. *A salad will suffice,* I think to myself. *In the back of my mind, I can hear the motivational speaker and author, Rachel Hollis, giving wise advice, "Eat the stupid salad!"* The chopping begins! Just as I finish throwing a salad together, the home phone rings. I typically don't answer my home phone. Too many political surveys and solicitors. Today, however, Caller ID transmits — "M Health Fairview." My heart precipitously drops into my stomach! It is the hospital calling.

"Hello," I eek out, with a crack in my voice.

"Good afternoon. May I speak to Laurel Fischbach?"

"This is she."

"This is Fairview Hospital calling about your COVID-19 test results."

"Yes. I've been expecting your call. Do you have some good news for me?" I ask, trying not to cough into the phone.

"Your test came back positive, Mrs. Fischbach. — I'm sorry."

A moment of silence ensues, lingering in the space between us for what seems like an eternity.

"Really? I'm positive? — I really didn't want to believe this pneumonia was the coronavirus," I respond ever so softly.

Reflecting on this experience, of course I could believe I had the coronavirus. In fact, logically, it seemed likely I had it and that's why waiting for my test result was unsettling. The symptoms I have experienced since returning from Vail were strikingly similar to those detailed in the letter from the Chicago mom. The few symptoms described by Tom Hanks also lined up. For days, my subconscious had been denying I was infected with this virus. Why was I working so hard to push the possibility out of my mind? I contend it's human nature. When you're frightened by the unknown, that's what you do. I didn't want to think I had a novel virus — one that wasn't understood by the medical community. I didn't want to think about the daily rise in positive cases. I didn't want to think about the staggering number of deaths in Italy. I didn't want to think I may have infected those I care about. I tried not to know what I instinctually knew!

The gentleman calling from the hospital is every bit of the word "gentleman." His voice is kind. He explains the new COVID-19 test and tells me I am the first patient to receive one at this hospital. He goes on to explain my results are considered "presumptive positive."

The moment I hear the word "presumptive," my immediate reaction is, "Oh, I still have a chance of being negative! What exactly does presumptive positive mean?" I optimistically ask.

"Presumptive positive means our lab in the hospital returned a positive result with SARS-CoV-2, the virus that causes COVID-19. The test gives us a 99% accurate outcome; however, your samples will be sent to the CDC in Atlanta today for additional testing. The CDC reruns all COVID-19 tests to be sure the labs are accurate. Until we receive the results from them, you are considered presumptive positive. We want you to treat your test result as if you're confirmed positive and follow the CDC's guidelines. You will be counted in Minnesota's positive case numbers, and you need to be prepared for a call from the Department of Health."

"Oh, the Department of Health is going to call?" I say, my voice quivering.

"Yes, but don't be alarmed. They will assign a case manager to help you with your quarantine, and they will be asking you some questions about your travels."

"OK," I reply, sheepishly.

"Please pay attention to how you feel. If you are having any difficulty breathing or feel compression in your chest — please call 911. We will want to see you immediately here at the hospital. Our staff is prepared to help you."

"I will, but can you explain what you mean by — compression in my chest?" I inquire, noticing my unusually tight grip on the phone.

"Yes. Compression may feel as though a weight is sitting on your chest, or your lungs may feel tight. If this feeling begins to happen, we will want to monitor your blood oxygen level."

"Right now, my lungs feel tight, I can't take a deep breath without coughing, and I'm winded while walking up stairs."

"I'm looking at your chart, and I see you had a chest X-ray showing pneumonia. Your symptoms are in line with bronchitis and pneumonia. You have one infiltrate in the lower right lobe. An infiltrate in this area of the lung is the most common site to develop a mass of fluid and inflammation, so the most important thing you can do is monitor how you feel. If you begin experiencing extreme shortness of breath with rapid breathing or if you have chest pain, then it's time to come to the hospital. Do you understand?"

"Yes, thank you."

"OK, do you have any other questions for me?"

I thank the doctor for his call, hanging up the phone in a daze.

The flood of emotions runs the gamut. How am I going to self-monitor my symptoms? Florida is out! What about all the people I've been around? Sitting at my kitchen counter, I feel stuck. *"Now what do I do?"* The phone rings again. This time, it's the Minnesota Department of Health.

"Hello," I answer with trepidation.

"Hello. Is Laurel Fischbach available?"

"This is she," I say, sounding like a child with a high-pitched inflection.

"Good morning, Mrs. Fischbach. This is Aaron calling from the Department of Health."

"Good morning. I was told someone from the Department of Health would be calling. I just hung up with the hospital."

"All right, so you understand you've tested positive for the coronavirus? I'm assuming your diagnosis

156

has been explained to you," Aaron says, shuffling papers in the background.

"Yes."

"OK. Well, I need to ask you some questions."

For the next 45 minutes, he asks a series of questions, going down a checklist, ensuring he ultimately covers all of his bases. The conversation flows, thanks to his gentle way of jogging my memory. When answering all of these questions, I imagine Aaron is taking copious notes.

"Who lives in your home with you?"

"My daughter and husband, oh... and our cat," I add as I watch her dart to the picture window with a squirrel in her sights.

"What is your daughter's age?"

"She's 16."

"OK, you mentioned you have a cat. Would you like to get a COVID test for your cat?"

A test for my cat? Did I hear him correctly? Bewildered by this question, I responded, stammering at first.

"Um... I don't know...I mean, I don't think I need a coronavirus test for my cat. Um...It's not that I don't love my cat... I do, I just think she'll be fine," I say with a weird feeling.

You can't make this stuff up! I imagined Aaron checking a box on a long-detailed list. "Family pet — Check. Cat — Check. Test for Pet — No." When you put this situation into context, all of my ski buddies in different states are home presenting symptoms, and 90% of them are told to just stay home because there aren't enough tests. Still, Minnesota has a coronavirus test available for my cat? Really? This makes no sense!

"OK. Next, I need to know where your daughter and husband are," Aaron asks.

"My daughter is at school and my husband is in New York City on business."

I hear an audible exhale from Aaron as he pauses.

"Your husband is in New York City? Can you tell me when he arrived and which airport he flew into?"

I give Aaron details about John's business trip and explain he is expected to fly home this evening. I gather Aaron is scrolling through a document looking for instruction or maybe some type of protocol for how to respond.

"OK. We need to get in touch with your husband before he goes to the airport. I also need to consult with the New York Department of Health to determine if he's allowed to board a plane. Your husband may need to quarantine in New York City. I haven't dealt with this type of situation, so please bear with me."

"I understand. Could he rent a car and drive back to Minnesota?" I ask, trying to stay levelheaded.

"Hmmm…I'm not sure about crossing multiple state lines. Do you know if your husband has any symptoms?"

"Last night before I went to bed, he didn't complain of feeling ill, but I didn't ask either."

"All right. I need to ask some questions about your daughter. What's her name, and where does she attend high school? Also, is she experiencing any symptoms?"

"Avery Fischbach. She attends Edina High School and no, she hasn't been sick."

"Next, can you tell me when you traveled to Vail, Colorado and the timeline for your trip?" Aaron inquires, while I envision a calendar splayed in front of him.

158

"Sure. I flew into Denver on Friday, February 21st, took a shuttle van to Vail and stayed exclusively in Vail village until March 1st."

"Did you fly out of Denver for your return on March 1st?"

"Yes, that's correct. Are you going to get in touch with the Colorado Department of Health?" I ask.

"No. We are most concerned with where you have been since you landed in Minneapolis," Aaron explains in a way that indicates we're moving on to details involving my exposure to others beginning on March 1st.

"Oh... but isn't it important for the Colorado Department of Health to contact the hotel where I stayed? Shouldn't the employees at the hotel know about my positive result? I had contact with several employees at the hotel," I say, feeling puzzled.

"No, our job is to contact trace here in Minnesota."

I had to excuse myself several times during our conversation to cough and try to squelch the nagging tickle that pulled at my words. It felt as though my lungs were debating about how my air intake should be divided between speaking and breathing.

"I need to retrace your steps since you landed on March 1st, so let's go through each day," Aaron says, sighing through the word — day.

"Oh, no! I don't want to tell you where I have been over the past week," I respond with a tentative tone.

"Why?" He asked, his voice rising an octave.

"Because, um... I do something — very unusual," I respond reticently.

A pause between the two of us creates an uncomfortable silence. Struggling to wrap my brain around the plethora of people dancing through my mind

159

during this silence causes every muscle in my body to tense.

"What is it?" Aaron asks, sounding curious but also hesitant.

"Um… I'm an amateur ballroom dancer. And — um…I just went to a dance on Sunday night. I danced for several hours with a lot of different partners."

All the air inside of Aaron's lungs escaped at once. At the end of the exhalation was a sound resembling shhh…

"Ohhhhh — that 'is' — very unusual."

"I don't even know who all of the men are that I danced with."

"Um, what? You don't know who you danced with?"

"Yes, I'm sorry."

"When did you say you went to this dance? I need to make some notes about where it was and get any names of partners you do know," Aaron asks, his fingers feverishly clicking on a keyboard in the background.

"Sure. I understand. Um…let me think. I attended the dance at Cinema Ballroom on Sunday night, March 8th. The Jerry O'Hagan band played from 7:00 p.m. to 9:30 p.m., preceded by an hour-long dance lesson at six o'clock. I didn't attend the dance lesson. I arrived right at seven o'clock and danced until the band quit. Oh — and during the evening, um…there was a mixer."

Aaron stops me before I can continue on with my recount of the evening.

"A mixer?" he asks, questioning the word, searching for its meaning.

"Yes, a mixer at a ballroom dance allows everyone to dance with many different partners for about 15 minutes. I probably danced with nine or ten different gentlemen, many of whom I don't know because the pairing of partners during a mixer is random."

Aaron was silent for an eternal moment. I assume he was grappling with the picture of ballroom dancers — waltzing rib to rib — faces inches apart. And — that would be accurate!

"Oh… there is one more thing I need to share with you." *I took a deep breath and paused as the words struggled to form.* — "Most of these dance partners at Cinema Ballroom are 65 and older."

Sigh… "Laurel, I'm going to need phone numbers of as many of these men as possible."

"All right. I'll do my best."

"I'm going to have to draft a letter to Cinema Ballroom. The owner will need to inform the attendees. Just so you know, all of this will be documented and placed on the Minnesota Department of Health website. But your identity will remain anonymous," Aaron promises.

"OK. Thank you for letting me know. I do have a question about giving people's cell numbers. I'm not comfortable with giving out phone numbers. Would it be possible for me to contact these men directly and give them your number?"

"Yes. As long as they contact me within 24 hours. Have them call my direct line. Now, I think we need to map out each day starting with when you landed on March 1st."

"OK. I landed in the evening around ten o'clock. My husband, John, picked me up, and we went directly from the airport to the house."

"All right, let's move on to Monday the 2nd."

"On Monday, Bob Sondag and I had a dance lesson at Cinema Ballroom with Grace."

"Got it. Did you have contact with anyone else there?" he asks.

"No, not really, only a brief hello with the receptionist when I checked in."

"What did you do with the rest of your day?"

"Oh boy," I say with a sigh — "I nanny for five-year-old twins daily after school."

"You nanny for a family — daily? How many hours are you with these kids?"

"Yes, I greet the twins at their house every day when the bus drops them off and usually stay for about three hours. When I finished my dance lesson, I drove directly to their house. You can make a note that I cared for the kids each day during the week of March 2nd."

Aaron is silent. I wait, holding my breath, thinking about the kids and their parents. The silence from Aaron gives my thoughts time to churn. Eventually, an exhaled breath breaks the quiet, communicating, *This woman's case is going to be complicated.*

"Who else were you in contact with during the daily care of these two children?" Aaron inquires.

"The twins' dad always gets home from work before their mom, and I debrief him about our afternoon."

"OK, were you caring for the kids after school the week beginning Monday, March 9th?"

"No, the kids had a stomach virus and stayed home from school on Monday, so I didn't go that day. Then my doctor diagnosed me with bronchitis and told me to stay home because I was contagious."

"The five-year-old twins had a stomach virus?"

"Yes."

"Did they see a doctor? Do you know if they were diagnosed with anything specific?"

162

"No, I'm sorry I don't know," I answer, feeling inadequate with this response.

"All right, back to March 2nd. What did you do that evening?" Aaron probes.

"Nothing much. I was exhausted from my ski trip and needed to be home since I had been away for nine days. I didn't go anywhere in the evenings until Sunday night the 8th for the Ballroom Dance."

"Good! That's helpful!"

"I do need to tell you I took four dance lessons with three different instructors at three different dance studios since returning from Vail."

"Why don't you go ahead and give me those dates and details."

"Let's see…Cinema Ballroom was Monday the 2nd; I already told you about that lesson. Dancers Studio was Wednesday the 4th. Char Torkelson (Howard) was Thursday the 5th. And my last lesson was at Cinema Ballroom on Monday the 9th. My dance partner at Dancers Studio was Bob Sondag, with Gordon instructing. On Thursday, I had a lesson taught by Char with a different dance partner, Dave Tsang, and when I arrived at Char's home, I socialized with a few students who just finished a group class. My last lesson this past Monday was with Bob and Grace at Cinema Ballroom."

"Wow — That's a lot of dance lessons!"

"I know, that's why having this virus is concerning. When I take lessons, the instructor and dance partner are only inches from my face. Dance frame lends itself to extremely close contact."

At this point in the conversation, 30 minutes have passed. I can only imagine how many pages of notes are splayed across Aaron's desk.

"Do you think you have covered all the details about your dancing? If so, I'd like to know about any other public places you visited in the last ten days."

I pull up my iPhone calendar to help jog my memory and try my best to remember each day. This is exhausting. I'm trying to see the details, remember the days, and retrace my steps. Sometimes when I try, all I see are shadows lost in a fog. I know I went to a grocery store, but I don't remember which day. I know I went to Walgreens and the doctor's office, and I think those details are noted and accurate. I hope they're accurate.

"Do you feel as though you have remembered everything?"

"Yes. Um… I think so."

"OK. I need to go over some specifics about your quarantine. You need to stay in your home for the next 14 days, only leaving to go to the hospital if you require medical attention. The Department of Health will provide groceries and pick up any medication that has been prescribed for you. It's imperative that you don't leave your home or have contact with anyone, so your family members will need to keep their distance from you within the house."

"If John can return from New York City, would it be OK if he and Avery go to a hotel?"

"Sure. If they can afford to do that, it would be ideal. As soon as we hang up, I'll contact the New York Department of Health."

"OK," I reply.

"For now, Mrs. Fischbach, I'll need you to start contacting everyone you've come in contact with since you arrived from Colorado. Give out my direct number, and ask them to contact me so I can instruct them about their suggested quarantine period."

"Wait! A quarantine period for everyone I've had contact with?"

"Yes. It's important to contain the virus to the best of our ability. I'll have questions and instructions for each of your contacts."

"All right. I'll try to get a hold of as many people as possible today. Oh, and one other thing, how do I get coronavirus tests for Avery and John?"

"The Department of Health can't order COVID-19 tests. You'll need to get in touch with your doctor and ask this question."

"Oh, I didn't know."

"I'll be back in touch with a plan for your husband's return to Minnesota."

Overwhelmed only scratches the surface of how I felt when I hung up the phone. My emotions were running high, and I knew I needed to call my best friend, Lori. For thirty years, when I'm struggling, she's been my confidant. As soon as I heard her consoling voice, my emotions released. Tears formed, my head dropped, and my body shook. I tried to speak but couldn't.

"Oh, Laurel, what's going on?" Lori asks, worried.

"I have to figure out how to get a hold of every single person I've had contact with since I returned from Vail. I just found out I'm positive with the coronavirus," I explain through coughs and simultaneous sobs. "I don't want to scare anyone with my news. What if someone gets really sick because of me? My God, what if someone dies? Oh, Lori — I just remembered something! One of the dance instructors I danced with this week has a pregnant wife. What if she ends up getting the virus from me? What if something happens to the baby?"

"Laurel, I need you to try to take a deep breath and slow down. Your test came back positive?"

"Yes. I just don't know where to start. I have to make a list of everyone I've had contact with. There are so many people to contact, and I don't want to give any of them this awful news," I say, grabbing a tissue and then a second one.

"I know this is frightening, but people will understand. You had no idea you were positive with the coronavirus."

"Lori, I'm concerned for the twins. I spent every day with them the first five days after my return from skiing, and now they're home sick with upset stomachs."

"I know this is daunting, but you'll get through it."

Lori's calm, comforting tone soothes me, and I can feel my best friend's love and concern. Bending her ear is cathartic, helping me muster the courage to dial the first phone number, the twins' parents. As soon as I hear the twins' father answer the phone, I say, "I don't want to scare you, but I need to inform you that I have tested positive for the coronavirus. I'm so sorry."

I repeated those somber words over and over for the next 48 hours. I now know how ulcers get their start. It's a miracle I didn't develop one from the sick feeling in my stomach. Often, I was met with measured silence on the other end of the phone. Ultimately when the content of the words sank in, an avalanche of questions began. I went to great lengths, trying to remember the multitude of dance partners from my evening at Cinema Ballroom. I called popular dance instructors around the Twin Cities, asking if they had contact information for gentlemen I didn't know very well. I found myself sitting at my desk for hours, calling and emailing for the next few days. I

166

made a list of friends my daughter socialized with during the past week so I could alert the parents, just in case. And, I made list, upon list, upon list.

Chapter 15

I decide it's best to call John only after the Department of Health has a plan for his return. This time allows me to scour my memory for Avery's whereabouts and to retrace my own over the past 10 days. I hope I won't miss anything. Surprisingly, Aaron calls back within an hour, so my time is cut short. I am relieved to learn the State of New York has no problem with John boarding a plane, and fortunately, there are no snowstorms in the forecast. I don't think my nerves could handle any delays.

Aaron asks for John's phone number. I oblige but request he wait a few minutes before calling him, giving me time to talk with him first. I immediately call, catching him between appointments. The moment he answers the phone, it's akin to the sound of a shot at the start of a race.

"John, I found out I'm positive with the coronavirus. I've been on the phone with the Department of Health, and they'll be calling you momentarily. I need you to…"

John interrupts me while I work to get everything out in one breath.

"Oh, when did you get a call?" John asks, surprised.

"The hospital called first a little while ago, and then the Department of Health called next. I have to quarantine for 14 days, and so do you and Avery. I think the two of you should go to a hotel if you feel OK. You still feel OK, right? Maybe you could ask the Department of Health if a hotel could be an option. I already brought it up and they thought it could be a possibility," my words tripping over each other.

"OK. Slow down, please! Laurel — I need you to take a breath."

"Easier said than done! Slowing down didn't feel like a viable option. Many people needed to be called, and conversing without coughing my head off will be challenging," I think.

"I wasn't sure if you were going to be required to quarantine in New York City. There was talk about you having to find a hotel for 14 days, and there was a possibility that you would be restricted from flying. The New York Department of Health has spoken with our Department of Health, and at the moment, you're cleared to fly. You don't have a cough, do you? I don't know if you should go to your next appointment. Maybe you should head straight to the airport? I wonder if I should call the high school and pull Avery out right now?" I fire at him without giving him a chance to respond.

"Laurel, I feel fine. I'm sure I'll be able to get back home. Calm down — please! Minnesota and New York are talking about me being able to fly?"

"Yes! John, there was discussion about you not being able to board a plane."

"OK. So, you're telling me as of now — I can fly?"

"Yes, and you're going to get a call from Aaron at the Minnesota Department of Health."

"All right. Now, what did you say about Avery? Something about pulling her out of school?" John asks, trying to follow my breathless sentences.

"Now that I know I'm positive, shouldn't she be pulled from school?"

"Avery only has a couple hours left in her day, so I don't think it will make any difference if she stays in

169

school. Pulling her out for the last few hours seems silly. She doesn't have school tomorrow, right?" he inquires.

"Yes, right, It's a teacher workday. There's no school," I express with relief at this well-timed day off.

"All right, I need to make some calls. I'll call you when I get to — Um — oh, someone is trying to call. I don't recognize the number. This could be the health department."

With an abrupt goodbye, John takes the incoming call.

Staring out the window into my backyard, I'm at a loss. Where do I go from here? The only thing I can come up with is pen and paper. Writing down names, dates, and locations for future check marks is the best strategy I can think of after my frenetic call with John. One call I knew was going to be awkward would be to Cinema Ballroom.

As I study my list, Cinema takes first place. Pulling in the deepest breath my lungs allow, I dial the number. A recorded message begins after one ring, "We open at noon." I look at the clock, go back to my list, and dial the next name in line. At exactly 12:00 p.m. Cinema's number is at the top of my list. I manage to get the receptionist. My goals are to inform the owner a letter is on its way from the Minnesota Department of Health and to get our instructor, Grace, on the phone as quickly as possible. She needs to know about my positive diagnosis. I am sure I sound a little frantic. The receptionist is slow to grasp my urgency for interrupting Grace's dance lesson. I can almost feel her consternation. The receptionist presumably had never dealt with a situation where a caller insisted a private lesson be interrupted. She finally agrees to pull Grace from the dance floor, and she promises me she will let the owner know what's

170

happening. I urge they check their email for the letter. As I wait on the line, I can hear a mambo playing in the background. This seems strangely out of place in light of the depressing news I am about deliver.

When Grace says hello, I begin with an apology. "Grace, I'm so sorry I have to interrupt your lesson. Please apologize to your student for me. The reason for my call is to let you know I tested positive for the coronavirus, and you could be infected."

After a long moment of silence, Grace eventually acknowledges my words with a simple response resembling, "Oh."

"I just explained to the receptionist a letter is on its way to Cinema about my attendance Sunday night. You especially need to be concerned, Grace, because I've had two private lessons with you since my return from Vail. The doctors feel certain I contracted the virus in Colorado."

"OK," Grace responds, barely audible.

"Again, I'm so very sorry. Please contact me if I can answer any questions for you," I say, feeling helpless.

"I will."

For the next two days, my life is an exhausting blur. Tedious routine consumes me: making lists, checking names, delivering news, answering questions, and sharing Aaron's direct line at the Department of Health. There is a constant feeling of underlying fear that I could be the source of future illness for each person on the other end of the line. These phone calls were gut-wrenching. Both of my regular dance partners and one of my dance instructors are over 60, so calling them was extremely difficult. It was clear that "age" was a significant risk factor, and I felt an especially heavy burden when I had to call Bob because I had danced with him the most.

There were times I considered creating an audio recording of myself. I thought about pressing the play button when the redundant questions began – right after the familiar gasp. The gasp induced by the impact of the words "positive" and "coronavirus."

"I believe I contracted the virus in Vail, Colorado. — Yes, I feel certain my symptoms started at the end of February. — Yes, my first symptom was tightness in my chest. — At this time, my family is not sick. — I suggest you call and inform your doctor you had contact with me. — I would ask your doctor to order a COVID-19 test for you. — I'm sorry, I don't have any more answers for you but feel certain the Department of Health will be able to help you. Here is the phone number."

Four o'clock in the afternoon arrives on the strangest Thursday of my life. Avery comes through the door with a spring in her step, knowing she is free from school for the next 10 days. Spring break has arrived! Moments after she sets down her backpack, I ask her to come into the TV room. When she approaches, I ask her to stop at the entry and promptly launch into my spiel.

"Avery, I found out today I'm positive with the coronavirus. You need to keep your distance from me. I've been on the phone with the Department of Health several times today, and Dad is trying to figure out what to do."

"Mom, are you going to be OK?"

172

"Yes. I'm doing OK, Honey. Don't worry," I say with a caring, calm demeanor, trying to give her a sense of security. "Avery, listen to me for a second. I need you to pack a suitcase with everything you might need for a two-week stay in a hotel."

"What do you mean?" she inquires, tilting her head.

"Dad is working on finding a place for the two of you to quarantine together. The Department of Health needs you and Dad to monitor yourselves for symptoms for the next 14 days. I really hope I haven't infected either of you, but the only way to know is to isolate and monitor yourselves. I'm going to ask my doctor to order COVID-19 tests for the both of you."

"When will Dad be home from New York City?" Avery asks, showing obvious signs of worry in her eyes.

"He should make it home sometime this evening."

"OK, Mom. I'll go pack."

"Thank you. I'm sorry you have to go through this. I love you and wish I could give you a hug," expressing myself as the tightness in my chest heightens, exacerbated by emotion.

"I know, Mom," Avery says as she looks over her shoulder with one hand on the handrail, her shoulders slumped forward.

At this moment, she and I know our spring break plans are canceled. Still, I focus my energy on getting in touch with my doctor's office and tracking down more people. I am effectively doing my own "contact tracing." I leave a message informing my doctor of my positive test and requesting COVID-19 tests for John and Avery. Not knowing what goes on behind the scenes in a public health crisis, I am surprised to learn my doctor had already been apprised. She calls me back within the hour and gives me some very disappointing news.

"Hi, Laurel. I understand you called about getting COVID-19 tests for your husband and daughter," Dr. Gamren says.

"Yes. I'm concerned I've infected them, and I would like them to be tested. Can you order the same test I received even though they aren't patients of yours?" I plead.

"Do they have symptoms?"

"No, they tell me they feel fine."

"Well, I'm sorry, but COVID-19 tests won't detect the virus if they don't have symptoms, so I can't order any. Also, I have started my quarantine, I'm returning your call from my home. I won't be in the clinic for the next 14 days."

"Oh, I'm so sorry you have to be on quarantine because of me, Dr. Gamren."

"It's OK, that's part of the job. I don't have any symptoms at this time, so that's good."

"What should I do if I need to see a doctor while you're in quarantine?"

"Just call the clinic. There is a note in the system giving instructions to assign you to another doctor. Be aware, you won't be allowed to visit the clinic. You can speak with a physician, but if you think you need to be seen by someone, you'll need to go to the emergency room," she explains while sounding as if these instructions were fresh from a CDC document she just read.

"OK, so there's no way I can get tests ordered for my family because they aren't showing symptoms? Right? What if I speak to someone at the hospital? Could I try that route?" I ask, grasping at straws.

174

"No. Again, I've been informed that tests are only given to symptomatic patients who have had contact with a known positive case. These tests won't be of any help to your family if they're asymptomatic," she explains.

"All right. Thank you for calling me back. Again, I'm sorry I've forced you into quarantine. Oh, I just thought of something… I've probably sent the X-ray technician and the nurse that saw me on Monday into quarantine as well. Haven't I?"

Dr. Gamren pauses. "Yes, they are both quarantined."

The number of people I came in contact with since I returned home, I think, is unfathomable! I have been in close contact with dozens of people. Anyone to whom I have passed the infection has likely been in close contact with dozens of different people. I have been home going about my day-to-day routine for nine days. How can we effectively contact trace? The numbers are staggering!

On March 11, 2020, the local, state, national, and worldwide news released one story after another showcasing me as a number on the television screen. Watching this — knowing I was one of those numbers associated with the "novel coronavirus" — was surreal. But — at least I made the top 10 in the state of Minnesota!

Pioneer Press Newspaper in St. Paul, MN:

https://www.twincities.com/2020/03/12/minnesota-coronavirus-cases-continue-to-climb-now-at-nine/

The Minnesota Department of Health reported 4 new COVID-19 cases Thursday

March 11th, 2020 bringing the total number of coronavirus cases statewide to nine. All of Minnesota's COVID-19 cases are related to travel in some way.

The CDC released the following information:

https://www.cdc.gov/washington/testimony/2020/t20200
311.htm

https://www.whitehouse.gov/presidential-
actions/proclamation-suspension-entry-immigrants-
nonimmigrants-persons-pose-risk-transmitting-2019-
novel-coronavirus/

On January 30, 2020, the World Health Organization (WHO) declared the 2019 Novel Coronavirus (2019-nCoV) disease outbreak a public health emergency of international concern.

On March 11, 2020 the Novel Coronavirus Disease, COVID-19, was declared a pandemic by the World Health Organization. On March 13, 2020 a national emergency was declared in the United States concerning the COVID-19 Outbreak.

Reading information released by the CDC on March 11th takes me back to the top of Gondola One on February 24th. This day marked the onset of tightness in my chest. You have to wonder — who suspected the virus was circulating in the U.S? The hospital in Ohio where Dr. Dave works was definitely on alert in the middle of

February, or they would not have required extensive PPE for an examination of a patient presenting concerning symptoms who actually had strep throat. The CDC confirmed the virus spread between two people on January 31st in the U.S., representing the first instance of person-to-person transmission within the U.S. That same day, the President issued Proclamation 9984 (Suspension of Entry as Immigrants and Nonimmigrants of Persons Who Pose a Risk of Transmitting 2019 Novel Coronavirus and Other Appropriate Measures to Address This Risk). Who else knew this virus was likely spreading silently during this infamous month in 2020? Why did the WHO wait 40 days to announce the novel coronavirus as a pandemic after the date they declared the disease outbreak a "concerning international public health emergency" on January 30th? Worldwide spread on a mass scale was needed for the label "pandemic" to be applied, but how is mass scale measured? What's the criteria? Was the term reserved until SARS-CoV-2 was documented in all continents except Antarctica? So many questions…

Thursday evening, March 11th… John lands at the Minneapolis airport from New York City and manages to make it home at a decent hour. I'm holed up in the TV room behind glass doors, so our conversation is brief. I remind him to wash his hands after touching anything in our house.

He shouts from the kitchen sink, "How are you feeling?"

"So far I'm doing OK."

"Is Avery upstairs? I have a hotel booked for us with separate rooms and an adjoining door. The hotel is close, just a few miles away."

"Yes, she's upstairs. I'm glad the Department of Health agreed to your quarantine in a hotel. This will give me peace of mind knowing you won't be near me, sharing the air. I sure hope the two of you don't end up getting this virus," I say, trying to sound upbeat.

"I'm going to pack a bag and tell Avery she should follow me in her car. The health department said Avery and I have to keep our distance from one another especially since New York City is becoming a hot spot."

"OK. There are masks on the mudroom counter. The hospital sent a few home with me the night I was tested."

Shortly after our brief conversation and bags are packed, my family leaves for the hotel. I wave from behind the glass accompanied by a sad, tired goodbye as I watch them leave. The sound of the garage door opening and then promptly closing marks the beginning of a long... lonely journey.

Chapter 16

A deep, unsettling cough shakes my body awake. Curled into the fetal position, I feel a raw, aching burn in my chest. It hurts. Once the cough calms down, and I catch my breath, I can't help but notice the stillness. My home feels eerie. Alone, my quarantine having just begun, I lie in bed, knowing once again phone calls will dominate my day. Lacking desire and motivation to pull back the covers, I lie there with my thoughts. *What is the coronavirus doing inside my lungs? When will my new antibiotic kick in? Who have I forgotten to add to my list? Where will Friday, March 12th take me?*

My vibrating phone interrupts the questions I can't answer. I reach across my pillow, pluck the phone from the nightstand, and scroll through messages from the ski group. An onslaught of pleas floods the screen. "Who's coughing their head off?" "Does anyone know which pain reliever I should take for body aches?" "Has anyone been able to get a COVID-19 test?"

Jill sent the text asking about getting a COVID-19 test, so I decide to respond directly. "Hey. Are you still having fatigue and stomach problems? I saw your question asking about a test."

Jill responds, "Yes. I'm a mess. I called my doctor's office yesterday, and they told me they don't have any tests. Their exact words were — 'stay home and isolate yourself because you most likely have the coronavirus.' They also said I can't come in because of my exposure to you and Jay, and if I start having difficulty breathing to check myself into the ER."

"Oh Jill, I'm so sorry. I wish there was something I could do for you."

"Thanks. So far, I haven't developed a cough, so that's a plus."

"Good! Stay in touch. I need to get myself out of bed and start calling people."

The moment I touch the "send" arrow, I imagine the nanosecond it takes for the message to fly through space before landing on Jill's screen. Channeling this invisible energy, I pull back the covers to start my day.

I go through my morning ritual, making a pot of coffee, feeding the cat, and turning on the TV. While listening to the news toss out new terminology, "pandemic" — "global health crisis" — "national emergency," my stomach knots with anxious energy. Watching my identity become reduced to a "number" lumped into the total of positive cases nationally and globally is freaking me out! I don't want to be freaked out! I try to tell myself not to be freaked out! But this strategy is not working. It's probably not working because right next to the number of positive cases worldwide is the number of deaths worldwide!

The coffee maker beeps, giving me the go ahead to pour a cup at the same time my home phone rings.

"Good morning. May I speak with Laurel Fischbach? This is Erica from the Department of Health."

"This is she," I answer with a froggy morning voice.

"Hi Laurel. I'm going to be taking over your case from Aaron."

"Oh… OK," I reply, not really knowing if this change is a good thing.

"We need to document all the places you've been since March 1st," Erica explains.

"Sure, I understand."

I pull up my iPhone calendar which provides a guide for the day-to-day recount she requires. At the end of our timeline discussion, I remember one more place to add.

"Erica, I just remembered that I took a barre exercise class at Lifetime in St. Louis Park on Sunday the 8th. Um…I think it was at noon."

"OK, did you just take the class, or did you use other facilities while you were at the gym?"

"I arrived about fifteen minutes early and went directly to the studio. I didn't use the locker room or machines."

"All right. Do you happen to know who taught the class?" she inquires, while sounds of her typing faintly fill in between her questions.

"Yes, I believe the instructor's name was… um… Leslie. Oh, and the class was full."

"Do you know who was next to you in the class?"

"Well, the good news is I had audio equipment next to me on my left, so I only had one person next to me. Unfortunately, I don't know who the woman was on my right, and the mats are very close together — so — this woman was probably only two feet from me."

Erica lets out an audible humph of exasperation, pausing for a moment but typing furiously.

"I will have to call Lifetime and send out a letter alerting them about your attendance as a positive COVID case." Then she switches gears. "Have you taken your temperature today?"

"No, I haven't. Should I have done that already?"

"You need to start taking your temperature several times a day and begin keeping a log for me. Each time I call, I'll need your readings. You can expect two calls per day."

"Got it. I've made a reminder note for myself."

"Now, do you need groceries or medicine? We'll provide anything you need because it's important you don't leave your house."

"I understand. No, I don't need anything right now. Fortunately, I have friends who have offered to grocery shop and run errands," I reply, feeling grateful as the corners of my mouth pull up into a small smile.

"OK. I'll check back with you toward the dinner hour," she assures.

I really don't know what to think by the end of this call. First, I am surprised my contact switched from Aaron to Erica. Secondly, I am surprised to learn my "new normal" includes two calls per day. While sitting at my kitchen counter, sipping coffee, wondering what to do next, Avery's dance studio pops into my mind. *Shoot, I've got to let Kirsten know what's going on.* My call passes directly into voicemail.

I had never given the familiar sound of a voicemail beep much thought until I tested positive for COVID-19. Not wanting to leave my diagnosis on voicemail, the beep became the signal for my canned spiel: "Hi. This is Laurel Fischbach calling. It's important I speak with you today. Please call me back at your earliest convenience."

Working my way through my contacts and then Avery's contacts was grueling. The problem was Avery could be positive. She wasn't symptomatic at this moment, but the Department of Health had placed her in quarantine. I needed to warn the parents of her friends, the administration at her school, and the students'

182

parents at her dance studio. Scouring my memory for the names of contacts since March 1st was taxing.

By mid-morning, the number of calls and text messages becomes unmanageable as word spreads fast among friends, neighbors, dancers, and neighborhood moms. I find myself continuously interrupting the person I am speaking with to take another incoming call. Pajamas end up being my outfit of choice because I never have a moment to change. By the time I gain a "moment" — I think, why bother. I sit in my kitchen for the longest time, taking one phone call after another. I finally take a breakfast break around one o'clock to fry a couple eggs.

One particular return call I am anxious to receive this Friday afternoon comes from Gordon at Dancers Studio. Gordon has five kids, and his wife is six months pregnant. Bob and I took a private lesson a few days after I returned from Vail. The thought of infecting him is weighing on me.

The first words that fly out of my mouth when I pick-up the phone is, "Gordon, how are you? Are you feeling, OK?"

The two of us talk briefly because he is preparing for a showcase dance starting in a matter of hours. Gordon receives my canned explanation about the virus and the Department of Health, along with a sincere apology. In the end, he assures me he feels fine, and it gives me comfort knowing today is the ninth day since we last had contact. In addition, I am relieved to hear his wife is doing well with her pregnancy.

When the eight o'clock hour strikes, my friend, Carol, calls to check in with me. She is responding to my frequent texts keeping her abreast of this unbelievable situation. Calling from a sleepy little town outside of

Toronto, she says, "I feel so removed from the world at large here in Orillia. How are you holding up?"

"Yes, I'm sure you do. I'm hanging in there."

She picks up on my hoarse, exhausted voice and asks if I have been on the phone all day.

"Yes. It's been nonstop."

"I can talk to you another time if that would be better," Carol says in her sweet natured way.

"No, it's OK. I'm thrilled to be talking to you because I don't need to give you the spiel that I may have infected you," I say with a chuckle.

Carol laughs and says, "Well, I guess it's a good thing I've spent the last month in Canada."

We talk for an hour, covering a myriad of details, when she finally observes, "Laurel, you seem exhausted, and your voice sounds raw. I think it's time you park yourself in front of the TV and veg out for a while."

"I agree. Thanks for calling. It feels so good to talk with you about all this craziness."

We say goodbye, and I follow her advice. While making myself comfortable, I send a text to John, updating him. We volley back and forth for a few minutes, and when our text conversation comes to a close, I click the silence button. I am physically drained from fighting pneumonia and emotionally drained by guilt that someone may become gravely ill. I know it's not logical to feel guilty for something I didn't think I had. However, this was little consolation for possibly infecting people, and most assuredly, having them locked into quarantine.

Engrossed in HGTV, my head begins to bob as I nod off in the chair. Falling asleep upright is never good for one's neck, so I lumber upstairs to my bedroom. I throw the decorative pillows off my bed and contemplate crawling in without brushing my teeth. My father's voice makes an appearance in the back of my mind as if I am a child again — the lecture coming in loud and clear. *You only get one set of teeth, so you better take care of them.* I make an about-face, go directly to the sink, and grab my toothbrush.

Sleep comes quickly, but it never lasts for long. All night, I am aroused hourly with coughs startling me, forcing me to sit up. I feel caught in a vicious cycle with no idea how to break out of it.

Waking to the light of Saturday morning, I am relieved the night is over. Two women from the social dance community reach out to me through Facebook Messenger, offering their help. Cindy offers to pick up anything I might need at the grocery store, and Sheryl offers to bring a meal. I am touched by their generosity. I reply to Cindy that I'd love a couple avocadoes, and she responds with a "thumbs up" emoji and delivery time. I text back, "I'm not going anywhere for a while — 13 days to be exact, so avocado delivery can happen any time — day or night."

Responding back to Sheryl, "Thanks for your offer to drop off a meal. Please call me to coordinate. Thanks." She rings me right away, and after a short conversation, she lets me know a lasagna will be on my doorstep before sunset.

This Saturday marks the beginning of an outpour of support. I spend the day receiving one kind message and gesture after another. My next-door neighbor leaves treats from the local bakery, a mom friend drops off a bouquet of tulips, and a family member drops off magazines.

When my doorbell rings midday, Cindy is standing in my driveway waving. Opening the door, I see two bags of groceries perched on my porch. Staring at them in surprise, I see four avocadoes on top. I stand in my doorway for the next fifteen minutes as we talk about all things involving the coronavirus. Cindy's big cheerful smile brightens my day as we chat "socially distanced" with fifteen feet or more between us. I leaf through the bags toward the end of our conversation, pulling items out one at a time, thanking her for such thoughtful selections. She offers her help during my two-week quarantine and tells me to reach out anytime. While unloading the groceries, I snap a photo of this covered kitchen counter and send it to Carol. My text caption reads, "Look at what our friend Cindy did for me today. Can you believe she bought all this? She really went above and beyond, especially since she lives an hour away! I feel so lucky to be part of the social dance community."

Carol responds, "I've been on a texting chain with Sheryl and Cindy discussing your situation, and everyone feels so bad for you. We all want to help in any way we can. I knew Cindy was going to shop for you today."

I text back, "You ladies are the best! Thank goodness I discovered social dancing. The entire dance

186

community has enriched my life more than I could've imagined."

The theme for my foreseeable future became generosity. Daily I was surprised with meals, books, magazines, cards, poems, flowers, instructional dance DVDs, offers for grocery runs, and gifts of toilet paper. Who knew how precious gifts of toilet paper would turn out to be?

The hours zoom by in a flurry during my third day in quarantine. As I check in with my family during the dinner hour, John asks me what I did all day. *My first reaction is, not a lot, but in actuality, I spent the day texting, calling, and writing thank you notes.*

My energy level is low as my body fights hard against pneumonia. Sleep calls for me at an unusually early hour, so I relent. Lying in bed brings on a heavy feeling in my chest, causing spastic coughing to erupt again. I try propping my head up, sipping water, and focusing on taking shallow, deliberate breaths. Nothing helps for what seems like forever as the coughing consumes me. I imagine this is what it feels like to be drowning. Utterly panicked, I bolt to the bathroom in fear of vomiting in bed. I stand hunched over the sink with my hands gripping the edge of the bathroom counter. My thoughts leap from, *don't throw up — to — catch your breath!* Eventually, the coughing calms down, leaving in its wake a sore, raw feeling deep in my chest. I shuffle back to bed, barely able to keep my eyes open. Knowing I need to try to sleep sitting up, I pull together a pile of pillows, creating a wedge onto which I ease my back. This strategy works. The next time I open my eyes, the bedroom is bright, signaling the start of day four of my quarantine.

Chapter 17

Do you remember the movie *Groundhog Day?* The 1993 comedy depicting a weatherman reporting about Groundhog Day, starring Bill Murray and Andie MacDowell? Bill Murray becomes trapped in a time loop, forcing himself to relive the same monotonous, repetitive, and often unpleasant day over and over. Welcome to my world! For the next two weeks, my life becomes the movie *Groundhog Day*.

On a daily basis, I update friends, family, and the Department of Health. The conversations always focus on my symptoms and progress. I log my temperature readings and update Erica from the Department of Health twice per day. Her phone calls are akin to a shotgun of direct questions. Sprinkled in throughout each of my personal "Groundhog Days" are check-ins with my ski buddies nationwide. The majority of my ski friends aren't able to get COVID-19 tests due to the shortage, so these check-ins center around comparing symptoms to help with self-diagnosis and self-medication. Hours of my days are absorbed by my phone.

Care packages, cards, flowers, and meals arrive daily from family, friends, and neighbors. The outpour of support, care, and concern showing up on my doorstep, in my mailbox, and in my messages is what makes the monotonous, repetitive days bearable.

Throughout my quarantine, restful sleep is in short supply. An unrelenting, dry cough cannot be calmed when prone. I lie in bed, unable to squelch the spastic coughs. Fear comes to life: internal heat flares, sweat beads form, and panic sets in. *I wonder...is now the time I should go to the emergency room? Is this what delirium feels like? My logical brain takes over. "Get a grip, breathe, slow your breath, don't panic, you'll be fine!"* These are the phrases I say to myself over and over again in the dark, quiet of my bedroom.

When morning comes, I call my doctor's office. I can no longer manage these nighttime coughing fits. At first mention of my positive diagnosis, the nurse asks to place me on a brief hold. I can almost picture what her face looks like at this moment.

"Hi, Mrs. Fischbach? I'm back, sorry about that."

"No problem. I know Dr. Gamren is in quarantine because of me, and she told me another doctor on staff would take over my care. I'm wondering if I could speak with Dr. Dell because he's my husband's physician."

"Um...yes, I see a note in your chart. I'll get a message to Dr. Dell and ask that he call you."

The one advantage of having the coronavirus at the onset of this pandemic is prompt medical care. Looking back on this experience, I can only imagine how strange the conversations must have been between the medical staff.

I don't wait long for a return call from Dr. Dell; the phone rings within twenty minutes.

"Hello. Mrs. Fischbach, this is Dr. Dell calling. I have some notes from the nurse that I'd like to discuss with you."

"Yes. Thank you so much for calling me back so quickly. I can't lie down, and my cough is uncontrollable at night," I expound desperately.

"All right. I see you're positive with the coronavirus, and your chest X-ray shows pneumonia in the lower right lobe. Also, I see here you're on an antibiotic, correct?"

"Yes."

189

"OK. A dry, spastic cough is typical with pneumonia, so I'm going to prescribe a couple of things to help you sleep and calm the cough."

Dr. Dell sends over prescriptions for Virtussin AC syrup and an Advair steroid inhaler. Both are ready for pick-up in a matter of hours. When the call comes from Walgreens, I text John, asking if he would pick them up and drop them on the porch. The request is met with an enthusiastic, "Absolutely!" *I have to believe he was thrilled to be leaving the hotel to run this errand for the simple pleasure of breaking up his own personal "Groundhog Day."*

The lack of restful sleep was taking a toll on me. My emotions ran the gamut. I found myself mostly cycling through frightened, sad, grateful, and lonely. Those are the four emotions I remember the most. At one point, my logical self could no longer keep the emotions in check. I needed help. I needed consoling. I needed my best friend. The moment Lori answered the phone, it all came pouring out of me — a vulnerable side I didn't know was lurking under the surface. Days and days of rattling around my house alone, sleep-deprived, emotionally exhausted, all while talking on the phone constantly, eventually prompted an intense need to honestly express myself. I hadn't been able to talk to anyone without feeling obliged to couch my words in confidence and optimism. It is so terribly wearing to tell caller after caller — "I feel pretty good" — "I'm sure I'll stop coughing soon" — "I'm not worried!"

"Lori, I'm a mess! I don't even know where to begin. I trust you and love you like a sister. I need to tell you that I feel so guilty accepting all of this generosity from so many people. I'm overwhelmed with so many offers for help. I feel grateful for everyone's care and concern, but at the same time, I feel bad. I don't know what's wrong with me?" I tell people I'm fine, but I don't feel fine. The truth is I'm scared and lonely. I don't know if the medicine will get rid of this cough. Tears cascade down my cheeks, dripping onto the kitchen counter, as I let go of everything inside of me.

I suspect from Lori's perspective I was pretty incoherent. When I dig deeper as I type this nine months later, I realize I experienced guilt from many angles. People were going out of their way to help me. I was a huge inconvenience for many. People were spending money and significant chunks of time on me. I brought the coronavirus to Minnesota, and any one of them could get it as a result of my vacation. Someone could die because of me! Yet, while I am genuinely grateful, part of me feels bad that I exude manufactured confidence.

I struggled to sort out my conflicted emotions. I needed to graciously accept this daily support. I had to affirm my many benefactors for their genuine thoughtfulness and generosity. I had to allow them to feel the "empowerment" that flows from acts of kindness. They had to know I appreciated and valued them. Nevertheless, accepting help is a two-way street — I needed to repay them by being upbeat and sunny. I had to try to allay the anxiety that most were feeling about the mysterious menace of the coronavirus. Depending on my physical and mental state at that moment, this was often extraordinarily taxing!

Lori stays on the phone with me for as long as she can, "talking me off the ledge," but it isn't enough. A half hour after our phone call ends, I break down again. I really can't get a grip. I call Carol, grateful she answers the phone! The mix of loneliness, sadness, guilt and fear cycles once again, this time up to Canada. Carol is a rock.

Listening with a compassionate ear while offering inspiring words of wisdom is Carol's gift. She paints a beautiful mental picture of the two of us dining and dancing at one of our favorite restaurants. Her mental imagery at Mancini's Char House pulls me back into a good place. She, too, "talks me off the ledge."

I struggled on and off with my emotions throughout the quarantine; however, once restful sleep returned, they leveled out. The cough syrup was a saving grace. Transporting me to a dreamland while calming the cough. I truly believe the combination of the steroid inhaler and codeine-laced cough syrup jumpstarted my recovery.

Two days after my emotional phone call with Carol, a package arrives from Amazon. Opening the padded envelope, I'm met with a note:

"I thought you could use a little laughter in your life. I am here for you if you need me.

Love your friend,
Carol"

I pull out a book and smile as I read the cheerful title, "Laughter The Best Medicine."

Quoted from the book:
"Looking for a little bit of laughter in your day? Drawn from one of the most popular features of Reader's Digest, this collection of jokes, one-liners, and other lighthearted glimpses of life is just what the doctor ordered."

I hadn't laid eyes on a *Reader's Digest* since I was a kid. At first sight, I am flooded with childhood memories of the magazines spread across the coffee table. I don't ever recall seeing my parents peruse *Reader's Digest* magazines. Still, I do remember playing with them as a child.

I call Carol straight away, greeting her with, "Hey, you want to hear a joke? Someone just sent a joke book to me!"

The two of us laugh, launching into stories about growing up with *Reader's Digest* magazines. I needed this book, and for the next few weeks, I find myself dog-earing pages for easy reference. Always wanting to have a joke ready for my next conversation with Carol.

My cathartic, emotional meltdowns with friends and reading jokes from a book were the moments that turned my quarantine into an unforgettable experience. Reflecting upon the time I spent alone — riding inside an emotional rollercoaster car — gave me perspective on how many wonderful people I have in my life. "Grateful" is simply not a strong enough word for what I felt.

Great literary works are often written about finding silver linings, finding light by wading through the darkness. I now understand at least one source of inspiration. Quarantining alone with an illness no one understands while watching the death toll climb daily — is a darkness I didn't know existed, but silver linings keep showing up...

Chapter 18

As the quarantine continues, I realize people seem to "need" detailed information about my diagnosis, prognosis, and what I'm learning from doctors, as well as my own experience with COVID-19. During a conversation with Carol, subsequent to my recent meltdown, she mentions a member of our social dance Facebook group thinks I should post about my symptoms. It was said I shouldn't have allowed so many days to pass without an update since Cinema Ballroom was shut down.

I am taken aback by this request, and I know Carol is caught in the middle. She never revealed who the request came from and made it clear I should not feel pressured.

"Carol, I'm exhausted, it's sometimes hard to think straight, and I'm not happy about someone asking you to relay this to me," I say, feeling a heat build in my gut.

On the one hand, I understand the request due to my insight into something frightening. On the other hand, I am perturbed. Crafting a well-worded Facebook post educating, updating, and calming others isn't something I have the energy for at the moment. My brain is not firing on all cylinders.

My dear friend quickly switches to support mode, "Yes, I understand. Your number one job right now is to rest and get better."

I ruminate for hours, ultimately heeding Carol's advice — letting the request from the unidentified social dancer lie by the wayside.

On one of the nightly calls to John and Avery at the hotel, I ask for his opinion about posting something in

Dance Friends on Facebook. He votes in favor of silence, uncertain about sharing medical information on social media. I feel vindicated, but the feeling of righteous indignation doesn't last for long. In a calmer and perhaps better rested moment, I recognize COVID is producing dramatic swings in my physical, emotional, and intellectual state. I somewhat begrudgingly conclude that my perturbed reaction was inappropriate and seriously overwrought.

I gradually become more and more embarrassed at my petulant response to a reasonable suggestion. After all, I had exposed, and could theoretically have infected, a large number of local dancers. I had exposed and shut down four different dance studios, and I had placed over a dozen people into quarantine. Of course, I "should" have made every effort to disseminate information about what I had been experiencing. Indeed, some people would take comfort from the fact that I was recuperating at home and not in the hospital.

So, when the energy and creativity presented itself on March 20th, I opened my laptop.

Private Group (Dance Friends) Facebook Post:
Laurel Valvano Fischbach
Admin · March 20

A message to all the dancers that are part of this page:
As many of you already know, I tested positive for the COVID-19 virus. I have been home in isolation, following the instructions given to me by the MN Department of Health as I fight off bronchitis and pneumonia. Unfortunately, my pneumonia is a byproduct of this virus

since it attacks a person's lungs. I'm taking antibiotics and an inhaler was prescribed to help me push through symptoms.

I know people have a lot of questions about symptoms and what to look for. The symptoms can be extremely mild or extremely severe. In my opinion, I've had mild symptoms up until the pneumonia took hold.

Here is what I can tell you -
    A slight tightness in your chest may be felt.
    A slight annoying dry cough that doesn't produce anything may begin.
    A fluctuating cough may present when talking or laughing.
    No cough may be present if inactive.
    One day you may feel normal while the next day you struggle with having enough energy.
    A low-grade fever may present itself. I don't know if I ever had a fever because I never took my temperature. I did experience achiness and shakes for several hours one evening.
    Not feeling well while skiing in Vail, CO didn't set off any alarm bells. Skiing in high altitude and not sleeping well were my rationales for feeling under the weather. I never suspected I had COVID-19.
    I have been home from Vail, CO since March 1ˢᵗ. Today I feel I am definitely at the tail end of fighting bronchitis, pneumonia, and

COVID-19. I will rebound and hope to build up immunity to keep me from ever getting this virus again. My husband and daughter have self-quarantined, and the two of them show no symptoms to date, so that is good news.

I hope this post helps everyone understand my symptoms with the virus. Again, I will say this is just how my body reacted to the virus and what I am going through.

To all of you dancers out there, do your best to take any and all measures to keep yourself healthy.

Laurel

Responses to my post are instantaneous. An outpour of well wishes, appreciation, and prayers was an unexpected surprise considering I was the cause of social dancing coming to a screeching halt.

A few Facebook responses to my post:

Sheryl wrote-
Thank you Laurel for sharing and so glad you are healing. Sorry you have had to go through this. Telling us your experience helps make it real for all of us and all the more reason for us all to follow the rules to stay home. We can all help do our part to help flatten the curve. Sending you continued healing prayers!

Addie wrote-
You have no idea how many people are happy to hear from you and have been praying for you.

Katie wrote-
Much love to you, Laurel. Thank you for sharing your story and educating us about symptoms. You are a jewel of the dance community!

Needless to say, these warm and encouraging posts leave me even more ashamed of my peevish response to the request Carol relayed to me a few days ago. I take comfort from the fact I am genuinely sick and sleep deprived.

I should also interject that COVID-19 has definitely been shown to interfere with "cognitive functioning." Degrees of "brain fog" are reported by many of the infected. For some, the "fog" is short-term. For others (a group of recovering doctors who formed a select support group comes to mind), the fog lingers for months. *As I write this, I believe I am fine today, but there were times in March, April, and May where I struggled mightily to think rationally — and there were times I clearly failed!*

Another Facebook comment soon after I posted was strangely encouraging:

Kian wrote-
Were you by chance at the Eagles Swing dance on March 6th or the First Saturday Swing on March 7th? The vocalist on both nights just tested positive this morning for COVID-19.

I recall learning about these dances when I returned home from Vail. They were on my calendar; however, I passed on both because I was too tired, and I certainly didn't want to cough on anyone with what I thought was a chest cold. Thinking if I rested and did the "right thing" by staying home, I could possibly attend the now infamous "Jerry O'Hagan Orchestra Ballroom Dance" at Cinema Ballroom on Sunday, March 8th.

You might be thinking, "What was encouraging about Kian's post?" Well, it's the fact that the lead singer for a popular local dance band was positive with COVID-19, and she didn't get it from me! This provides me an odd sense of relief. Also, I am not the only COVID-19 positive person responsible for exposing dancers, canceling dance lessons, and shutting down dance venues.

Several nights later, during my daily conversation with my quarantined family, John and I discuss the subject of them coming home. It has been eleven days, and neither of them has symptoms. They are tired of living in small hotel rooms, and I am lonesome. John is confident they are fine and certain they haven't caught the coronavirus from me. I, too, am beginning to believe I may not have infected them.

"I would like to bring Avery home tomorrow, but Avery is concerned. She hears you coughing through the phone every evening," John cautions.

"Yes, it's difficult for me to carry on a conversation for any length of time in the evening without spurring coughing fits."

"She told me she's worried about being around you, and she's wondering if the virus is living on surfaces."

"I don't blame her," I respond with a heavy heart.

200

"Personally, I'm not very worried at this point, but I need to make sure Avery is comfortable and mentally prepared. Maybe your cough will be better in a day or two?"

"OK. I will think about how best to stay apart from you two when you decide to come home. I think we should research disinfecting surfaces and how long the experts think the virus can survive on them. Maybe you could give Dr. Roettger a call and ask him what he knows."

"Sure. That's a good idea," John agrees.

Well, this was typical of the COVID roller coaster. I was feeling great, my family hadn't developed symptoms, and then I was deflated to learn my sixteen-year-old was afraid of me. Avery's concerns were reasonable. I wasn't able to carry on a conversation for more than fifteen minutes without coughing. It was probably a little worse in the evening when I was more fatigued. Compounding the problem was the great uncertainty regarding how long the coronavirus would survive on surfaces. It wouldn't have been enough to avoid coughing in her presence. I could be continually coating the house with new viruses. Experts offered so many differing opinions. One doctor's suggestion was to carefully disinfect each item brought into the house after grocery shopping. I remember him emphasizing that even the paper bag itself was a threat! Then there were the news clips from South Korea. A small army of South Korean workers walking down the streets in hazmat suits spraying sidewalks, parking meters, crosswalks, and small animals. (Just kidding! No animals were actually sprayed!)

The thought of spraying disinfectant on every surface that could have my aerosolized virus droplets is daunting. Do I have the energy? Do I have enough bleach? How long do viruses stay "alive" on doorknobs, appliance handles, and microwave buttons? Is the house big enough for us to stay at a safe distance? What if we all wear masks and gloves? Thinking about all of these questions and scenarios is exhausting.

Chapter 19

Sunday, March 22nd, is the last day I awake in the house alone. I have developed a plan for my own "new normal," which includes constant disinfecting and physical distancing from my family. I spend Sunday morning scouring surfaces with a concocted bleach and water solution, hoping this will eliminate any chance they might have of contracting the virus. They have assured me they will help with the daily sanitizing, wearing gloves and masks.

The time has come to barricade myself in the TV room. When John and Avery walk into the house and greet me through the glass doors, I feel unexpectedly grateful for the glass. I am happy they are home, but my nerves keep me on edge. This new normal does not resemble "normal" at all.

Once again, an old movie comes to mind. Do you remember the 1970s classic *The Boy in the Plastic Bubble* with John Travolta? The boy is restricted to a protective bubble-like room where he lives due to a compromised immune system. Well... I'm *"The Girl in the Plastic Bubble"* — speaking to my family through glass doors. Who knew this approach would become accepted as the only way families could visit their loved ones in nursing homes?

Operating under these strange rules in my house involves wearing a mask each time I emerge from my cocoon. It also involves using the kitchen as little as possible and relegating myself to my own separate bath. John and Avery share her bathroom, and the three of us intentionally keep our distance from one another. The measures we put in place seem to be working as neither of them has developed symptoms.

The Department of Health continues daily check-ins to log my temperature readings. Erica rings on Tuesday, March 24th, to see how I'm feeling. I thank her for calling daily but mention I'm still coughing. To my delight, she announces my quarantine is over! Then, she proceeds to warn me about my over-taxed immune system.

"Laurel, you need to take precautions when leaving the house. Your immune system has been compromised, so you're more susceptible to other illnesses. I highly recommend you stay at home for another 72 hours. Also, you should follow-up with your doctor about that lingering cough."

I followed her instructions. Calling T.C. Family Physicians became a regular occurrence in my life. As soon as receptionists or nurses heard my name, they made it evident they knew exactly who I am and directed me accordingly. Strangely, my name became famous at the clinic. The name synonymous with — get this COVID-19 patient transferred to Dr. Dell.

"Hi, Dr. Dell. This is Laurel Fischbach calling. The Department of Health suggested I follow-up with you because I can't seem to shake this lingering cough. I've been released from quarantine, but my case manager said my immune system is most likely compromised. She recommends I stay at home for three more days."

"You've been released from quarantine even though you're still coughing?" Dr. Dell questioned.

"Yes."

"I'm going to have to speak with the Department of Health about your release. If you're still coughing, I don't think you should be released from quarantine. The

204

lingering cough you're dealing with is referred to as a "post-infectious cough," and it's caused by inflammation in your lungs. The steroid inhaler you were prescribed and another round of antibiotics should help ease the cough. I'm going to call in a second round of antibiotics, this time increasing the dosage to 14 days. This second round will make sure you don't develop a secondary infection. Laurel — I do want to stress it's important that you keep your cough covered at all times."

When will this virus ever be done with me? My first symptom, tightness in my chest, started on February 24th — it's now March 24th!

I comply with Dr. Dell's orders and Erica's caution, continuing to live inside my TV room bubble — limiting my exposure to people and their germs. I spend large portions of each day checking on friends, fearful someone will say, "I just tested positive." Fortunately, the news is great! Not a single gentleman I danced with at Cinema Ballroom developed symptoms during his 14-day quarantine. The good news continues when I learn all three of the dance instructors also remained symptom-free. "Whew!" It appears everyone has dodged my coronavirus bullet.

So, here I am — still coughing during the last week of March. I'm no longer officially in quarantine, but I continue to keep myself isolated. Daily walks around Lake Harriet and Lake of the Isles become my mode of recreation — and my only excuse for leaving the house. I am hopeful the exercise and fresh air will aid in my recovery. But truly, I find the walks to be a godsend for my psyche.

I am starving for social interaction, and my friends know it. If you thought the coronavirus was simply about becoming ill, getting tested, monitoring symptoms, and resting, I can tell you it wasn't. As one of the first nine cases in Minnesota lumped into the first 1500 cases in the U.S., it was also psychological. To give you an analogy — think, "leper." Leprosy has evoked fear since antiquity — it is depicted in the Bible as the "disease of outcasts." There were many times in the coming weeks when I thought, "How long will people continue to be afraid of me?" It is one thing to be in isolation for a definitive period of time (14 days). It is an entirely different thing to feel fear from family and friends once you are released. I'm an outcast.

Some of my best quarantine memories were made with friends who took the time to visit me while standing on my front stoop. Having a face-to-face conversation felt luxurious, even though twenty feet separated us. Other great memories during this otherwise dreary time were "Zoom" happy hours with friends. These virtual gatherings gave me something to look forward to. I was so grateful to have friends who cared about my plight, who made efforts to include me, and who understood why I felt like a "leper." As the weeks progressed, I continued my self-quarantine. March turned into April, friends continued to keep their distance, and ever so slowly, my cough finally improved.

April 3rd is an important day for the fight against the coronavirus. The FDA releases a statement about the study and use of convalescent plasma.

For Immediate Release:
April 03, 2020

https://www.fda.gov/news-events/press-announcements/coronavirus-covid-19-update-daily-roundup-april-3-2020

The U.S. Food and Drug Administration today announced the following actions taken in its ongoing response effort to the COVID-19 pandemic:

The FDA announced that it is leading an effort, working collaboratively with government, industry and academic partners, to develop and implement a protocol that will provide convalescent plasma to patients in need across the country who may not have access to institutions with clinical trials in place. Convalescent plasma has the potential to lessen the severity or shorten the length of illness caused by COVID-19. This collaboration, involving BARDA, the American Red Cross and the Mayo Clinic will allow for a simplified process for health care providers that will help ensure patient safety while allowing for the collection of needed information about product efficacy. The FDA anticipates that the effort will be able to move thousands of units of plasma to patients who need them in the coming weeks. https://www.redcrossblood.org/donate-blood/dlp/plasma-donations-from-recovered-covid-19-patients.html

Having friends who are doctors, I already knew convalescent plasma programs were beginning to ramp up in March. Amanda sent a link to me from the National COVID-19 Convalescent Plasma Project spearheaded by Michigan State University. This website was launched for two reasons. It provided doctors a place to register their ICU patients who might benefit from a convalescent plasma infusion, and it provided a place for recovered COVID-19 patients to enter into the nationwide donor database. Once the website had the donor's information, it matched the registrant to the nearest donation site. Without hesitation, I complete the donor registration. I am assigned to Mayo Clinic, the premier, world-renowned hospital in Rochester, Minnesota. The Mayo is designated by the FDA as the industry leader in convalescent plasma research, and I am fortunate it's only a ninety-minute drive from my home. I am one of the first COVID-19 survivors to be matched.

I will forever remember Sunday night, April 5th. Getting ready to call it a night, I take my first step to head upstairs when John says, "Laurel, I just finished watching a news story about Mayo. You have to donate plasma and be part of this research. You have something very few people have right now."

Freezing on the stairs, I look over at John, caught off guard by the tone in his voice.

"I know, John. It's amazing to be able to offer my antibodies."

"You need to sign up for this study program right away and get an appointment as soon as possible."

"I've already signed up, and Mayo has accepted my registration. Now it's just a waiting game."

"You can't let this go too long. You need to contact Mayo if you don't hear from them within the week," John pressed, emphatically.

"Good idea. I'll let them know I can make the drive down there any time."

The conversation with John was a bit odd. He surprised me with his obvious sense of urgency. He seemed to be pleading with me, and I wondered where this was coming from. Maybe he was scared for his parents, who are in their mid-eighties. I didn't need pushing to offer myself for medical research; I wanted to help in any way possible. Giving blood and plasma to the medical community to make advances in understanding this bizarre virus was a priority for me. What I didn't know on this Sunday night was how many hoops I would have to jump through to actually sit in a chair and donate.

Chapter 20

"Convalescent plasma" is the liquid portion of blood taken from formerly sick individuals, who generate protective antibodies while successfully fighting off and recovering from a disease. About 55% of our blood is plasma, and the remaining 45% comprises red blood cells, white blood cells, and platelets suspended in plasma. Generally, the convalescent plasma donation involves taking blood from a recently recovered patient, separating the plasma from the blood, and then returning the donor's red blood cells and platelets along with a saline solution. The convalescent plasma contains antibodies the recovered patient's immune system generated to neutralize a pathogen (often a virus). The hope is the donor's antibodies will attack the pathogen in the seriously ill patient. This technique has been used in some form for over 100 years, including with respect to the Spanish Flu in 1918.

For more information see the NIH website at: www.ncbi.nlm.nih.gov/pmc/articles/PMC7289739/

Generally the convalescent plasma use during the Spanish influenza A (H1N1) pneumonia (pandemic of 1918–1920) has been reported as its first application [3], [4], [5], [6].

The simple extraction of convalescent plasma from blood has been touted as an incredible lifesaving gift. Watching the coronavirus death toll tick upward daily on the news, it's disheartening to know I have antibodies that could help someone but no way to donate them just yet. I desperately want an email or phone call from Mayo Clinic. I am determined to accomplish my mission — save at least one person with my convalescent plasma and help the medical community understand this virus.

The latest news headlines show New York City and the Tri-State Area being ravaged by the virus:
Latest coronavirus updates in New York: Sunday, April 5, 2020
By: PIX11 Web Team

https://www.pix11.com/news/coronavirus/latest-coronavirus-updates-in-new-york-sunday-april-5-2020

> **4,159 people have died from the coronavirus as statewide cases climb to 122,031 Gov. Cuomo said.**

Monday, April 6th, I feel confident the steroid inhaler and antibiotics have done their jobs. No secondary infection — Hallelujah! After six weeks of enduring unhappy lungs, I can finally take a deep, full breath. I am starting to feel like myself again, and the good news continues when an email from Mayo lands in my inbox.

From: Convalescent Plasma-Mayo Clinic:
To: Laurel Fischbach
RE: [EXTERNAL] Documentation for registered plasma volunteer

Hello Laurel,

Thank you for your patience. Please see the information below and respond to the survey if interested.

We are part of the Convalescent Plasma Project Team under the direction of Dr. Michael Joyner at the Mayo Clinic in Rochester, Minnesota. We received your information and potential interest in our study on treatment for COVID-19.

The purpose of this study is to determine whether your plasma (the liquid part of your blood) which contains COVID-19 antibodies that your body produced to fight off your infection, could be given to other people who are sick with COVID-19 as a treatment therapy.

If you are interested in potentially donating your plasma we are asking you to please fill out the donor screening survey found-here:
https://redcap2.mayo.edu/redcap/surveys/?s=9FFA8YNT9X

We will review your responses to the survey and a member of our team will contact you with more information.

Please also visit our website https://ccpp19.org/ which is being updated daily with more information on national efforts regarding convalescent plasma.

Thank you for your time and consideration, The Convalescent Plasma Project Team at Mayo Clinic

Screening Survey Completed:
 From: Laurel Fischbach
Sent: Monday, April 06, 2020 12:59 PM
To: Convalescent Plasma-Mayo
Subject: [EXTERNAL] Documentation for registered plasma volunteer

Laurel Fischbach
50 years old
Blood Type O negative
Regular blood donor at Memorial Blood Bank - Have not donated in the year of 2020
No travel outside the USA for the past 12 months

Tested Positive for COVID-19 on 3/11/2020 at M Fairview Southdale Hospital in Edina, MN

COVID-19 test confirmed by the CDC lab on 3/21/2020

Physician seen to diagnose the pneumonia:
T.C. Family Physicians - Allina Health
Dr. Beatrice R. Gamren MD

This email brings hope that I will soon be able to make a difference. Weeks of suffering with pneumonia will not have been in vain. I will repay the many kindnesses bestowed upon me during quarantine by "paying it forward."

As days go by, my inbox fills with emails from friends asking about my recovery and wanting an update about when I will donate convalescent plasma. Because Mayo Clinic is close by, it's constantly in the news. Typical questions — "Did you hear from Mayo? When will you make the drive to donate?" I badly want to respond, "I'm going down tomorrow!" but I hear nothing. These daily questions inspire my desire to explore other options.

Even in the best of times, I am not known to be particularly patient. And this is far from the best of times! I have been sick for six weeks — and primarily isolated for most of those weeks. I have been worthless to the world, to say the least — a burden on friends, family, and the local medical community. I now have something of value: antibodies that need to be shared and studied. I was tempted to drive to Mayo and knock on Dr. Michael Joyner's office door. Instead, knowing this was a dumb and impetuous idea, I researched other plasma study programs in bordering states. Illinois became my next pursuit.

I find what I am looking for at the University of Chicago. A convalescent plasma project just opened up for registration. In less than 24 hours, I receive a response.

Email from the University of Chicago:

Plasma [SUR]
To: Laurel Fischbach
Convalescent Plasma Project

Thank you for your interest in the University of Chicago Medicine Convalescent Plasma Project.

We are looking volunteers who have recovered from COVID-19 for a research study for people currently sick in the hospital with COVID-19. People like you may have substances in your plasma (the liquid part of your blood) called antibodies. We are studying if these antibodies can be collected in the form of plasma and then given to those who are ill with COVID-19 infections. We do not know if infusing your plasma in people who have COVID-19 may help them improve faster. This type of treatment is called "convalescent plasma therapy." It is being explored as a possible treatment in several medical centers throughout the United States.

You may be eligible to participant if you are age 18 or older, eligible to donate blood, and recovered from COVID-19. If you are interested in being a convalescent plasma donor, please complete this questionnaire https://is.gd/donateplasma. Be sure to include a current daytime phone number. If you are eligible after completing the questionnaire, a member of the study team will call you to do an additional screening questionnaire. If you qualify and want to participate, we will provide you with information on how to donate your blood.

You will receive light snacks for your help. If you drive to the University of Chicago to donate, you will also receive parking vouchers.

We are happy to answer any additional questions about the project or plasma donation process. To get more information, you can email us at plasma@uchospitals.edu.

Thank you so much for your interest and willingness to help those in need!

Sincerely,
Maria Lucia Madariaga MD and the Convalescent Plasma Team

One more iron in the fire to help expedite my donation, I think to myself while reading this email and filling out the attached questionnaire. Giving friends and family the good news about my registration with the University of Chicago is met with surprise and plenty of questions.

One common reaction is — "You're going to drive all the way down to Chicago to donate plasma?"

My standard response is — "You better believe I am! A seven-hour drive to aid in the study of this disease and possibly save a life is a small price to pay."

In actual conversations, I offer a longer explanation, frequently following-up with a logical argument revealing hard data:

"Only about 330,000 people in the U.S. have tested positive for COVID-19 as of April 6th. I am one of the few who has both recovered and has gone more than 28 days since my positive test result without a fever. The medical community put in place a 28-day waiting period to help ensure as a donor you would no longer be contagious. Think about how few candidates there are who can donate right now. The criteria to offer plasma has so many factors: symptom-free, general good health, no travel outside of the U.S. for the past twelve months, 28 days since your positive coronavirus test, and certain medications cannot be in your bloodstream. If you backtrack 28 days from now, there are only 2,800 potential donors who meet this specific 'criterion.' I am one of only 2,800 people in the entire U.S. that can donate plasma and help scientists study this virus right now. Then when you subtract the number of people who are not in good health, who have traveled outside the U.S., and who take medication on the prohibited list, the number shrinks again. This is extremely important to me — however the medical community chooses to use my plasma and blood."

So, when friends and family comment about the long drive to Chicago — all I can think is — when will I finally be given the green light to hop on the freeway?

In the midst of researching plasma study programs, I am compelled to get in touch with Dr. Michael Osterholm at the University of Minnesota. His regular appearances on CNN and MSNBC spark my interest, so I track down his email and number in the University of Minnesota staff directory and promptly fire off a letter.

Laurel Fischbach
To: mto@umn.edu
Re: Survivor of COVID-19

Dr. Osterholm,

      My name is Laurel Fischbach. I was one of the first people diagnosed with COVID-19 in Minnesota. I live in Edina, and I have been released off quarantine by the Department of Health. I feel certain my first symptom started with tightness in my chest on Feb. 24th, so I am now past 30 days. As the universal donor, having O negative blood, I would like to offer my blood and plasma for medical research. If you could help me navigate this donation process, I would appreciate any advice.

      On another note, I have a variety of unique circumstances regarding my timeline spanning two different states, my

218

interactions with people, and the symptoms surrounding this virus's infectious period. I believe this could be helpful information for you.

Please feel free to contact me.
Regards,
Laurel Fischbach

In addition to emailing Dr. Osterholm, I call his assistant, explain my situation, and provide details about my last six weeks. She clarifies that he is doing large scale research and most likely will not be looking at individual cases. Nevertheless, I offer to help in any way possible, hoping she will persuade him to contact me.

I never did hear back from Dr. Osterholm, but on Saturday, April 11th, I did hear back from Mayo.

Email from Mayo Clinic:
Convalescent Plasma-Mayo
To: Laurel Fischbach
Reply-To: Convalescent Plasma-Mayo
Plasma Donor Requirements

Thank you for your willingness to help in these efforts. It appears that you **may** be a potential candidate to donate plasma.

However, to be an eligible donor you must meet the following criteria:

1. A positive COVID-19 lab test **and**

2. A follow-up negative COVID-19 lab test <u>and</u>

3. No longer have COVID-19 symptoms
Unfortunately, at this time our team is unable to order this follow-up lab test for you, but we direct you to the care team that provided your initial COVID-19 test.

If at any point you are able to obtain this second test or have a plan to do so through your employer or other means, please answer these additional questions in this supplemental survey and our team will stay in touch with you to confirm when you are eligible - <u>Mayo Clinic COVID-19 Plasma Donation Supplemental Survey</u>

If our ability to offer testing or requirements of donor eligibility changes, we will be in contact with you in the future.

If you believe you have received this message in error and in fact are currently eligible, please respond to this e-mail to get in contact with a member of our team to confirm your eligibility.

You may open the survey in your web browser by clicking the link below:
<u>Mayo Clinic COVID-19 Plasma Donation Supplemental Survey</u>

If the link above does not work, try copying the link below into your web browser:

https://redcap2.mayo.edu/redcap/surveys/?s=IJWJtM77wM

This link is unique to you and should not be forwarded to others.

We look forward to hearing from you soon!
The Convalescent Plasma Project Team at Mayo Clinic

Reading this email brings excitement but also discouragement. How on earth am I going to get tested for COVID-19 a second time? Mayo is obviously not offering to test me. Yet, they won't let me volunteer for their own study unless I can find someone else to test me? The news is full of reports about shortages of swabs and reagents (the chemicals used to detect DNA linked to SARS-CoV-2). In fact, daily news headlines are awash with coronavirus testing shortages at the very time I need to prove I am negative.

All I could focus on for the next 36 hours was my back-up plan in the event my doctor couldn't order a second test for me. The more I hear about testing shortages, the more I realize a tenacious resolve will be needed to secure this second test.

References - The true historical origin of convalescent plasma therapy

3. Brown B.L., McCullough J. Treatment for emerging viruses: convalescent plasma and COVID-19. Transfus Apher Sci. 2020 doi: 10.1016/transci.2020.102790. [PMC free article] [PubMed] [CrossRef] [Google Scholar]

4. Cao H., Shi Y. Convalescent plasma: possible therapy for novel coronavirus disease 2019. Transfusion. 2020;60:1078–1083. [PMC free article] [PubMed] [Google Scholar]

5. Tiberghien P., de Lamballiere X., Morel P., Gallian P., Lacombe K., Yazdanpanah Y. Collecting and evaluating convalescent plasma for COVID-19 tratment: why and how? Vox Sang. 2020 doi: 10.1111/vox.12926. [PubMed] [CrossRef] [Google Scholar]

6. Rajendran K., Krishnasamy N., Rangarajan J., Rathinam J., Natarajan M., Ramachandran A. Convalescent plasma transfusion for the treatment of COVID-19: systematic review. J Med Virol. 2020 doi: 10.1002/jmv.25961. [PMC free article] [PubMed] [CrossRef] [Google Scholar]

Chapter 21

Monday, April 13th, I call my doctor's office. (You're probably wondering if I have T.C. Family Physicians on speed dial? I don't — but probably should.) As usual, I speak with a nurse who promises a call back from the doctor. Answering the phone, I'm pleased to hear my primary doctor's voice.

"Dr. Gamren, you're back! Thank you for returning my call so quickly."

"Yes, I'm back to seeing patients. What can I help you with?"

"I have a letter from Mayo Clinic requesting a second COVID-19 test. The letter instructs me to ask my doctor for a second test. This is a requirement in order to participate in the new convalescent plasma study to prove I'm negative."

Without pause, Dr. Gamren explains why she can't order a second test. "The clinic tried to set up a drive-thru testing facility, ultimately scrapping it due to test kit shortages. The current protocol is to reserve tests for the severely ill. I'm sorry. I can't help you."

Disappointed, I entreat, "Well, is there someone at the hospital you can refer me to?"

"My hands are tied, Laurel. I don't know who would talk to you since the testing shortage is so severe. Hospitals are forced to be extremely judicious right now," she explains.

"I understand. Thanks for the return call," I say, exhaling a sigh, feeling deflated.

During the past 36 hours since I read the Mayo email, I anticipated potential roadblocks. Obtaining a second test was definitely outside the norm, so I allowed myself to feel deflated but not defeated. I summoned the energy to help me find a solution.

I make a pot of coffee, grab the phone, and dial hospital number one. For the next several hours, I sit at my desk calling hospitals around the Twin Cities. My approach, for want of a better idea, is to start with each hospital's emergency room, and when I hit a roadblock, ask for the hospital's administration. (Technically, I did a lot less talking and a lot more holding.) Unfortunately, my efforts are consistently met with resistance even though I offer to send a copy of my Mayo Clinic letter requesting the test. I am not convincing anyone, at any hospital, to entertain any of it. The enthusiasm I channeled earlier toward finding a solution is waning, irritation now taking its place. I think to myself… *How could anybody be part of this plasma study if Mayo Clinic isn't prepared to administer the second COVID-19 test? How does Mayo expect me to get a second test with a nationwide shortage of test kits and PPE? This is insane! I need to put the onus on Mayo.*

Suppose you have never had an experience with Mayo Clinic. In that case, the one phrase I will use to sum it up is "extraordinary customer/patient service." Mayo Clinic employs 65,000 people and cares for more than one million people per year for all fifty states and nearly 140 countries. It is indeed an extraordinary nonprofit organization committed to clinical practice, education, and research.

When I dial Mayo's main number to start navigating through the system to solve my dilemma, I am treated as their top priority. I'm not going to tell you I didn't spend an hour on the phone bouncing around from one department to the next because I did. What I will say is that every person who spoke to me made it known they

224

would do their best to help me find a solution. Eventually, I am handed over to a nurse whose sole job is to help those who believe they are positive with the coronavirus. I explain my situation, offer a copy of the letter from Dr. Joyner, and let her know the Twin Cities hospitals lack an adequate supply of tests. The nurse knows precisely what this letter entails and offers her thanks for pursuing participation. She outlines a process that I need to follow and asks me to hold a minute.

"OK, Mrs. Fischbach, I'm back. First things first. We have to create an account for you and generate a Mayo Clinic patient number."

"I'm happy to give you any information you need," I respond, beginning to feel hope.

Once my patient number is created, the nurse begins asking questions. "You're a recovered COVID-19 patient?"

"Yes, and I'm unable to obtain a second test from my doctor or local emergency room," I say, hoping she will appreciate my urgency.

"I understand. The medical community is in constant flux with ever-changing protocols. I can see this would be an impossible requirement to fulfill."

"Yes, impossible! I knew someone at Mayo would understand my frustration."

"If you're willing to drive to New Prague, I can order a test for you at our drive-thru testing location," the nurse offers.

"That would be wonderful. I'll be happy to do that," I answer.

"OK, I've placed the order for a COVID-19 test in the patient portal under your new Mayo Clinic number. All you have to do is show up before five o'clock today and give them your name and patient number. I'll give you the address and information you need."

"Perfect. Thank you again for all your help," I reply, grabbing pen and paper.

Armed with what I need, I hang up the phone and make a quick calculation about timing. I suddenly realize half the day has disappeared, so I scarf down some lunch and head to New Prague. Test #2 — here I come!

Never having visited New Prague, I use my iPhone navigation to find the drive-thru location. Oddly, the voice commands direct me past the business district into a residential neighborhood. I pull over to check the directions, thinking I must have mistyped the address. The address from the nurse matches the one I typed in, but clearly, there is a mistake somewhere. I begin Googling "Mayo Clinic satellite office New Prague 212 10th Ave. NE." The navigation appears to reset but doesn't give me different directions, so I drive back to the small main street and keep my eyes open for signs and numbered avenues. After wandering for a few more blocks, I see a red sign that says COVID-19 TESTING with an arrow pointing toward a large white tent. Whew, I made it! With no cars in line, I pull right up to the tent. I expected to wait in line for up to an hour, so this is a pleasant surprise.

Under the tent is an empty table and a door to the back of the clinic. Unsure of what to do upon arrival, I just sit in my vehicle, taking in the stark surroundings. The clock on my dashboard gives me a reminder that it will be the dinner hour when I make it home. Of course, my thoughts turn to food as I try to remember what's in the refrigerator. My mind flips through a mental Rolodex of

recipes as I ponder what to prepare. These salivating thoughts abruptly end when I observe what appears to be a human emerging from the clinic door. The PPE required to test someone for COVID-19 is so "all-encompassing" that it leaves me wondering what this person looks like and how they can move in that get up. I quickly roll down my window while watching the sizeable yellow robe approach. The nurse introduces herself and asks me if I have an appointment and a mask.

"Oh, yes, I do have a mask. Sorry I forgot to put it on," I say, fumbling through my purse.

"No problem. Do you have an appointment? If so, I'll need your name."

"Yes, Laurel Fischbach. Also, I have a Mayo patient number if that's helpful," I say, grabbing my note with all of the pertinent information given to me by the kind nurse who understood my predicament.

"The patient number would be great. Thanks."

The nurse excuses herself, walking back into the clinic, while my mind returns to dinner. (Musing about food rather than how to acquire a second COVID test is a welcome change.) A few minutes later, she returns with paperwork and explains what to expect next.

"Dr. Kaur will be coming out to swab you and ask a few health questions."

When the doctor emerges from the clinic, I wonder whether she is a doctor or an astronaut. The PPE she is wearing takes personal protection to a new level. Sporting a helmet with a face shield encircled with a fabric hood covering every inch of her chin, neck, and head reminds me of the movie *Contagion*! A thick black flexible tube poking out the back of the helmet connecting to a battery pack and air purification filter. *I later learned she had on a PAPR (Powered Air Purification Respirator).*

"Good afternoon Mrs. Fischbach. I'm Dr. Kaur. I need to ask you some questions."

"Sure," I reply, looking like a deer in the headlights as thoughts of leprosy surface again.

"Do you have a fever, or have you had a fever in the past 24 hours?"

"No."

"Do you have a cough or a sore throat?"

"No. Just slight wheezing if I take a deep breath," I say as I unconsciously take a deep breath, testing my lungs.

"Have you vomited or had diarrhea in the past 24 hours?"

"No."

"OK. I'm going to take your temperature and then swab your nose, so I'll need you to remove your mask," the doctor explains.

I remember the advice given to me during my first COVID-19 test. Wiggle your toes when the swab enters your nose. I have to say, it's a helpful little trick. I close my eyes knowing what to expect, wiggle my toes, and listen to the doctor count to ten. Each swabbing triggers my eyes to water, and I try my best to hold back the urge to cough. As soon as she's finished, she places the long Q-tip in a vile held by the nurse. Next, she advises me to check the patient portal in 48 hours for an update and explains a positive result will warrant a call.

"Only negative results are posted in the patient portal at the time they are confirmed," the doctor explains.

I nod my head to confirm that I understand. She then asks if I have any questions, so I take this opportunity to inquire about my throat. "Will you be swabbing my throat next?"

"No. We stopped swabbing the throat a few weeks ago. We found most of the virus to be detected in the nasal passages. Swabbing the nose is all we need for an effective sample."

"Oh, OK," I reply, surprised.

"Take care, keep yourself isolated as you wait for your results, and drive safely," she says, like a concerned mom.

Pulling out of the parking lot, I take a deep breath, exhale, and think — *I did it! I figured out how to get a second COVID-19 test. Soon I will be called to Mayo to give the doctors, scientists, and researchers what they need to begin unlocking the mysteries behind COVID-19. Little do I know the joy and relief I felt on my drive home would be crushed within 48 hours.*

Chapter 22

April in Minnesota can feel like spring one day and winter the next. Fluctuating weather can bring wicked snowstorms or a stretch of mid 60s. Flexibility for what mother nature may deliver is paramount; therefore, comparing my emotions to spring weather at times seems fitting.

Forty-eight hours doesn't seem like a very long time in the grand scheme of life, but it is when waiting for COVID-19 test results. I am anxious to participate in the plasma study program. Several times per day, I log into my Mayo Clinic account, looking for an update or "negative" test result. The anticipation is intense. Wednesday, April 15th, at approximately 1:30 p.m., my anticipation and anxious curiosity are quelled.

The house phone rings. I see the word "Mayo" on Caller ID and immediately know this phone call is going to be distressing.

"Hello?"

"Good afternoon. Am I speaking with Mrs. Fischbach?"

"Yes, this is she."

"Mrs. Fischbach, this is Dr. Kaur calling. I performed your COVID-19 test on Monday. I'm calling to inform you that your test result has come back positive for the coronavirus."

I crumple over the kitchen counter, cup my forehead in my hand, and let out an audible gasp. "I can't believe I'm still positive!"

"Still positive? What do you mean by, 'still positive?'" the doctor asks.

"This is my second test. My first one was done at the hospital in Edina on March 10th. I contracted the virus in Vail, Colorado, back in February. How can I still be positive almost two months later? Something is wrong!"

"I didn't realize this is your second test. Hmmm…I don't have any notes in my system."

"I received a letter from the Convalescent Plasma Team headed up by Dr. Michael Joyner with instructions to be tested a second time in order to participate in this new plasma study."

"I see. You're the first patient I've had test twice. Can I place you on hold for a minute?"

"Of course, no problem," I say on the verge of tears.

While I say, "No problem," in the typical mindless and perfunctory way, this is actually A BIG PROBLEM! I am positive? I still have an active virus? I feel so much better, and I thought I was OK? I thought 28 days was the magic number. I thought now I could contribute antibodies to help others… Do I need to go back into quarantine? Am I still contagious? This can't be happening! I feel like a spring storm just dumped a foot of heavy wet snow on top of me. I feel buried — stuck — lost in a whiteout.

"Mrs. Fischbach, I want to go over your health history for the past two months," says Dr. Kaur, interrupting my mental panic attack.

With a crack in my voice, I eek out, "Sure."

For the next ten minutes, Dr. Kaur asks a slew of questions. She is extremely thorough, examining my timeline with this virus and asking about each symptom I have experienced. Scanning my medical records from the hospital, she also notes the dates medications were prescribed.

231

"Laurel, based on everything you've told me and tracing your first symptom back to February 24th, I don't believe you are contagious any longer even though you have tested positive. Let me explain my reasoning. The COVID-19 tests are extremely sensitive and use what we call "PCR assay" which stands for "polymerase chain reaction." It's a specific type of test created to detect minute traces of genetic material associated with SARS-CoV-2. I believe the test is picking up dead fragments of the virus that are still shedding in your body. I don't think you have a live, active virus in your body, so I don't believe you're contagious," she asserts with certainty.

I am desperately trying to process all of this. "If you don't think I'm contagious, then are you saying I won't need to go back into quarantine? I shudder to think about putting anyone at risk of contracting this virus from me."

"No, I don't see a need for you to begin a second quarantine. You've recovered from the cough which indicates to me you no longer have an active virus. You reported some slight wheezing with deep breaths, but this is associated with residual inflammation. The wheezing should improve quickly at this point, and you'll return to normal deep breath sensations soon."

"Thank you for explaining all of this to me."

"I'm going to place a call to the epidemiological team and discuss your case with them since you are our very first patient to test positive twice. Also, I'm going to recommend you be included in the convalescent plasma study program despite your second positive test result. If you don't hear back from me, then you can expect a call from the Convalescent Plasma Team."

"I appreciate it...um..." I try to ask one more question, but I can't get it out.

After a brief silence, I hear Dr. Kaur clear her throat. "If I were you, I would just go live your life."

She senses the heaviness I am feeling. Those final words ease my mind and stick with me.

Notes in my Mayo Clinic Portal from Dr. Kaur after our phone conversation on April 15th:

Name: Laurel A. Fischbach
DOB: X-Oct-XXXX
MCN: XX-XXXX-XX
Patient Copy

Mrs. Fischbach was contacted to inform her of the positive SARS Coronavirus-2 RNA positive test.
She underwent the test to be considered for convalescent plasma donation at Mayo Clinic.
The patient reports that she may have contracted the infection while she was in Colorado at the end of February.
Her initial symptoms began on 2/24/2020 which were chest tightness, fever, loss of smell and pink eye.
She returned to MN and saw her local provider on 3/9/2020 as symptoms, especially the chest tightness was not improving. Chest Xray confirmed an infiltrate. She underwent Covid-19 PCR testing on 3/10/2020 which was positive.
She was in self isolation until 3/25/2020 after which she was released by MDH.

Her PCP advised her to use Advair 2x/day for the chest congestion/bronchitis, which she is currently using.

At present she denies any symptoms except for a feeling of "wheezing" when she takes a deep breath.

She denies dyspnea, chest tightness, cough, fever, GI symptoms. She is back to her usual activities. She works from home.

She lives with her husband and teenage daughter who are asymptomatic and have not been tested for Covid-19.

Will consult with the CFCT team regarding further recommendations for this patient.

Informing my husband, family, and friends about the latest test result is a part-time job. Everyone has a thousand questions. I calculate the number of days from my first symptom in Vail to the day I test positive a second time — 50 days! It's remarkable I'm still positive! *When will it be gone? When will I finish shedding fragments of this dead coronavirus?* I work hard to not allow negative thoughts about the virus — or its fragments — to continue holding me captive. The difficult task of pushing the thoughts away is exacerbated by the reactions of others. A typical response after my bombshell is dropped sounds like this, "Well, don't you think you should keep yourself isolated until you can get a test proving you're negative?" My rebuttal always includes direct quotes from Dr. Kaur: "no live virus" — "just dead fragments" — "If I were you, I would just go live your life." Honestly, though, I do wonder what it means to shed fragments? Could this be like a forest fire where the main blaze is well under control, but where embers still glow the blaze could reignite? Could I actually still have a live virus? I don't know how my body's virus-fighting immune system works. Mayo seems to have been taken by surprise that I was positive! But ultimately, I have to trust Dr. Kaur — I certainly want her to be right. Besides, if I have to figure out how to obtain a third test, I will lose my mind! I don't know if I could find the fortitude.

The positive result from my second COVID-19 test started yet another waiting game for me. This time, I am waiting for Mayo Clinic's Convalescent Plasma Project Team to contact me. *Will they accept me with a second positive test result?* I am hopeful Dr. Kaur will argue my case with conviction, but there are no guarantees. The other waiting game stemming from a second positive result is tied to my friends. Everyone is uncomfortable being in my vicinity, and I don't blame them. Daily walks around the lakes will continue, but sadly, I will be walking alone for weeks to come.

Tuesday, April 21st, brings an end to one of my waiting games — the most important one. Seeing Mayo on Caller ID, once again, my chest tightens. *Will this be the call from Dr. Kaur telling me my second test result prohibits my participation in the study, or will it be the Convalescent Plasma Project Team at Mayo asking me to drive down to Rochester?*

I tentatively answer, "Hello."

"Good morning. This is Mayo Clinic calling to speak with Laurel Fischbach. Is she available?"

"This is she."

"Mrs. Fischbach, this is the scheduling nurse for the blood donation bank calling to request an appointment for you to donate convalescent plasma."

It takes a moment for me to realize the last three weeks of persistence has finally paid off.

"Yes…um … Great! I'm so happy to hear from you. I was wondering if I was going to get a call."

"We apologize for the delay in getting back to you. Once the Mayo received approval from the FDA, our program took a little longer to ramp up than we expected. We appreciate your patience; I see you were one of the first people to register."

"Yes. I caught the virus back in February, so when I saw the news about Mayo spearheading efforts to study the disease, I wanted to offer my help. Especially since I live just a short drive away."

"We appreciate your willingness to participate. Can we find a convenient time for you?"

"Of course. I'm a stay-at-home mom, so I have a lot of flexibility."

"Perfect! We are wide open with our schedule, so you tell me what works for you this week or even this afternoon if you would like to donate today."

"Um…let's see," I say, grabbing my iPhone to pull up the calendar as I think about my own personal logistics with donating.

A quick side note - I have been a blood donor for many years. My O negative blood type is "universal" which means my blood is accepted by everyone regardless of their blood types. Since O negative is sought after, and the blood bank regularly contacts me to donate, I try to donate as often as possible. Knowing the procedures that surround a blood donation, I remember the finger prick to test the blood iron count. I typically have low iron, so I always take a supplement several days prior. Guessing a plasma donation will have similar standard procedures, I make a split-second decision not to accept a same-day appointment, even though I would have preferred it.

"How about Thursday the 23rd?" I ask, sounding apologetic.

"You name the time on Thursday. We don't have any appointments that day."

"OK, one o'clock?"

"It's yours. I have the appointment set in the system, so you'll see a confirmation in your patient portal."

"Thank you," I reply, feeling relief knowing I now have forty-eight hours to increase my iron count. The last thing I want is to be rejected for low iron in my blood. It is such a simple fix with an over-the-counter supplement.

"I need to go over a few items with you. We have strict guidelines that need to be followed at Mayo. First, you'll need to wear a mask when you arrive. If you don't have one, we'll provide one. You'll need to check in and be screened prior to entering the elevator. Your temperature will be taken, and it's important that you don't keep your appointment if you're feeling sick," she explains, sounding like she memorized these instructions.

The nurse goes on to give me specific details about where to park, which door to enter, and how much time I should allow for paperwork during check-in.

For the next two days, I swallow iron supplements and eat spinach salads for lunch and dinner. Googling "iron-rich foods" gives me the idea to incorporate currants into my diet, so I add them to my oatmeal. Who knew currants would make the iron-rich food list? *Any little bit will help.*

On Thursday, April 23rd, I call my best friend to start my day. "Lori, can you believe I'm finally driving down to Mayo? What a journey this has been the last two months."

"Yes, you've definitely been through the ringer. I'm so glad you're finally over the pneumonia. What a battle your lungs endured."

It was nice to hear her voice, share my excitement, and catch up about what was going on in her world down in Florida.

"What time are you leaving to start the drive?" Lori asks.

"In a few hours — probably 10:30 a.m. That should give me plenty of time to find the building, park, and get checked in."

"Give me a call when you're driving home. I want to hear all about it. I've never donated blood or plasma."

The drive to Mayo is easy. I open my audible account, select a book, and become engrossed. When I arrive at the exit, I wind my way through downtown Rochester, navigating the confusing one-way streets and construction detours. Leaving early is now proving to have been prudent. Once I find the Hilton building, parking is easy, and the walk to the entrance is short. Following the nurse's instructions, I put on my mask, enter the building, and get checked in. A nurse, who ultimately ends up drawing my blood, greets me at the check-in table just inside the door. She introduces herself and escorts me to the blood donation department, where I am handed an extensive questionnaire. I sit in a spacious lobby socially distanced from others and start in on page one. I find myself consistently referring to the calendar on my iPhone. The form is awash with questions about specific days involving symptoms and doctors' appointments. Soon after handing it to the receptionist, I am escorted back to the only room designated for plasma donation. Once the curtain is drawn, the nurse tells me I may remove my mask if I choose.

"Really, it's OK? I assumed I'd have to wear it the entire time."

"It's just the two of us in this room, and I'm not concerned about you infecting me. You wouldn't be here if the doctors thought you were contagious. I have to leave mine on, but if you're more comfortable without yours, feel free to take it off."

Wow! It feels fantastic to have a medical professional demonstrate such confidence that I cannot infect her!

"I need to give you a finger prick for your hemoglobin count. Which finger would you like to give me?"

"The left one please."

A quick prick producing a small sample for the test strip is collected and then placed off to the side. The preparation for donation takes some time, including checking my weight, blood pressure, and inspecting my veins. I am nervous when the nurse asks me to step on the scale. One hundred ten pounds is the minimum to donate plasma, and I wasn't sure if I had dropped below this cut-off. The digital number appears immediately: 112. *Whew! I made it by the skin of my teeth!* The nurse notes my weight and then returns to the test, processing my hemoglobin number.

"Your iron level is a half point below the reading we need for donation. I'll need to get clearance from my supervisor."

No way! A half point? Could there be any more obstacles thrown at me? I sit in this medical chair, watching the nurse type on the computer with the phone up to her ear, patiently waiting for her supervisor to answer. Thinking about the iron-rich food I've eaten over the last two days combined with the iron supplements, I am stunned. *Why isn't my iron level within range? If I am turned away because of a half point…*

Listening intently to the nurse's responses leads me to believe my hemoglobin number is going to pass muster.

"My supervisor gave the OK for your donation. I figured under these extraordinary circumstances, he would approve. Especially since it's not even a full point below the cutoff," she says with crinkled eyes suggesting she is smiling under her mask.

The last hurdle has been cleared! The nurse walks over to the machine preparing it for my donation.

Feeling relaxed is never easy when I am about to have a needle inserted into my vein; however, at this moment, I do feel relaxed. My persistence has paid off. The goal of sitting in this chair, being able to help others, has finally come to fruition.

The nurse and I chat the entire time she's setting up the machine. We talk about the likelihood of contracting the coronavirus from a surface, the contagion factors, and the facts Mayo recently learned from the first donor earlier in the week. I thoroughly enjoy hearing her viewpoints. It's fascinating to listen to someone who spends her days surrounded by world-renowned medical professionals.

Everything is in place, and my blood begins to fill the tube. Listening to the machine churn as it extracts, I remind myself to take deep breaths to keep the blood flow consistent. Everything is going smoothly — until it isn't. A loud beeping emanates from the equipment, alerting the nurse that something is going wrong.

Chapter 23

The beeping sound from the plasma apheresis machine is loud but not piercing. It's similar to an oven timer alerting you to check on your food before it burns. The constant beeping signals the nurse to make a manual adjustment on the computerized touch screen. She succeeds in quieting the alarm and then promptly moves to my side, pausing to examine my arm; then she checks the needle and adjusts the tube filling with my blood.

"Is everything OK?" I am not feeling anything out of the ordinary, but her actions indicate that something is not quite right.

"Yes, it's OK. The machine is drawing at a vigorous pace, and your small vein is having difficulty keeping up. This happens sometimes and requires manual adjustments during the donation," the nurse explains while rolling the needle slightly between her pinched fingers.

"Oh, this is a bit different than my past blood donations," I respond with my eyes focused on her fingers and the needle.

"Yes, it is. This machine is brand new, and I was just trained on it last week."

With curiosity and undoubtedly raised eyebrows, I ask, "Did Mayo purchase this equipment specifically for this plasma program?"

"Yes, we had to. We pulled one out of storage and scrambled to set it up. We called the medical device sales representative asking for calibration and training, but he said the equipment was too old and no longer supported. Mayo immediately ordered a new machine and had its delivery expedited."

241

"I would not have thought Mayo would be in need of updated medical equipment," I commented.

"We're not in the business of extracting plasma here. The Red Cross and plasma banks specialize in it. They have rooms lined with multiple machines and nurses trained to make the process extremely efficient. We have our blood donation department but not specifically a plasma department, so we were thrown into a predicament. I think you are the third person to donate plasma with this machine."

"Well, this explains why it took three weeks from the time I first heard about the study. I remember hearing on the news that Mayo was chosen as the lead hospital by the FDA to study convalescent plasma in early April. I see why you needed so much time before accepting donors."

"Yes, exactly."

The beeping sound fills the room yet again, so the nurse quells it in the same manner. She does not appear concerned as she pushes the needle a bit deeper into my arm.

While I can't remember the name of this incredibly nice nurse, I can see her kind eyes while writing this. She was very personable, and the conversation naturally bounced around. While some of you may get a chuckle out of this, our conversation switches to hair.

"I never realized, until now, how important my hairdresser is to me," the nurse remarks.

"Oh — I completely agree! My hair is a disaster. It's living in a constant ponytail," I laugh.

"Yes, me too. Feeling good about the way I look is tied to my hair having regular cuts and color. This is something I didn't know about myself until the pandemic.

I haven't seen my hairdresser since the beginning of February."

"I'm in the same boat."

"Although I will say, since I am living behind a mask, I'm saving a lot of money on lipstick."

The conversation ebbs and flows from one subject to the next. The nurse asks me questions about how I thought I contracted the coronavirus, how the symptoms have affected me, and whether I have experienced anything out of the ordinary since my recovery. In turn, I ask her many questions, I enjoy learning what she knows about the continually changing discoveries with COVID. Never leaving the room, constantly monitoring my donation, she continues to make adjustments to the needle, giving my small vein help to work with the new machine.

I felt fortunate to be cared for by so many outstanding nurses and doctors during this pandemic. All of the frontline medical workers — starting with my primary doctor to the hospital staff to the nurse at Mayo — have been consummate professionals. My respect for and appreciation of them was a big reason that I became determined to give back. Perhaps one of them might become infected in the line of duty and need my antibodies.

The nurse is pulling out all the stops to work with my uncooperative body — evidence of her experience and patience. I am in good hands, so when she looks at me and tells me we may need to change course with my donation, I know she has exhausted her expertise.

After perhaps an hour, she states matter-of-factly, "Your vein collapsed. The machine has stopped drawing your blood. I'm going to call my supervisor and discuss a different course of action."

"Oh, no! I don't feel anything strange or painful."

"This sometimes happens with small veins. I'm not able to dial in your exact weight and size with this machine. Unfortunately, this model is designed for the average size person. You are definitely not an average size. The force of the draw is difficult for you."

Again, I listen to one side of the phone conversation, feeling disappointment set in. The call ends with, "OK, I'll ask for her consent to donate a quarter pint." The second she hangs up, she turns to me and asks, "The epidemiological team would like a 'whole blood' donation from you. Is that OK?"

"Absolutely!"

"We'll only be taking a quarter pint, and we won't be using the plasma machine. We'll extract from your other arm so it won't take long and shouldn't be a problem."

"Great. Hopefully this will aid in their research."

"Yes, it will, and they'll also use the small amount of plasma already extracted from you in their research efforts," the nurse explains as she places stickers on empty vials.

"It's going to take me a few minutes to print off some paperwork and get everything set up."

Soon vials begin filling with my blood while the nurse talks about the Red Cross. "I encourage you to seek donation with the Red Cross. Mayo will be working closely with them, and they have better plasma apheresis machines with more sophisticated settings. Their machines can be adjusted to a patient's body weight and size, allowing the extraction to be tailored to you. In your case, the pull on your vein could be calibrated to help keep it from collapsing."

"Thanks. I've donated through them before. I will give them a try. I'd really like to put my antibodies to work somehow."

The nurse switches out one vial after another, placing each one in a tray with my patient number clearly displayed.

"I'm not sure if they are ramped up with their program yet, but if they aren't, they will be soon," the nurse says, placing the last vial of my blood in the tray.

The curveballs thrown at me in the "baseball game of life" definitely had me feeling off-balance at times. When I walked out of the clinic — did I feel like I hit a home run? No, because I wasn't able to fill a bag to the brim with plasma. I felt like I hit a ground ball, and now I needed to run as fast as possible to first base.

On Friday, April 24th, the day after my trip to Mayo, the research begins. I start by calling the downtown Minneapolis location on River Parkway, knowing this is the Red Cross Region Headquarters for Minnesota, North Dakota and South Dakota. I bounce around from one department to another, eventually connecting with a woman who understands exactly what I need to do.

"Are you able to pull up a website while you're on the phone with me?" she asks.

"Yes. I'm sitting in front of my computer, so please go ahead."

The accommodating and knowledgeable Red Cross employee walks me through a newly created webpage for convalescent plasma donation. She explains it's essential I provide proof of a positive COVID-19 test. *Well that certainly isn't a problem because I have two of those from two different hospitals!* I think. She thanks me for taking the time to figure out the donation process.

Her last words are, "Hold tight, and don't get discouraged if you don't hear back from someone right away because the Red Cross is just getting started with this new donation program. I promise someone will contact you as soon as the program gets ramped up."

I let her know her help has been invaluable and that I'm happy to be patient. In a matter of hours, I receive confirmation I'm in the system and a request for a scanned copy of my positive COVID test.

April 24, 2020 at 2:17pm
Durica, Justyna
To: lafischbach@xxxxx
Cc: American Red Cross Convalescent Plasma Covid-19
Re: Red Cross Convalescent Plasma Follow Up Request – Last Day Symptom and Test Result

Dear Laurel,
Thank you for your continued interest in helping others through the Convalescent Plasma Program. While reviewing your submission the team determined some additional information was needed. Can you please provide a copy of your test results with your full name visible, or a letter from your physician indicating the test results that confirmed your diagnosis of COVID-19 for participation as a donor in this program.
In addition, can you please provide the date of your last COVID-19 related symptoms (MM/DD/YY) to include any fever, cough and shortness of breath and the date of your test.

You can attach the test results or letter and submit via email to Conv_donor_plasma@redcross.org or fax it to 800-886-7024. If you need to submit this documentation by US mail, please send it to the following address:

Donor and Client Support Center
American Red Cross
9013-J Perimeter Woods Drive
Charlotte, NC 28216
ATTN: J Hall Convalescent Plasma

Regards,
 American Red Cross
Convalescent Plasma Program

Responding is quick and easy. Now the onus is on me to exercise patience once again.

Chapter 24

Today is the last day of April, and I am out for my first bike ride of the year. For someone who loves physical activity, riding my bike through the neighborhood, breathing in the smell of spring, feels extraordinarily exhilarating. My long stretch of inactivity has created an abundance of pent-up energy, and I am anxious to test my lungs. *This will be interesting to see how much my cardiovascular system has suffered.* Halfway up my first challenging hill, breathing hard, my phone rings. I would not dream of stopping on this incline, so I peddle harder to crest the hill. When I hit the top, I look down at the phone mount and see a number I don't recognize. I contemplate letting it go to voicemail but decide to answer it on the very last ring.

"Hello," I answer, breathing heavily.

"Good evening. May I speak with Laurel Fischbach?"

"This is she," I say, sucking in air simultaneously.

"This is the Red Cross calling about your registration with the convalescent plasma donation program. We received your documentation, and I'm calling to find out if we can schedule you to donate at one of our locations?"

"Yes, oh — I'm sorry— whew, I'm out of breath right now. I'm on my bike — my first ride of the year."

"No problem, I can call back another time if that would be more convenient for you," the woman offered.

"No, it's fine, let me place you on speaker phone so I can check my calendar."

"Sure, just let me know when you're ready."

"OK, would it be possible for me to donate on a weekend?" I inquire.

"Yes, a few of our locations are open on weekends. What's your zip code? I'll search for the closest location and times available."

I settle on Sunday afternoon, May 3rd at the Bloomington location.

"Thank you for scheduling with me this evening. You'll receive a confirmation email with some instructions about what to do prior to your donation."

"OK, I'll keep my eye out for it."

"If you have any questions, or if you need to reschedule, please call the number in the email."

"Thank you. I will," I say, feeling energized to take on the next hill.

The remainder of my ride feels great. I walk in the door announcing my good news to the family.

"That's terrific," John says.

"I know! Can you believe how quickly the Red Cross got back to me? I hope their equipment has an easier time extracting the plasma from my 'skinny' vein. I have to make sure I ramp up my iron intake, so my hemoglobin count is where it needs to be," I babble, noticing my mind and mouth are speeding along at a hundred miles an hour.

Waking up on Sunday, May 3rd, my stomach feels nervous. I begin thinking about my weight, iron count, and need to pump up my veins. Determined to rid myself of this nervous feeling, I walk downstairs to my basement home gym and start my workout music. *This will get me in the mood to sweat.* For the next hour, I push myself hard on the treadmill. Then I move to lifting weights — switching rapidly from arms to chest to shoulders to back. My hope is that strenuous exercise and drinking some extra fluid will give me the "weightlifter pump" so my veins will be ready for pricking. Knowing the pre-donation instructions suggest you eat prior to arriving, I cook a hearty brunch to keep me satiated.

I arrive early for my appointment, check in at the front desk, and get a surprised look when the receptionist notices on her calendar that I am here for a convalescent plasma donation.

"Oh — um — you're scheduled for a convalescent plasma donation, correct?" she asks, sizing me up.

"Yes, I am," I respond, becoming used to people having strange reactions around me.

"Oh — OK — um — I'm going to need you to fill out some special paperwork before you can be called back," she says while fumbling through a file folder.

"No problem," I respond, standing six feet away, giving her space to feel comfortable.

"You can take a seat anywhere you'd like, and I'll bring the forms to you as soon as I find them."

I choose a large table, make myself comfortable, and notice how the residential furniture gives the clinic a warm, inviting feel despite the sterile environment that waits just past the lobby. The receptionist doesn't take long before handing me a clip board with a stack of forms mixed with questionnaires. I thumb through the pages and think, *it's a good thing I got here early.*

"You can bring the completed forms back to me at the front desk when you're finished."

"OK, will do."

Just as I am completing the last form, a woman approaches me. "Hi. Are you Laurel Fischbach?"

"Yes, I am," I reply, looking up at her.

"I'm Sue Thesenga, Red Cross External Communications Manager. I was told there would be a

250

convalescent plasma donor here today. I wanted to personally meet you and thank you for coming in to help aid in the research with convalescent plasma. The medical community believes it can help to save lives."

"I was just at Mayo a little over a week ago, and they encouraged me to reach out to the Red Cross."

"Oh, glad to hear it. I was hoping I could sit down with you for a few minutes before you're called back for the donation. I'm interested in writing a story about you, how you contracted the virus, and why you're donating. Would you be willing to let me publish a story about you?" Sue asked.

"Sure. I'd be happy to help you," I reply, surprised she is taking time on a Sunday afternoon to interview me.

"Let me explain why I'm interested in writing a story about your donation. The Red Cross is not receiving enough registrations for convalescent plasma donation. We need to promote the ease of signing up and donating plasma. The Red Cross has an overwhelming number of requests for convalescent plasma from doctors. We can't get close to meeting the need right now."

"Yes, I've heard there aren't very many of us survivors donating right now. Mayo had a lot of open appointment times available."

"I'm hoping your story and a photo of you donating will encourage others to sign-up to donate," Sue says, sounding optimistic.

Sue made me feel at ease as she asked a lot of questions. She was particularly interested in how it felt knowing a life or lives could potentially be saved with my plasma. I need to emphasize the word "potentially" because there was no absolute certainty that convalescent plasma would alleviate severe COVID-19 symptoms in every case. We had just enough time to get through her questions and talk about my recent donation at Mayo.

A nurse approaches the table. "We're ready for you, Laurel, whenever you are," she says, motioning her hand toward an examination room.

"Perfect timing! Sue and I are just wrapping up our conversation."

"If it's OK with you, Laurel, I would like to take a few photos of you sitting in the chair donating to include with the story," Sue mentions.

"Sure, that's a good idea."

"OK, I'll organize my notes while you get prepped."

I follow the nurse to the examination room as I mentally prepare myself for the finger prick. *Please, please, please, let my iron count be within range!* The nurse is organized, and everything she needs to prepare me for my donation is ready. I start by getting the same 112-pound weight on the scale. *Whew! The first hurdle is out of the way.*

"I need your index finger for a prick to check your iron count."

It's always a quick and painless prick, but I am sweating it. I sit in suspense while the test processes my iron count.

"Your iron count is good: 13.5," the nurse comments, typing the number into my chart. "Now, I need to go through some questions with you, and then we'll walk back to find a chair for your donation."

The first question she asks goes in one ear and out the other. My thoughts are off in a sea of relief. *I have just leapt over the second hurdle with a 13.5 hemoglobin reading. Hallelujah!*

"I'm sorry, could you repeat that first question?" I ask.

When the litany of questions is answered, the nurse escorts me back to a row of medical recliners and introduces me to a colleague. I'm briefed about what will take place next. I take a seat in the one available recliner. The clinic is busy but unfortunately not with convalescent plasma donors — only regular plasma donors. The team of nurses goes to work setting up the machine, preparing my arms for vein selections and ultimately figuring out if they will use one vein or two. Trying to use two veins, one in each arm, quickly proves unsuccessful. It takes two nurses extra time to get my donation started because the needle needs to be adjusted at a very specific angle for the blood to start flowing. One of the nurses has a lot of experience and assesses my situation accurately — small, finicky veins. With a little extra attention, the blood begins to flow nicely. The machine begins separating the plasma, and I see my golden yellow liquid trickle into the bag. Watching the flow of blood and the plasma separation begin, I think, *I've now leapt over hurdle number three, and I'm sprinting to the finish line!*

Sue walks toward me with a fleece blanket in her hands, the American Red Cross logo plastered over its entirety.

"May I lay this blanket over your legs before I take the photo? Would you like a blanket?"

"Sure. Thanks. I get cold easily."

"I'm going to take a few photos at different angles. I'll send the best one to you," Sue explains while backing up.

"Thanks. I want to send a photo to my daughter, so this works out perfectly. I'll send a text to you with my email address."

"All right, I have what I need for the story. You've been a huge help. As soon as I finish it, I'll send a link to you. I'm planning on posting it on Facebook and Twitter."

"Wonderful! I look forward to reading it."

Having one hand and one arm free from a needle and tubing gives me the opportunity to read a few things on my phone. I relax in the comfortable chair, scrolling through emails. Shortly after opening an email, a text message arrives from Sue with the photo she just took. Delighted to have it, I text Avery, giving her a real-time account of my donation. I also text it to a few friends, and Amanda texts back from Michigan, "That's awesome! I'll have to look into donating, too."

The plasma apheresis machine drawing my blood at the Red Cross is having a much easier time than the one at Mayo, just as the nurse predicted. I feel grateful for her suggestion to pursue the Red Cross.

I am not sure how long I sat connected to the machine. The nurses were constantly checking on me, asking if I was comfortable or if I needed anything, always noting the fluid collection progress. I was extremely impressed with this clinic; it ran like a well-oiled machine.

One of the nurses is examining the needle placement in my vein when she notices something that needs attention.

"Hmmm, I need to get my co-worker. I'll be right back."

What now? Please don't let whatever needs attention end up being a big problem. A couple of minutes pass as I study the needle in my arm, wondering if it is doing what it's supposed to be doing.

Two nurses approach, and the most experienced one says, "OK, let's get a look at what's going on here."

She removes some tape on my arm and adjusts the needle slightly. It only takes her a moment to reach a conclusion. "You've clotted," she says, looking up at the blood and plasma bags hanging from hooks on the machine.

"I've clotted? What does that mean?" I ask, feeling confused.

"We've taken everything we're going to get from you today."

I also take a second to look over at the bag containing my plasma.

"Oh, so I'm finished donating today? Were you able to get enough plasma from me?" I ask.

"Yes, we definitely got enough to process and send off. You gave enough plasma to help at least one patient, and your plasma will be studied, too. So, that's good," the nurse explains.

"Well, that's a relief. Why did I clot before I could completely fill the bag?"

"It's hard to say. You definitely have very tiny veins," she observes, shrugging her shoulders.

The entire experience with the Red Cross was positive, despite my inability to completely fill a bag with plasma. The facility, staff, and sophisticated medical equipment used are top notch. I walked out of the clinic knowing I made a difference, and this gave me a sense of accomplishment I would hold close to my heart.

May 6, 2020

no-reply@givebloodtoday.redcrossblood.org

To: Laurel Fischbach
Reply-To: American Red Cross
Thank You For Giving Convalescent Plasma.

Thank You.
Not too long ago, you fought COVID-19 and won. Then, you made an incredible choice to donate convalescent plasma and help others who are currently fighting the disease.

On behalf of COVID-19 patients in need, THANK YOU. Your generous gift may be just what a grandmother, an uncle or an immunocompromised child needs to survive this virus. While we don't yet know how effective COVID-19 Convalescent Plasma treatment is, we will find out thanks to donors like you.
There's a lot of hope around this new, experimental treatment. We are so grateful you're a part of it.

Thank You,
Your American Red Cross

P.S. If you're willing to help more patients in need, please consider giving again in the weeks ahead. You can give plasma every 28 days.

Please call (833) 225-8017 to schedule your next appointment. Convalescent Plasma scheduling staff are ready to assist you Monday through Friday: 9:30 a.m. to 9 p.m. EST or Saturday and Sunday: 9:30 a.m. to 2 p.m. EST.

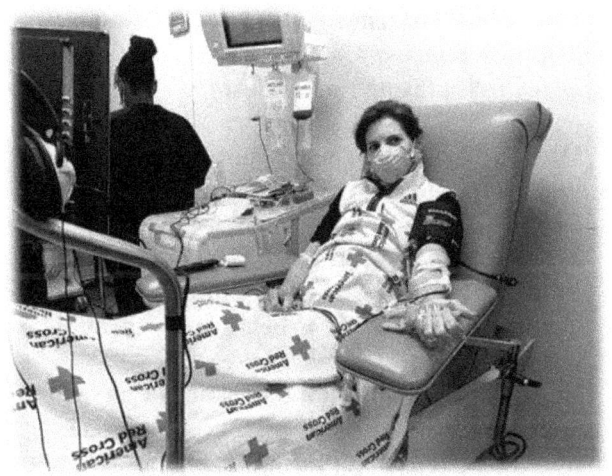

Chapter 25

Within 24 hours of meeting Sue Thesenga, I receive an email from her. I assume she is working on massaging a rough draft for the social media story and needs answers to finish it.

> **May 4, 2020**
> **From: Sue Thesenga**
> **To: lafischbach@XXXX.XXX**
> **Red Cross plasma donation story**
>
> **Hi Laurel – it was a pleasure meeting you yesterday and hearing about your COVID-19 story.**
> **I took a stab at writing it up – see attached. Feel free to make any edits you want or give me a call at the number below to go through the changes you want to make.**
> **Here are a few additional questions I have:**
> - **How was your experience donating plasma?**
> - **How long did the donation take?**
> - **Would you donate again in 28 days?**
>
> **Thanks again for sharing your story and your time to do the donation.**
> **Sue Thesenga**
> **External Communications Manager**

I email back with affirmative answers to all of her questions. Of course, I will donate again. Two days later, she sends links to the Facebook and Twitter posts.

> May 6, 2020
> From: Susan Thesenga
> To: Laurel Fischbach
> RE: [EXTERNAL] Re: Red Cross plasma donation story
>
> Hi Laurel – I just posted the following. It wouldn't let me tag you so go in and you can share it too.
> Thanks again! Stay Safe!
> Sue Thesenga
> External Communications Manager
>
> Facebook – American Red Cross - Minnesota
> https://www.facebook.com/photo?fbid=101 57530350554164&set=a.168634939163

"When I found out about donating my plasma to help others who were critically ill w/#COVID-19, I thought it was my civic duty to give it, said Laurel Valvano Fischbach from Edina. "It feels amazing – kind of like an invisible Superwoman!" Learn more about convalescent plasma: rcblood.org/2XH3zAR

Twitter @RedCrossBloodNC
https://twitter.com/RedCrossBloodNC/status/125804 6568692961282

Wanting to springboard off this social media post from the Red Cross, I reach out to a local TV station, KARE 11. I leave a message with the receptionist about my need to speak with someone regarding a story to promote convalescent plasma donation. She assures me my message will make it into the right hands, and it does.

KARE 11 Reporter, Kent Erdahl, contacts me to request an interview. Our first phone call lasts almost an hour, and I am happy to provide the details he is seeking. He is already working with Dr. Michael Joyner at Mayo Clinic, gathering as much information about plasma therapy as he can while he constructs a story. Kent is sure my donations will enhance his feature nicely.

"I am here to help, so just let me know when you want to meet. If it would be convenient for you, we could meet on my deck in the backyard."

"Yes, that may work well, Laurel. I really appreciate your quick response and flexibility. Thanks. I'll be in touch."

What a pleasant young man, I think to myself after hanging up. He ends up scheduling three or four different interviews with me before one finally sticks. Each time, Kent texts, "I'm so sorry, but I got assigned to another story, so I have to cancel with you. I apologize for the last-minute notice." I understand his day-to-day duties, thanks to my internship at a local news station way back in my college days. News is an extremely time sensitive business, and a reporter often finds himself pivoting on a dime. When Kent and I finally connect, my deck is the easiest location for him to comply with the news station's COVID response policy. The goal of the story is to educate the viewers about Mayo Clinic's FDA-approved Convalescent Plasma Study program. Watching the story air on the ten o'clock news that evening, I feel he succeeded in combining my personal experience with Mayo Clinic's broader efforts. His story details how Mayo will use convalescent plasma not only to study COVID-19 but also to treat the severely ill. The gift of convalescent plasma is essential, and hopefully this news story encourages many people in the Twin Cities to consider donating.

KARE 11 TV Minneapolis, May 25, 2020:

Author: Kent Erdahl
Published: 11:10 PM CDT May 25, 2020
Updated: 11:10 PM CDT May 25, 2020

With more Minnesotans gaining access to coronavirus testing, the Red Cross and Mayo Clinic hope it leads to more donations of convalescent plasma.

"It's not doing any harm and we believe we may be doing some good," said Dr. Michael Joyner, who is leading a national convalescent plasma study at the Mayo Clinic. "We're going to try to figure out exactly how much good we're doing, and under what circumstances, in the coming weeks and months."

Hospitals across the country have been asking recovered COVID-19 patients to donate plasma since April. The effort caught the attention of Laurel Fischbach, who began experiencing COVID-19 symptoms during a ski trip to Vail, Colorado in March.

"I started uncontrollably coughing, and that unfortunately went on for approximately two months," she said.

Fischbach was among Minnesota's first wave of recovered COVID-19 patients to donate plasma for the Mayo Clinic study. She tested positive for antibodies and found a donation site through the Red Cross.

"It's really about heading this virus off in the best way we can," Fischbach said.

A **trial this month** showed convalescent plasma transfusions are safe for COVID-19 patients. Dr. Joyner says another trial now underway will help determine its effectiveness. In the meantime, hospitals are reporting encouraging results and plasma's history is on their side.

Dr. Joyner: "Historically, if you look at the use of convalescent plasma prior to World War II, a huge amount of it was prophylactic."

Kent Erdahl: "So, based on the history, there's good reason to believe that it could be used to prevent COVID?"

Dr. Joyner: "Correct, or to suppress outbreaks."

Even if it proves effective, Dr. Joyner says plasma poses a logistical challenge, due to its reliance on donations. Thankfully, he says increased testing and cooperation across the country are making him feel optimistic.

The study has logged more than 12,000 transfusions nationwide, and 500-600 people are now donating plasma each day.

"Seven or eight people could be helped by one person," Dr. Joyner said. "What we've done so far probably exceeds even the most optimistic expectations by two or three-fold."

As the trials continue, Fischbach says she's happy to do her part.

"They just actually called me last week and I'm on the books to donate again on June 2nd," she said. "Give people some peace of mind as we go forward that there are many, many people out there that have already been through this and have survived. We're all in this together."

Chapter 26

Fast forward to Wednesday, July 29th. Heidi Wigdahl from KARE 11 News calls at ten o'clock in the morning, and fortunately, I am home to take the call. I am sitting outside on my deck, about to go for a walk in the neighborhood.

"Hello. Is Laurel Fischbach available? This is Heidi Wigdahl from KARE 11 News calling."

"Yes, this is Laurel speaking."

"Oh… hello, Laurel, I'm calling because I saw you recently did an interview with Kent Erdahl."

"Yes, Kent interviewed me last month about my convalescent plasma donation."

"I've been assigned the task of finding a convalescent plasma donor to interview, and I am hoping to use you. I'm working with the Red Cross to produce a story about their need to encourage more COVID-19 survivors to donate," Heidi explains.

"Yes. I am aware it's been a struggle for the Red Cross to fulfill the requests from doctors for convalescent plasma."

"I'm working on this story today and hope I can find a convenient time for an interview. Would you be willing to meet with me?"

"Absolutely, Heidi. Would you like to interview me on my deck? Kent found my backyard to work well for his interview."

"Yes, that would be great. Thanks."

"OK, I can be ready in an hour. Feel free to come by anytime that works best for you," I told her.

"That's terrific! I'll see you in an hour."

My walk will have to wait, but I don't mind. Having a second news story air about the critical need for convalescent plasma is important. I dash upstairs to shower and pull myself together for Heidi's arrival.

When Heidi pulls up to the house, I show her to the backyard and offer to move deck furniture to help her set up for the interview. She is prepared with her tripod and camera in tow.

"Thank you so much for giving me an interview on such short notice. I didn't expect to be doing this an hour after I called you — but boy is this helpful!" Heidi said excitedly.

"I explained to Kent that I have a little understanding about your day-to-day as a reporter because I have a communications degree. I know you have deadlines and pressure to produce a story quickly."

"That's true. Right after we finish, I have an interview at the Red Cross," Heidi adds.

"I'm thrilled to hear that. Is your interview with Susan Thesenga?" I ask.

"Yes, it is."

"You'll enjoy working with her. She interviewed me for stories she posted on the Red Cross social media sites. Her sole purpose was to communicate the ease of plasma donation and the desperate need for convalescent plasma. She is passionate about her work."

"I'm glad to hear it, and I look forward to meeting her."

The entire interview with Heidi takes only twenty minutes. Once again, KARE 11 demonstrates it employs conscientious, excellent reporters. Heidi asks thoughtful questions and produces a compelling story.

Author: Heidi Wigdahl
Published: 5:39 PM CDT July 29, 2020
Updated: 5:54 PM CDT July 29, 2020

Red Cross in need of plasma donations from COVID-19 survivors amid shortage.

An increase in COVID-19 cases has led to an emergency shortage of convalescent plasma, according to the American Red Cross.

MINNEAPOLIS, Minnesota — The American Red Cross is experiencing an emergency shortage of convalescent plasma, a potentially lifesaving treatment for COVID-19 patients.

"Convalescent plasma is a blood donation collected from individuals who have fully recovered from COVID-19 and it has antibodies in it that will help patients who are currently fighting this virus," explained Sue Thesenga, communications manager for the American Red Cross.

According to the Red Cross, an increase in COVID-19 cases across the U.S. has led to the shortage. The nonprofit is looking for more people who have fully recovered from the disease, willing to donate their plasma.

"I can't say enough about the Red Cross and how they handle the whole process. Making you feel comfortable through the entire experience," said Laurel Fischbach of Edina.

266

Fischbach contracted COVID-19 while on a ski trip in Vail, Colorado.

"February 24th was my first symptom. Tightness in the chest. But of course I just chalked it up to the altitude and skiing," Fischbach recalled.

Fischbach became one of the first in Minnesota to recover from the disease and donate her convalescent plasma for a Mayo Clinic study. She also gave to the American Red Cross and plans on donating again.

"It just warms your heart. It just makes you feel like you have something to give, something to give back," she said.

Thesenga said they're hoping for more people, like Fischbach, who are willing to donate their plasma. In the last month, demand for convalescent plasma more than doubled. Plasma products are now being distributed faster than donations are coming in. With each donation, survivors can help up to three patients recover from the virus.

"As this crisis continues, I think this is a time where we need to remember to care for one another and this is a way that you can turn a negative into a positive," Thesenga said.

Those who have fully recovered and have received a verified COVID-19 diagnosis can sign up to see if they're eligible to donate, here.

Additionally, the Red Cross is also in need of blood donations.

https://www.google.com/amp/s/www.kare11.com/amp/a rticle/news/health/coronavirus/red-cross-in-need-of-plasma-donations-from-covid-19-survivors-amid-shortage/89-223a61b2-70f4-4b36-97bc-20ee21c72b76

Participating in a news story which shows COVID-19 survivors how they can make a difference gives me a feeling of accomplishment. After posting the news links on my personal Facebook page, I find out a few months later that I inspired two COVID recovered social dancers to donate. This solidifies for me that taking the time to post onto my social media account can often wield good.

On November 6th, Mayo Clinic sends an email asking if I would participate in a new research study. They seek my DNA for research on why some individuals develop severe symptoms while others don't present any.

November 6, 2020
Mayo Clinic Health Tapestry: Genomic
Sequencing in Clinical Practice
> IRB: 19-000001
> PI: Dr. Konstantinos Lazaridis,
M.D., and Colleagues

Dear Laurel Fischbach,

As the COVID-19 pandemic continues, researchers at Mayo Clinic remain committed to the search for discoveries that may result in the prevention, earlier diagnosis, or better therapy to treat the virus. As part of this effort we have modified our existing trial to incorporate COVID-related research. These changes include the addition of a COVID survey that will be used in conjunction with DNA sequencing data to assess hereditary factors that may affect susceptibility, transmission, and outcomes.

We invite you to participate in the Tapestry study, whose goal is to understand how patient care may be impacted when results from DNA sequencing are in the medical record. Participation in the study can be done entirely from the comfort of your home, and no blood collection is needed. To learn more about the study and what you can expect, hear from our genetic counselor, Teresa Kruisselbrink, M.S., CGC, in this brief video (less than 5 minutes).

269

To participate in the study, <u>visit the Tapestry website</u> and <u>complete the eligibility form</u>.

Study participants will receive results from the screening test for familial hypercholesterolemia (FH), hereditary breast and ovarian cancer (HBOC), and Lynch Syndrome (hereditary colorectal cancers). Results will be placed in the medical   record.

More information is available by clicking on the links below.

- <u>General Information</u>
- <u>Participation Information</u>
- <u>Helix</u>
- <u>Results</u>
- <u>Data Privacy, Insurance, and Discrimination</u>
- <u>Tapestry Genomic Registry</u>
- <u>Tapestry Documents (brochure, example consent form, etc.)</u>
- <u>Related links</u>

Your participation in this research study is voluntary. Your current or future medical care at the Mayo Clinic will not be jeopardized if you choose not to participate.

If you do not want these genetic test results in your medical record, you should not participate in this study. To speak with

270

the study team about any concerns, you may contact them at <u>TAPESTRY@mayo.edu</u>.

If you do not wish to participate in this study, <u>complete the refusal form</u>.

This is a no-brainer. I immediately agree to participate in the Tapestry DNA Sequencing Research Study and then contact Kent Erdahl. I brief him with all I know about the study, and he is thankful for the opportunity to run a story about it.

"Let me get a hold of my contact at Mayo and let you know about setting up a meeting," Kent texted. I assume Kent needs to get clearance to release information about this new study.

"OK, no problem. I'll wait to hear back from you."

Within 48 hours, Kent and his cameraman are in my driveway interviewing me as I spit in a tube for the camera. The goal of this story is to get the word out to COVID-19 survivors that their DNA is needed for research. Kent pulls together a terrific story featuring Dr. Konstantinos Lazaridis, M.D., speaking about scientists' need to understand if specific DNA is linked to patients' outcomes. One way to study the DNA from recovered COVID-19 patients is to capture their saliva. It's a simple way to contribute important research. Once again, I am hopeful another news story will alert others, encouraging them to donate.

KARE 11 News November 17, 2020:
https://www.google.com/amp/s/www.kare11.com/amp/article/news/local/breaking-the-news/mayo-clinic-dna-study-aims-to-unlock-mystery-surrounding-covid-19-outcomes/89-03a5f334-5b49-4472-bf4c-ffaaa757d525

Thank you for accompanying me on my journey. One that sent me down many paths. Looking back on it, I realize how lucky I am. I never ended up in the hospital, I had exceptional medical care, I felt constant love and support from friends and family, I have avoided the lingering symptoms that continue to plague the "long haulers," and I had the opportunity to write this book.

If there is one thing I would like to leave with you — it's this: Think hard before rejecting the vaccine. Battling the coronavirus can be a tough road, and I wouldn't wish it on you or on anyone close to you.

Epilogue

2020 was a very strange year for all of us. It did not end well for many — for those who lost love ones, who lost jobs, who lost educational opportunities, and/or who lost businesses that they had built through years of great effort and great sacrifice. For me — I was very lucky. For me — 2020 ended incredibly well!

I wanted to write about my experience so that I would never lose track of it. I spent much of 2020 feeling sick, confused, frustrated, and fearful — but not just from COVID-19. This memoir focuses on my struggle as one of the first Minnesotans to become infected with the coronavirus. What I do not relate is the fact that three months after contracting the virus, and after largely recovering from it, I was found to have a bone spur pressing on a nerve in my neck. Initially, I wondered if the pain and numbness was a residual effect from the coronavirus. Perhaps it was just another of the wide array of seemingly disconnected COVID symptoms? It was not. A slowly growing bone spur had become large enough to press on a nerve. It created a problem for me that was much more serious than that caused by the coronavirus. I worried that I might have to live with chronic and debilitating pain. I feared that the active life I had always lived was over!

As it turned out, a physician, Dr. Michael McCue, recommended the least invasive procedure that was theoretically possible for my spine. On July 21st he made a small incision on the back of my neck, drilled a tiny hole, and carefully navigated through the microscopic structures in my spine to relieve the pressure. In the prior eight weeks of frantically completed tests, scans, research, and consultations, various orthopedic surgeons had recommended different, more invasive approaches to that suggested by Dr. McCue. I am grateful to all of them for their patience and knowledge. Yet, it was Dr. McCue who returned me to a normal life.

Thus, fate threw two curveballs at me in the first half of 2020. Each experience was challenging, stressful, and sometimes overwhelming. Yet, what I take away from this time is awe. I am in awe of doctors and of scientists — those who are experts in epidemiology and those who are experts in the human spine. I am in awe of the kindness of my friends and neighbors. I am in awe of the ability of my closest friends to say the right words, at the right time, to calm my anxieties. And I am in awe of the incredible warmth I have felt from a large group of fellow dancers who could have chosen to shun me, but rather, without exception, lifted my spirits regularly.

Although I am not "a crier," I found myself in tears many times during 2020. I cried at times because I was so sick from COVID that I could see no end. I cried at times because the pain in my neck, back, shoulder, and arm was so severe that I could foresee no relief. And, of course, I cried with friends who lost their parents. In truth, however, there is nothing remarkable about such tears.

What is remarkable, at least to me, is that I cried so often from pure gratitude. I was given time, effort, affirmation, and care so often and from so many. My friends and family saw me through my darkest days, while the dance community lifted my spirits with constant encouragement.

I ended the last chapter with a plea that readers trust the vaccine. In this epilogue I want to encourage you to find your place in a community of people with whom you share a passion for some activity, cause, hobby, or sport — something that will connect you to others and bring joy to your life.

Acknowledgements

I am fortunate to have a long list of names to type onto this page. When the phrase "It takes a village" is heard, we think of raising children. I'm here to tell you it also refers to writing a book.

For the sacrifice of ridiculous amounts of time, thanks to Tanya Dmowski, Carol Malecha, Bob Sondag, and Todd Weber. This book would not exist, be readable, or have any punctuation without all of you.

Tanya, your attention to detail was incredible, and your ability to verify something quickly was impressive. The late nights with you at your kitchen table were invaluable and enjoyable.

Carol, your willingness to look for extra spaces, extra periods, and extra anything was an offer I couldn't refuse. Thank you.

Bob, your insistence that I pay attention to sentence structure and watch Great Courses lectures on writing was the kick in the pants I needed. I learned so much from your edits, comments, and suggestions. In addition, your unwavering patience as I questioned one suggestion after the next was noticed and appreciated.

Todd, your offer to edit my chapters while juggling your practice and a house full of three active boys was generous. Please tell Amy I thank her for your time.

Next, I have to thank John and Avery, whom I forced into quarantine. Thank you both for spending twelve days in a hotel, calling me daily, and caring for me during my recuperation.

I thank my friends who listened to me talk about my book for months: Joanne Bergstedt-Junker, Michele

Bruning-Way, Tanya Dmowski, Brad Fredrickson, Kathleen and Doug Hokemeir-Seim, Patti Katz, Carol Malecha, Candy Quinn, Kelly Rickard, Larry Skeie, Theresa Sladek, Bob Sondag, Kathy Tran, Dave Tsang, and Lori Yacalavitch.

I am grateful for all the friends, family, and neighbors who took the time to cook, shop, call, and send gifts to cheer me up: Joanne Bergstedt-Junker, Andy and Michele Bruning-Way, Karen and Dave Carl, Marit and Greg Corniea, Tanya Dmowski, Rick Earnst, Brad Fredrickson, Kathleen Hokemeir-Seim, Jeanne and Tom Hunt, Chris and Dawn Keith, Gary Knigge, Amy Landelle, Emma Marshall-Cerqueira, Cindy Nowlan Gottschalk, Catherine Machak Groat, Helena Orth, Kelly Rickard, Lori and Rob Roettger, Michelle and Craig Rowe, Kim Sabow, Kim Schlender, Theresa Sladek, Bob Sondag, Kate Stites, Heather and Tony Succio, Laura Thrane, Kathy and Doug Tran, Larry Trebelhorn, Dave Tsang, Ann Vogt, and Sheryl and Jason White.

A big thank-you to my friends who "talked me off the ledge." You know who you are.

More thank-yous go to:

The Twin Cities dance community, whose members bring passion, purpose, and joy to my life.

Char Torkelson (Howard), for publishing expertise and encouragement.

Kathy Tran for her willingness to turn my ideas into artwork. I love the book cover.

Annie Frazer for suggesting the DNA strand.

Gail Gavin for accepting a last-minute request for editing help.

Kelly Rickard for answering my random punctuation questions.

My ski buddies, who push me each year to new heights and keep me young.

My book club, the Litwits, whose invitation to join the club five years ago was the start of a rewarding new activity in my life.

My little brother, "Nate the Skate" Valvano, who has more patience than I can ever hope to have.

For love and encouragement, I thank John, Avery, Nancy and Anthony Valvano, Donna and Carl Valvano, Lori Yacalavitch, and especially Bob, Carol, Tanya, and Todd. You believed I could write a book when I felt I had no idea what I was doing.

My friends visiting me from afar while I stand on my front porch during my quarantine.

Handmade get-well cards from Perrie and Myles.

BOOKS TO EXPLORE:

Apollo's Arrow

The profound and enduring impact of Coronavirus on the way we live.

By: Nicholas A. Christakis, MD, PhD

https://www.amazon.com/Apollos-Arrow-Profound-Enduring-Coronavirus/dp/0316628212

Ten Lessons for a Post-Pandemic World

By: Fareed Zakaria

https://www.simonandschuster.com/books/Ten-Lessons-for-a-Post-Pandemic-World/Fareed-Zakaria/9781797118093

For a list of current and forthcoming books with a clear and direct emphasis on the coronavirus look to: Pandemic in Print –

"Scott McLemee highlights the considerable number of current and forthcoming books flagged as pertinent to COVID-19 and its impact, or to pandemics more broadly."

https://www.insidehighered.com/views/2020/11/20/roundup-spring-2021-university-press-books-covid-19

CPSIA information can be obtained
at www.ICGtesting.com
Printed in the USA
LVHW031249280321
682728LV00004B/816